THE HUNTED

Also by Matt de la Peña

Ball Don't Lie

Mexican WhiteBoy

We Were Here

I Will Save You

The Living

THE HUNTED

Matt de la Peña

Delacorte Press

Text copyright © 2015 by Matt de la Peña
Jacket art © 2015 by Philip Straub

All rights reserved. Published in the United States by Delacorte Press,
an imprint of Random House Children's Books, a division of
Penguin Random House LLC, New York.

Delacorte Press is a registered trademark and the colophon
is a trademark of Penguin Random House LLC.

Visit us on the Web! randomhouseteens.com

Educators and librarians, for a variety of teaching tools,
visit us at RHTeachersLibrarians.com

Library of Congress Cataloging-in-Publication Data
de la Peña, Matt.
The hunted / Matt de la Peña. — First edition.
pages cm
Sequel to: The living.
Summary: After surviving the earthquake and tsunami, Shy manages to
make it back to land but he is far from safe because a secret his cruise ship co-worker,
Addie, shared with him is one that people have killed for, and now
that Shy knows, he has become a moving target.
ISBN 978-0-385-74122-4 (hardback) — ISBN 978-0-375-98436-5 (el)
ISBN 978-0-375-98992-6 (glb)
[1. Survival—Fiction. 2. Natural disasters—Fiction. 3. Diseases—Fiction. 4. Cruise
ships—Fiction. 5. Mexican Americans—Fiction.] I. Title.
PZ7.P3725Hun 2015
[Fic]—dc23
2014036148

The text of this book is set in 11.75-point Goudy.

Printed in the United States of America
10 9 8 7 6 5 4 3 2 1
First Edition

For my old man,

who showed me how to see the world

MAN: . . . but I'm not lost like that no more. I got a purpose. My family. [*Coughing.*] When everything crumbled around me that night, and I was almost burned to death in that fire . . . I guess you could say it's when I was born.

DJ DAN: It changed everyone. We're talking about the worst disaster in our country's history. [*Pause.*] My listeners are more interested in why you're here today. The warning you have. Why don't you start by giving us your name?

MAN: Already told you, mister. I'm not going there. Last thing I need is for this to finally come to an end and they turn around and throw me in jail. Just for spreading a message. Let's leave it at this: I'm part of the Suzuki Gang. That's what you all call us, right?

DJ DAN: You ride around on the same type of motorcycle acting like you have some type of authority.

MAN: Look, I know you don't spend all your time sitting in this little box. You've been out in the world. You've seen it. Folks are bleeding out of their eyes. Little kids, even. They're scratching off their own skin. Bodies are piled in the streets, rotting.

DJ DAN: Of course I've seen it. I started this radio program as a direct response to the things I've seen.

MAN: I remember hearing this one story a few weeks back, not long after the earthquakes. These two young parents were carrying their sick daughter through the streets of West Hollywood. She was in bad shape, I guess. A man guarding the entrance of an elementary school felt sorry for them and opened the gate, gave them food and water. Said he could only let them stay, though, if they kept to a shed off the soccer field, clear across the school from everyone else. But it didn't matter. A week later every single person staying in that school was either dead or dying. Over six hundred, I was told. That's how quickly this disease spreads. All of them wiped off the face of the earth because some dummy had a soft spot in his heart.

DJ DAN: But what does this have to do with—

MAN: I'm not done yet. [*Coughing.*] See, mister, that was back when things were mostly new. When none of us really understood shit, and everyone still had hope. But it's different now. Just yesterday I witnessed a similar situation. [*Coughing.*] A mom was wheeling her sick kid in a grocery cart, and she stopped in front of a community center in Silver Lake. She turned to look at all the faces watching her through the windows and she crumpled to her knees, sobbing and pleading for help.

DJ DAN: Let me guess, no one came out this time.

MAN: Shit, they came out, all right. Two men in dry suits. Dragged the mom and kid out of view by their shirts and hair and shot 'em in the street. Two bullets each, in the back of the head. Like it wasn't nothing. Another guy came out and torched the bodies. Left their charred remains as a warning to anyone else who wandered by.

DJ DAN: Jesus.

MAN: [*Scoffing.*] Call his name all you want, mister, but he ain't answered not one of us yet. [*Loud fit of coughing.*] This cough, by the way. It's not 'cause I got that disease. It's all the smoke I inhaled. I burned my lungs, I think.

DJ DAN: That's reassuring.

MAN: Point is, things are different now. We can agree on that much, I hope. And while most folks are still sitting around waiting on some savior from the other side to come riding in on a white pony . . . me and the guys, we've decided to get out there and do shit for ourselves, try and help our fellow man.

DJ DAN: Look, it's true, none of us know how much we can trust the government at this point—

MAN: Can't trust 'em at all.

DJ DAN:—but you're going about this all wrong. Take this interview, for example. There's absolutely no reason to be waving a gun in my face.

[*Sound of a gun being cocked.*]

MAN: Why, mister? Does it make you uncomfortable?

DJ DAN: What do *you* think?

MAN: In my experience, people are at their best when they're uncomfortable. See this burn across the side of my face? [*Pause.*] Shit's ugly. I know it is. But it's also a symbol of my rebirth. I never felt so humbled in my life as when I woke up on fire that night.

DJ DAN: Do you *honestly* think I need a gun in my face to feel fear? [*Sound of hand slapping desk.*] Fear is finding your wife crushed underneath your living room ceiling. Fear is witnessing your six-year-old daughter getting run over by a truck. Right outside the Sony lots. We're all scared, asshole. Every minute of every day.

MAN: Careful, mister. [*Pause.*] Here's what you don't get. I'm not just aiming this gun at you. I'm aiming it at everyone out there listening, too. Like I told you from the beginning, I've been sent here to issue a warning.

[*Rustling sound of the mike being grabbed.*]

Listen up. All of you. Doesn't matter if you're sick or healthy, man or woman, grown person or child . . . you need to stay where you are. No more traveling from zone to zone. For any reason. Or there will be consequences. Understand? [*Coughing.*] And I'm also looking for a kid—

DJ DAN: What consequences?

MAN: Hang on. [*Rustling.*] The kid's name is Shy Espinoza. Seventeen, with short brown hair and brown skin. Sort of tall and thin. Anyone can give me information on this boy's whereabouts, there'll be a reward. Just get in touch with DJ Dan here, and I'll keep checking back.

DJ DAN: What are the consequences for moving from zone to zone? And who will issue these consequences?

MAN: Us, man. We're out patrolling the streets, like you said. There's hundreds of us now, up and down the coast. And from this point on, if we catch your ass wandering around . . . we reserve the right to shoot you dead. No questions asked.

DJ DAN: Don't you hear what you're saying? You're talking about killing innocent human beings.

MAN: No, mister, I'm talking about saving them. If we don't do something to contain this disease, starting from right this second, it's gonna infect every last one of us. And then what? Huh, Mr. DJ Dan? Who would listen to your radio show then?

THE HUNTED

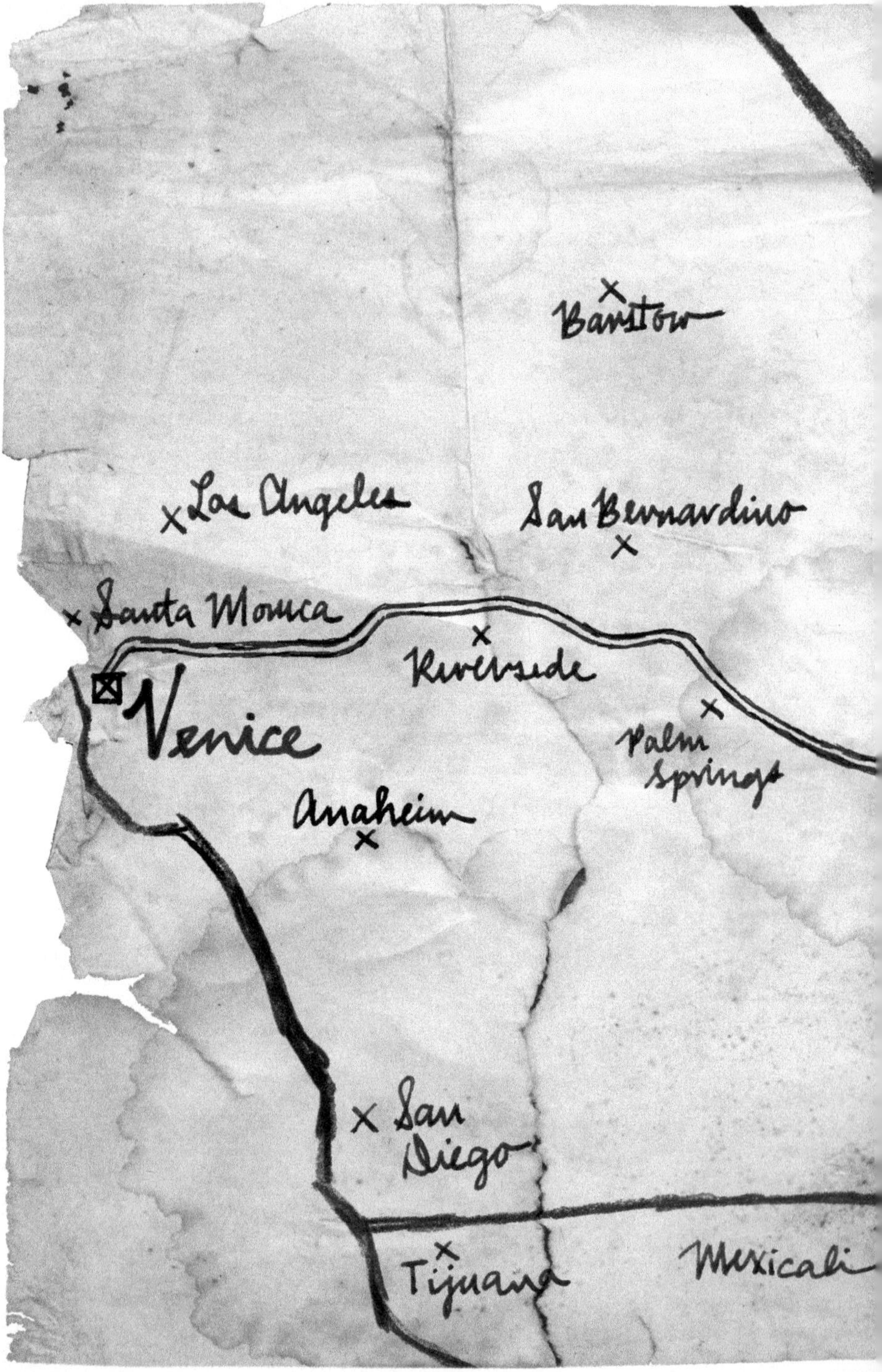
Barstow
Los Angeles
San Bernardino
Santa Monica
Riverside
Venice
Palm Springs
Anaheim
San Diego
Tijuana
Mexicali

x Las Vegas

Disease Border

AguaFria River ⊠

x Blythe

Phoenix

Yuma
x

Day 44

1
The Judge

The four of them stood near the bow in silence as their battered sailboat inched through the Pacific Ocean, toward the ruined California shoreline.

Shy pulled his shirt off his head and stared in awe—they were close enough now that he could make out the devastation caused by the earthquakes. Buildings flattened. Abandoned cars half submerged in parking lots and drifting in the tide. Palm trees snapped in half, and sand caked through the streets. Everything charred black.

Makeshift tents had been erected on the rooftops of the few burned-out structures that still stood, but Shy didn't see any people. Or any movement. Or any signs of electricity.

The place was a ghost town.

Still, his heart was racing. He thought he might never see land again. But here it was.

According to the staticky report they'd heard on Marcus's radio when they first left the island, the earthquakes that leveled the West Coast were more massive than any ever recorded. Entire cities had been wiped out. Hundreds of thousands had lost their lives. But worst of all, the earthquakes had caused the deadly Romero Disease to spread like wildfire, infecting nearly a quarter of the population in California and Washington and Oregon. In parts of Mexico.

Shy swallowed, his throat dry and scratchy, and fingered the diamond ring in his pocket, thinking about his mom and sis. His nephew, Miguel. Throughout the month he'd spent on the sailboat, Shy held out hope that his family might still be alive. But now, seeing a portion of the destruction firsthand, the idea of hope seemed stupid. Like living in a little-kid fantasy world.

He turned to Carmen, who was trembling and covering her mouth with her hand. "Hey," he said, touching her arm. "It's okay . . . we *made* it."

She nodded but didn't look at him.

He stared at the side of her face, recalling how fine she'd looked back when he met her on the cruise ship. The sun had just starting setting, like now, and his eyes cut right to her beautiful brown legs. The buttons on her white blouse straining to keep it from popping open. But what got him most of all was her face. It was way closer to perfect than some Photoshop shit you'd see in a magazine. He was so shook that first day, he could barely speak. The poor girl had to ask his roommate, Rodney, if he was a deaf-mute.

Now Carmen was weathered-looking and too thin.

Her entire body covered in a thick, salty film.

It was the same for all three of them, the result of spending thirty-six days at sea in a small sailboat—each day marked on the inside of the hull in black dye. They'd baked in the relentless summer sun, then rotated sleepless nights at the helm holding Shoeshine's compass so they wouldn't veer off course in the black of night. They'd survived on loaves of stale bread and the few fish they managed to catch. Shoeshine had allowed each of them only a few sips of water in the morning and a few more at night, and all Shy could think about now was bum-rushing somebody's front lawn and sucking down tap water straight from the hose.

He turned back to the beach. "Please tell me this shit's not a mirage."

"No mirage," Shoeshine answered.

"I keep rubbing my eyes," Marcus said. "Make sure my ass isn't dreaming."

Shy watched Marcus's long-lost smile come creeping back onto his face as he tried powering up his portable radio for the two thousandth time since it had stopped working.

Still nothing.

Not even static.

Back on the cruise ship, Marcus was a hip-hop dancer. Gave dance demonstrations twice a day and freestyled late night in the club. On the sailboat, though, Shy learned that Marcus ran deeper than the Compton cliché he played in front of rich passengers. He was halfway through an engineering degree at Cal State LA. Wrote video-game code in his free time. A few of the big tech firms were already dangling jobs for after he graduated.

But did those companies still exist?

Did Marcus's college?

"Breathe it into your lungs," Shoeshine told them. "You all just made it back from the dead." Laughing, he kissed his homemade compass and slipped it into the duffel bag by his feet.

A helicopter was visible in the distance, flying low over the beach. An emergency crew, Shy hoped, his heart suddenly pounding. Maybe they could just hand over the vaccine they'd carried off the island, and the letter, and that would be it.

He was so relieved as their sailboat approached the shoreline that a lump climbed into his throat. He'd imagined this moment for thirty-six straight days. He'd dreamed it every night. Now here they were.

But he was nervous, too. The entire stretch of beach was gutted. They had no idea who was dead or alive, or what they were walking into.

"Where you think we are, anyway?" Marcus asked.

Shy coughed into a closed fist. "Gotta be LA, right?"

"Venice Beach," Carmen said.

The three of them turned to her. First words she'd spoken in three days, even to Shy. She pointed at the shore, to the right of their boat. "See those graffiti walls?" She glanced at Shy. "That's where Brett asked me to marry him."

Shy cut his gaze away from Carmen's and focused on the untouched walls. The mere mention of Carmen's fiancé brought reality crashing back down on his head. Throughout their time on the sailboat, Carmen had been his salvation. He'd battled hunger for her. Dehydration. The crazy-person thoughts that kept creeping into his brain: *You should jump right now,* culo. *Feed your ass to the sharks and be done with it. Why couldn't you have just died on the ship like everyone else?*

But no matter how far Shy slipped into schizo territory, Carmen was always there to reel him back in. And he'd done the same for her.

Now that they'd made it back to California, though, it was time to face facts.

Carmen was engaged.

Carmen would be searching for her man.

"It *was* Venice Beach," Shoeshine said, steering the sailboat toward a clearing between two flagless poles. He glanced at the distant helicopter. "We don't know *what* it is now."

Shy scanned the stretch of beach again. His old man had taken him to Venice a handful of times during their year together in LA. But he didn't recognize *anything*.

"Whatever it is," Marcus said, "I guarantee it's better than floating our asses around for a damn month."

"That's the truth," Shy added.

Shoeshine shrugged, his wild gray hair blowing nappy in the wind. His braided chin beard still perfectly intact. "Time will be the judge," he told them.

2

Pack of Masked Bicycle Riders

When they got closer to shore, Shoeshine hopped over the side of the boat and splashed into water up to his chest. "We need to keep our eyes and ears open," he said, taking hold of the rope that hung from the bow. He began pulling them between the two flagpoles.

"No shit," Marcus said. "*Look* at this place."

Shy saw the way the tide washed over what was left of the pier and several fallen buildings, then sucked back out, carrying with it unidentifiable chunks of debris. Up and down the coast, it was the same. Crumbled beachfront houses and scorched earth. No sign of life aside from the distant helicopter.

"It's not the disasters themselves we need to worry about," Shoeshine warned. "It's the way folks may have adapted."

As if on cue, Shy sensed movement to the right of the boat. He turned and saw a pack of bicyclists emerge from behind a charred storefront, pedaling in the direction of the sailboat. He counted five of them. Just kids. Oversized medical masks covering their noses and mouths.

"Whoa, whoa, whoa," Marcus said, backing away from the edge of the boat. "What's the story *here*?"

"It's fine," Carmen said. "They're young, look."

The bikers stopped about ten yards from shore and watched as Shoeshine tied the sailboat to a thick metal stake extending out of the water near what looked to have been a lifeguard tower.

Shy stared at the kids, trying to get a beat on things. They were dressed in ragged jeans and sweatshirts, even though it was warm out. Their heads were shaved. One of them made some type of hand signal and they all lined up in a neat formation with their bikes. The way they were just staring at the sailboat creeped Shy out.

Marcus returned to the edge of the boat, calling out to them: "Hey!"

No answer from the kids.

"Yo, is this Venice Beach?" Marcus tried again.

Nothing.

They weren't even talking to each other.

Shy went from creeped out to pissed off. He was incredibly weak from spending over a month on a cramped sailboat, with barely any food or water. And these punk kids couldn't answer a simple question?

"Watch when I fire a damn flare at 'em," Shy mumbled. "That'll wake their asses up."

"Easy," Shoeshine said, securing the knot he'd just tied. He looked up at Shy. "Think of it from their side, young fella. Tattered boat like ours, coming in from the sea."

"What's up with the masks, though?" Marcus asked.

"And the shaved heads?" Shy added.

Carmen smoothed a section of her thick, tangled hair behind her left ear. "They're probably scared of the disease, right?"

That was it, Shy realized.

The disease.

He remembered watching his grandma die in the hospital back home. And he remembered Rodney's motionless body on the island. Their eyes red. Skin cold and flaking. Hearts no longer beating. He'd been on the sailboat so long he'd almost forgotten how bad it was.

"I'll speak to them once we get to shore." Shoeshine held his hand out for Carmen, helped her step down from the boat, into the waist-high water. "But not a word about what's in the duffel bag, understand?"

"You told us like fifty times already," Marcus said.

"And I'm telling you again."

Shy pointed to the sky. "Why can't we just hand it over to whoever's in that emergency helicopter?"

Shoeshine paused to stare at Shy. "Who was operating the last one you saw?"

Shy looked away. It had been Addie's dad, Mr. Miller. The man who'd created Romero Disease in the first place. The man who'd planted it in Mexican villages along the border to try to scare Americans into coughing up money for his meds.

Shoeshine had a point.

Shy handed the waterproof duffel over the side of the boat, and Shoeshine pointed at him and Marcus. "Wrong person finds out what we're carrying and soon everyone knows. And then it's gone."

Shy turned back to the masked kids.

Still just sitting on their bikes, staring.

They had no way of knowing that he, Carmen, Marcus and Shoeshine had already been vaccinated. That they had seven more shots tucked safely inside the duffel, shots that could save seven lives—or the lives of everyone, if they were able to get the syringes into the right hands.

Shy and Marcus hopped out next, and the four of them waded through the tide until they were safely on dry land, where they collapsed on a patch of sandy concrete.

Shy lay on his back, staring up at the helicopter, which was framed by a perfect sunset. He held the ground around him to try to stop the world from spinning, but it wasn't working. His legs felt like Jell-O. His stomach was twisted with nausea and hunger and thirst. He'd lost his shoes before they set sail from the island, and his bare feet were blistered and raw.

But they'd made it.

They were back in California. On land.

He allowed a relieved euphoria to settle over him as he slowly closed his eyes and breathed in the crisp coastal air. Forty-four days ago he'd set off on what he believed to be his final voyage as a Paradise Cruise Lines employee. He was only supposed to be at sea for eight days. *Eight!* Then he'd be back home with some cash in his pocket and two full weeks of doing nothing before his senior year.

So much for *that* plan.

He pictured his mom and sis and nephew again. He'd give anything to know they were somewhere safe right now, waiting for him.

But what if they weren't?

"Yo!" Shy heard Marcus shout. "Where the hell you going?"

Shy sat up quickly, his brain still floating on the water. When his eyes adjusted, he saw Marcus was standing. Then he turned toward the kids on bikes.

They were riding away.

3
Home Versus Arizona

"I'm not asking for no welcoming party," Marcus said, "but damn." He waved the kids off and sat back down.

Shy saw that they were sitting on a long patch of sandy cement, like a wide sidewalk or a basketball court. A fallen stretch of chain-link fence was visible in the tide to the right of them. Beyond the fence sat a wrecked Honda Civic, water rushing in and out of the busted windshield. Behind them, all the seller stalls were scorched and a bunch of chained-up food carts were tipped on their sides and already showing rust. The only thing Shy halfway recognized was the blackened remains of Muscle Beach to their left, where he'd once stopped with his old man to watch a group of 'roid heads tossing around free weights.

He turned to Carmen. "So how we supposed to get down to San Diego from here?"

She shrugged. "There's gotta be buses still running. Or trains."

Marcus frowned. "You're kidding, right?"

"What?" Carmen said. "There could be limited service or whatever. Like, just on freeways."

"Look at this place," Marcus told her. "Ain't limited *nothin'*."

Were there still buses? Shy wondered. What about food stores and hospitals and gas stations? And then another question occurred to him: was Addie out here somewhere?

She'd left the island on that helicopter with her dad, but where had they gone? And what would he do or say if their paths crossed again?

Shoeshine lifted their last jug of water out of the duffel. He uncapped it and held it out to Carmen. When she was done drinking, she passed the jug to Shy, who took a few desperate gulps of his own. He could feel the cool liquid settling in his stomach as he moved the jug along to Marcus.

Once they'd killed the water, Shoeshine capped the empty jug and looked around. "I plan to track down a few supplies tonight and get my bearings," he said. "First thing in the morning I'll start east."

"How?" Marcus said.

The man unlocked his journal with the key around his neck, flipped through several pages and used his teeth to uncap his pen. "Trust I'll find a way," he said.

Shy watched Shoeshine start writing.

Their monthlong journey in the sailboat had been filled with a whole lot of nothing. The sun rose and fell. The ocean whispered. Their tattered boat crept through the water, leaving a subtle wake that Shy would stare at for hours. They took turns fishing and steering and manning the sail. They spoke in quiet voices, and often didn't speak at all. But there was one topic they kept coming back to: what would they do if they actually made it back to California?

Shoeshine wanted to get the syringes into the hands of scientists as soon as possible. According to the report they'd heard, groups of them had gathered somewhere in Arizona to try and create a vaccine they had no idea already existed. Shy understood how important it was that the duffel get to Arizona—hundreds of thousands of lives were on the line—but he wanted to see about his family first. In case they needed him. It was the same for Carmen and Marcus.

After some back-and-forth, Shoeshine settled it by agreeing to take the duffel to Arizona himself. "No one said we had to stay together forever," he'd told them, looking directly at Shy.

When Shoeshine was done writing, he slipped his journal back into the duffel and zipped up. "Not much daylight left," he said, climbing to his feet.

"Maybe we should go with him," Carmen said to Shy and Marcus. "Just for the night."

"We need supplies, too," Shy said, struggling to stand. He didn't understand how he could feel more seasick on land than he'd ever felt on water.

"We can split up in the morning," Marcus added.

This was what they were all saying, but Shy knew the truth: they wanted to stay with Shoeshine as long as possible. He was the only reason they were still alive.

The farther they moved into town, the more devastation Shy saw. He studied the battered fish restaurant they passed on a street named Windward Avenue. The roof was caved in, and all that was left of the windows were long, blackened shards. The place next to it was burned beyond recognition. The poles holding up street signs were all tilted at odd angles, and many were spray-painted fluorescent green. Everything smelled of burned plastic and charcoal and brine. A small battered boat was on its side in the middle of the street.

Shy studied the fluorescent-green street signs, wondering who was going to fix all this. And how. What if they had to level the entire city and start from scratch?

He tried to imagine his own neighborhood back home, then thought better of it and focused on his surroundings.

They were halfway through the first cross street, Pacific Avenue, when Shy spotted the kids on bicycles riding back into view. Only this time they were followed by a handful of adults. Some on bikes. Others on foot.

Shy stopped in his tracks when he noticed something else.

Two of the men were carrying rifles.

4
Fair Trade

The group spread out around Shy and his crew, forming a crude semicircle of masked faces. All of them had shaved heads or wore hats, and they were too far away for Shy to make out the look in their eyes, especially in the fading daylight.

One of the men with a rifle lowered his medical mask slightly and called out: "Turn around slowly and head back where you started." This man was naturally bald, it looked like. And thin. His voice raspy.

Shy looked to Shoeshine, but he was already turning around and walking the other way.

Carmen and Marcus were as wide-eyed as Shy.

"Go on now," the bald man said, motioning them forward with his rifle. "Walk."

Before Shy even understood what was happening, the four

of them were retracing their footsteps, past the battered fish restaurant and all the other damaged buildings. He kept his eyes partially on the asphalt in front of him, stepping around sharp objects with his bare feet and trying to think. Who were these people? And why did they have rifles?

As soon as they were back on the sand-covered boardwalk, the bald man called for them to stop.

Marcus nudged Shy as the four of them turned around. "Shit, I woulda lost it if they tried to get me back on that boat."

"Still might," Shy said, watching two of the masked men pointing out toward the sea.

The bald man spoke again: "Who are you? And where'd you come from?"

A guy dressed in overalls and a straw hat lowered his mask, too. "Everyone knows you're supposed to stay put," he said. "You're lucky it was us who caught you and not the Suzuki Gang."

"Our cruise ship wrecked," Carmen blurted out. "We're the only ones who made it back."

The men looked at each other, their masks making it impossible to read their reactions. One of the kids on bikes was staring directly at Shy. He wore a filthy-looking gray sweatshirt. Hood up. Baggy jeans tucked into combat boots. He held a large white jug by its handle.

Shy was first to look away.

"What's happening here?" Marcus asked. "Is everyone really dying from that disease?"

The leader ignored Marcus and pointed out toward the water instead. "Who owns that boat?"

"*We* do," Shy said. "We got it off an island way out there."

"What island?" someone asked. "Catalina?"

"Jones Island," Shy corrected him.

Another man lowered his mask and said to the leader: "It doesn't add up, Drew. They just told us they were on a cruise."

"They look sick," one of the kids said. "They probably got kicked out of somewhere else before it spread."

"Make 'em go back where they came from," another kid said.

"No, we gotta shoot 'em," the first kid said.

Shy stared at the pack of kids in shock.

A guy in a Dodgers cap cocked his rifle suddenly and raised it.

"Yo, man!" Marcus called out, shielding his face with his hand. "Slow down! Damn!"

Shy cowered along with Carmen and Marcus, spooked, but Shoeshine just stood there, unfazed.

The guy in overalls dropped his bike, walked over to the man in the Dodgers cap and lowered the barrel of the rifle. "That's not who you are, Tom."

"They can't even answer a simple question!" the man shouted.

"Who cares what they say," someone else blurted out. "Leave the gun alone, Mason. You know what we have to do."

Shy's heart pounded. These people were actually arguing about whether or not to *shoot* them.

The guy named Mason made sure the barrel stayed aimed at the ground. "Explain how you got here," he said. "We don't allow outsiders to wander into our zone."

"What 'zone'?" Carmen said. "We don't even know what that means."

"We claimed this entire stretch of beach weeks ago."

"It's marked on all the signposts," someone else said. "There's no way you could've missed it."

Shy remembered the fluorescent-green spray paint he'd seen on many of the street signs. Had the entire state been marked off into zones? Had his neighborhood in Otay Mesa?

Carmen was first to step up again. She told the masked group how the four of them had been working on a luxury cruise ship bound for Hawaii. How the earthquakes had created a massive tsunami that wrecked their ship. How they had to bail into a dark, stormy ocean on lifeboats and life rafts with no sense of where they were or what they were supposed to do.

Shy listened to Carmen rattle off details about finding the half-flooded island, climbing the stone steps up to the hotel where they found food and water and shelter, where they survived for days.

"Less than a hundred of us made it there alive." Carmen was talking so fast she had to pause to catch her breath. "Us four . . . All we wanted to do was see about our families. So we fixed up that broken sailboat out there."

"And now here you are," the leader said, glancing at the men beside him. He didn't seem impressed.

"We just wanna go home," Carmen said.

"Home," someone scoffed. "Good one."

Shy was glad Carmen had left out the rest. If she'd told the men about the pharmaceutical company, LasoTech, razing the entire island to cover up its connection to the disease, it would only have led to more questions. And those questions might've led to the syringes stashed in Shoeshine's duffel bag.

The guy in the Dodgers cap turned his gun on Carmen. "I don't believe you," he said. "I think you came here from Santa Barbara. We've all heard about their recent outbreak."

Shy instinctively stepped in front of Carmen. "Everything she said is the truth." He turned to the leader. "Come on, man. We were just struggling out there for thirty-six straight days. With barely anything to eat or drink. And now you wanna point a gun at us?"

"It's *you* who are pointing the gun at *us*!" the leader shouted at Shy. "Don't you get that? If one person brings the disease into our zone, we all die."

"We don't care about your stupid zone," Carmen said. "We just wanna go find our families."

"You'll leave the sailboat with us," the leader announced.

"Take it," Shy told him. "We never wanna see that piece of shit again."

Shoeshine stepped forward. "We'll need something in return."

The guy in the Dodgers cap grinned as he turned to the rest of his group "The old man speaks."

"In exchange for the boat you can have your lives," the leader said. "How's that for a fair trade?"

Shy heard the kids behind the man snicker through their masks. The guy in the Dodgers cap pointed at the duffel hanging off Shoeshine's shoulder. "Why don't you tell us what's in the bag."

Shy froze.

The syringes. The letter that documented how LasoTech had created Romero Disease. Their only item of actual proof.

"Water and a few shirts," Shoeshine answered. "Some paper to write on."

"Let's see," the man said.

Shoeshine didn't move.

"Go on, unzip it."

Shy's eyes grew wide as Shoeshine unzipped the duffel and held it open. Even though these guys would have no idea what the syringes were for, or how important the letter was, they'd demand them, too. Shy was sure of it. And what would Shoeshine do *then*? Explain everything?

The man with the Dodgers cap slid his mask back over his face and set down his bike. He took the white jug from the kid holding it and started toward Shoeshine. "Toss it on the ground, old man."

Shoeshine set the duffel down, and the man motioned him away.

Shy watched nervously as the man began sifting through the bag's contents with the tip of his rifle. He nudged a couple of shirts out of the bag and doused them with liquid from the white jug, which smelled like bleach. He did the same to the empty water container. And the compass. He even poured bleach on the beat-up leather cover of Shoeshine's journal.

He was trying to disinfect everything, Shy realized.

The man reached down to flip open the journal's damp cover, but stopped when he saw it was locked. He folded over the top of the cover and kneeled down to read the few lines that were visible.

Shy still had no idea what Shoeshine wrote in his book. Nobody did. Marcus had asked on the sailboat once, but Shoeshine only gave a cryptic answer. "It's a study of human beings," he'd said without looking up. "A way of recording our path in the new world."

The man tossed down the journal and kicked the bag open wider. Holding it open with the butt of his rifle, he doused the whole thing with bleach. "Any more bags we should know about?" he asked.

"Just the one," Shoeshine said.

Shy didn't understand why the man hadn't pulled out the syringes or the letter. How could he have missed them?

The man turned to Marcus next. "What about the radio?"

"Doesn't work," Marcus told him, flipping on the power button and pulling up the antenna to prove it. The radio didn't make a sound.

"Empty your pockets," the man demanded.

Before Marcus could reach for his pockets, though, the leader said: "That's enough, Tom. We've got the boat. Now let's get them out of here."

The two men stared at each other.

"We can't just let them go," someone else said. "What if they come back?"

"They won't come back," the man named Mason said.

"We should shoot them right now!" someone shouted. "We have that right!"

The leader yanked his mask down and faced his group. "Listen to yourselves!" he barked. "I refuse to sit here and watch us turn into the Suzuki Gang!"

Shy breathed a sigh of relief as the man in the Dodgers cap finally lowered his rifle and started back toward his bike, shaking his head in disgust.

"Gregory. Chris." The leader pointed at two of the kids. "Go disinfect the boat. Now!" When the kids dropped their bikes and took off toward the water with the bottle of bleach, the leader turned back to Shy and his crew. "You will never set foot in our zone again," he said. "Understand me? Next time the consequences will be much greater."

Shy nodded with the others.

"Mason," the leader called out to the guy in overalls. "Follow them. Make sure they leave our zone completely and understand the borders." He turned to the man in the Dodgers cap. "Tom, give Mason your rifle."

Tom pulled down his mask, revealing a look of disgust. "Are you shittin' me, Drew?"

"Now!" the leader demanded.

The man spit to the side of his bike before tossing the rifle to Mason.

Shy watched them all secure their medical masks over their faces again, readying themselves to leave.

Mason kept his distance from Shy and his crew, saying: "Head straight down the street in front of you. Go on."

As Shy started toward the road, he glanced over his shoulder at the rifle in Mason's left hand, then at Mason's expressionless eyes. What if "follow them" was code for something far worse?

5
The Disease

Shy trailed Carmen, Marcus and Shoeshine as they moved through a roundabout called Windward Circle. He looked back. The man following them, Mason, motioned with his rifle for Shy to keep going.

He turned forward again and focused on what he could still see in the fading daylight. A decorative gondola in the middle of the roundabout was broken in half and burned, and there was a large red X painted on the concrete beside it. Shy wondered if that had something to do with people's zones, too. A van had crashed into the front gate of the postal annex, and there was mail scattered everywhere. Most of it was burned beyond recognition, but Shy reached down for one postcard that seemed oddly untouched.

Venice Beach was written across the front, the words transposed over a perfect breaking wave that reminded Shy of the massive wall of water that had crashed into the cruise ship, sending them into this whole mess. He flipped over the postcard and read the message as he continued walking:

Grandpa Barry,

We finally made it to LA! It's so incredibly beautiful here, I wish you could see it for yourself. Hugs to everyone back home!

Love,
Chloe

Shy Frisbeed the card back onto the sea of burned ones. "Beautiful" LA was now a disaster zone where people threatened you with rifles. The girl who'd written the postcard had probably died in the earthquakes. Or the fires that came after. Or she'd been infected with Romero Disease.

"Take Grand up ahead," Mason called out.

Another helicopter emerged in the distance, flying close to the shore. Shy peered down several quiet roads where most of the houses no longer stood. The air smelled of ash and decay. He spotted a group of dead rats near an overturned trash receptacle. Two dozen, maybe. Little empty holes where their eyes should have been. "Animals can get the disease, too?" he wondered out loud.

Carmen turned away from the rats, covering her mouth.

"Keep walking," Mason called to them.

There were abandoned cars everywhere, some left in the middle of the street with their doors wide open or their windshields bashed in. Storefronts were boarded up and charred black. Shattered glass was strewn about the sidewalks so recklessly Shy had to be conscious of each step. Some buildings had been reduced to mounds of blackened rubble that spilled out into the street.

Even if they found a car that worked, Shy didn't see how they'd be able to maneuver it through all the crap in the way. Between that and everyone stressing out about their stupid zones, he wondered how he and Carmen would get even *close* to San Diego.

Mason called for them to stop near a street named Riviera. He coasted forward on his bike, stopping a good fifteen feet away and putting one foot on the ground for balance. "Keep east of this street and you'll be fine," he told them through his mask. "North of Rose and south of Washington. You'll remember that, right?"

Shy nodded with everyone else.

Mason glanced at the destruction on the opposite side of the street. "Have you guys really been on a boat all this time?"

"Swear to God," Marcus told him.

Shy motioned toward his own weathered face. "Can't you tell by looking at us?"

Mason tipped back his straw hat and lowered his mask past his chin. "You think we look any better?"

There was just enough sunlight left for Shy to see the details of the man's face. His cheeks sagged like he'd recently lost a lot of weight. There were bags under his eyes. His hair looked recently buzzed, but thick gray and black whiskers covered his face and neck.

"Watch yourselves out there," Mason told them. "We're humanitarians compared to others you may run into. Those guys from the Suzuki Gang shoot first and ask questions later."

"What's the Suzuki Gang?" Carmen asked.

"Group of vigilante types on motorcycles." The man turned his handlebars back and forth, staring across the street.

Shy followed Mason's eyes to the other side of Riviera. A large chasm had opened up in the concrete between two collapsed buildings. Five feet wide at least, with a few cars sticking up out of the thing. A driver was still inside one of the cars, and he wasn't leaving anytime soon. Shy had to look away from the bloated, rotting corpse.

Mason turned his bike around like he was going to leave, but he just sat there, looking back toward his own zone. "And this disease going around . . . it's awful. The infected only survive a couple days, but when it's someone close to you . . . when it's your own *son* . . . it stays burned in your memory forever."

"We're sorry for your loss," Shoeshine said.

Shy recalled watching his grandma suffer at the hospital. Her eyes blood red as she tore at her skin. Back then hardly anyone knew about Romero Disease. The only cases on record were in Mexico and a few border cities on the American side, like where he and Carmen lived. It didn't spread north until after Shy started working for Paradise Cruise Lines.

"Isn't the government helping?" Carmen asked. "Or the Red Cross or someone?"

Mason pointed to the distant helicopter. "They make food and water drops near the big red Xs painted on some intersections. Other than that, we're on our own."

Shy couldn't believe it. Any time he'd seen a disaster on the news, the government was there right away. How could they just abandon everyone?

Mason pulled his mask back over his face. "Like I said, keep east of Pacific. A couple of those guys back there . . . they really will shoot you." He then kicked forward on his bike, started riding back the way they'd come.

"Wait!" Carmen called to him. "Are there trains or buses running?"

Mason gave a halfhearted wave with his rifle and continued pedaling.

After the man rounded the corner, out of sight, Shy turned to the others. But no one said anything right away. It was all too overwhelming. A sick thought crept into Shy's head: what if the government secretly *hoped* the entire population of California died off?

"We're screwed," Marcus said, breaking the silence.

"Where we supposed to spend the night?" Carmen asked, squatting down in the middle of the street. "It's almost dark already."

Shy looked across the road again, at the corpse inside the car. Then he turned to look back into the zone they'd just left. The colors hovering over the Pacific Ocean were beginning to slip away. Carmen was right, in ten or fifteen minutes they'd be wandering around in the dark.

Shy pointed at the duffel hanging from Shoeshine's shoulder. "Why didn't that guy back there take the syringes?"

"Can't take what you can't see," Shoeshine answered.

Marcus set down his radio. "He was digging all through the bag, though."

Shoeshine pulled the duffel off his shoulder and unzipped it. Shy watched him take out the shirts and the compass and the empty jug and his journal. When he held up the empty bag, the powerful bleach smell burned Shy's nose and eyes.

The syringes were gone.

So was the letter.

"Where the hell'd they go?" Marcus said.

Shoeshine pointed at a stitched area in the gut of the bag. "Sewed in a couple extra compartments while we were on the boat."

Shy looked at Shoeshine in awe.

So did Carmen and Marcus.

How was it that this man saw everything before it happened? It had been that way since back on the island. Back on the cruise ship, even. Shy wondered if he would ever learn who Shoeshine really was. He knew the guy had been in the military. That he'd shined shoes on the ship. But there had to be something else, something beyond what Shoeshine was telling them.

"You know how to sew, too?" Marcus asked.

Shoeshine shrugged and looked up into the sky. "Best we start walking."

A strange feeling came over Shy as he followed the man across the street. When tomorrow came and they went their separate ways, Shy, Carmen and Marcus would be even more lost than they were now. And more vulnerable. Because Shoeshine was the only one who knew the way. Shy could never be like that.

6
Truth

It grew darker with each passing minute.

Buildings and fallen trees went from clearly defined things to dull shapes that seemed to stagger across the road. Shy could no longer see well enough to avoid stepping on rocks or pieces of debris, and the soles of his raw feet burned.

There were no more helicopters, but stars began to reveal themselves in the sky, reminding Shy of all the cold nights he'd just spent on the sailboat. That was the one thing he could never forget. The stars. Distant pinpricks of light that followed the boat wherever it went. Followed *him*. He'd stare up at them for hours, aware that they'd been there millions of years before he was born and would be there a million more after he was gone. They proved how small he was. How insignificant. Which somehow made the idea of death less threatening.

* * *

They continued east, navigating their way around discarded cars in the near dark, random pieces of blackened furniture and downed power lines, which Shoeshine warned them away from. They passed gutted apartment buildings and half-crumbled houses. Shy occasionally felt eyes on his back, but whenever he spun around to check, he'd find no one.

In one intersection he spotted a pile of bodies in the street that gave off a powerful smell of bleach and rot. Carmen and Marcus quickly turned away, but Shy stared. There was something he wasn't grasping. Some deeper meaning or truth to it all. An answer.

When would it sink in?

As they passed an empty schoolyard Shy tripped over something in the street. He squatted down to study it. A single high-top. He held the shoe up to his face and inspected it more closely. No holes in the sole. Seemed sturdy enough. But the other one was nowhere to be found.

Carmen turned around, hissing: "Come on."

"I'm coming." Shy slipped his foot into the high-top and laced up. He glanced into the schoolyard as he started after Carmen, Marcus and Shoeshine. He spotted a lonely swing vibrating in the subtle wind, and for some reason he imagined his nephew climbing onto it. Imagined him kicking himself as high as he could. Jumping off into the thick sand and turning to see if Shy had been watching.

"I saw it," Shy mumbled as he caught up with the others.

Carmen glanced at him, but he didn't meet her eyes.

Long after they passed the playground, Shy was still picturing his nephew on that swing.

* * *

When they turned onto a wide street named Lincoln Boulevard, Shy spotted a small group of middle-aged women climbing out of the busted front window of what had once been a convenience store. "Look," he whispered, motioning for the others to stop.

Shoeshine kneeled down to watch the women.

Even in the dark Shy could see they were extremely thin, just wisps of human beings wearing soiled sweatshirts and loose jeans. Hospital masks covering their noses and mouths.

"Let's go talk to them," Marcus whispered.

"Now?" Carmen whispered back.

Shoeshine placed his hand on Marcus's arm. "Best leave them be."

Marcus turned to look at the man. "Why?"

"We have our business, they have theirs."

Shy could see that the women's hands were full. They were carrying things out of the store. But he agreed with Shoeshine: they should be left alone. There was something wild about the way they were slinking around in silence.

One of the women looked up suddenly and saw that she was being watched. She clicked her tongue at the others, who all looked up, too, and froze in their tracks. The smallest was still halfway in the window.

"We're not sick!" Marcus called out.

None of the women answered.

Shy heard a motorcycle far off in the distance, but when he turned his ear toward it, the sound disappeared.

Carmen took a small step toward the women, holding up her empty hands as if to show she was unarmed. They immediately scurried away from the store, down the middle of the road, cutting into the remains of a fallen hotel.

"What the hell?" Carmen said, turning to Shoeshine. "I didn't even do anything."

Shy and Marcus cautiously followed the women and peered into the wreckage, but they were gone. Or they were hiding. Shy couldn't see far enough into the maze of rubble to know which.

"Everyone thinks we got the disease," Marcus said. "We have to tell the truth. Or else no one's gonna help."

Shoeshine was beside them now, holding a flashlight. "What truth?" he asked Marcus.

Marcus turned to the man and opened his mouth as if to speak, but no words came out.

"Where'd you get that?" Shy asked, pointing at Shoeshine's flashlight.

"Under a Dumpster a few blocks back."

Shy didn't remember Shoeshine near any Dumpster.

"Does it work?" Carmen asked.

Shoeshine shined the light on the ground in front of them, then quickly cut it off. "Come on," he said, and he started walking ahead.

Shy heard the sound of the distant motorcycle again. They needed to get off the streets as soon as possible.

"What the hell we supposed to be doing, anyways?" Carmen said. "Just wandering around aimlessly?"

"Getting supplies," Marcus said. "Then me, you and Shy are going home."

"And Shoe's going to Arizona," Shy added.

"I know *that*," Carmen snapped. "I'm talking about *now*. Right this second."

No one answered.

As Carmen and Marcus followed Shoeshine, Shy reached

down for a half-rotted potato that one of the women had dropped. He turned it over in his hands, studying the small craters in its thick, wrinkled skin. It had been a little more than a month since the earthquakes hit, and already people were desperate enough to loot rotting potatoes.

7

Old-Man Strength

A few blocks south they found a small sporting goods shop. Shoeshine illuminated the boarded-up front door while Shy and Marcus took turns trying to kick it in. Through a crack in the foundation, underneath one of the barred windows, they could see that there were supplies inside. But the wood barring the door was thick and well secured. All Shy's kicking managed to do was jam his foot.

After a few minutes of furious kicking, Shy and Marcus were exhausted. They stopped and bent over, hands on knees, staring at each other, sucking in breaths.

"There's gotta be another way in," Shy said.

Marcus spit at the ground. "Yo, I need to get my ass some damn protein."

Shy turned to the boarded door again, trying to call up some extra strength, but he had nothing left in the tank. Marcus was right, they needed food.

"Keep trying," Carmen said, peering through a small crack in the door. "I see sleeping bags. And jackets."

"Hold up," Marcus said, pointing down at Shy's feet. "Are you rocking one shoe right now?" He snatched the flashlight out of Shoeshine's hand and aimed the beam at Shy's lone high-top.

"Better than nothing," Shy told him.

Carmen laughed. "Poor Shy," she said, kicking at his shoe. "Always a day late and a dollar short." She patted him on the shoulder. "It's kind of adorable."

Shy peeped his high-top, then looked back up at Carmen. Here they were, in a ruined city with nothing to eat or drink and nowhere to go, with dead bodies all around, and what was Shy doing? He was trying to interpret the way Carmen had said the word "adorable." Did she mean it in a real way? Like two people who could possibly end up together one day? Or did she mean it in a brother-and-sister sort of way?

Marcus tossed the flashlight back to Shoeshine, saying: "Why don't you two get married already? For real, I could perform the ceremony right here on this broke-ass street. Shoe could be the best man."

"Grow up," Carmen barked, landing a blind punch to Marcus's midsection.

"Dude, you need some new material," Shy said. Marcus had already gone to the marriage joke a dozen times on their boat ride back to California. It was played out. So what if Shy secretly watched Carmen's reaction every time?

"Why don't you make yourself useful?" Carmen told Marcus. "Start back in on that door. Shy's doing better with one shoe."

"I don't see *you* kickin' shit," Marcus fired back. "That women's lib BS works both ways, girl."

As Carmen and Marcus went back and forth at each other, Shy noticed Shoeshine moving toward the boarded-up door and squaring his shoulders. The man pulled in a long breath, then blasted straight through the wood with a single kick.

Shy stared at the shattered boards, baffled.

"What the hell?" Marcus said. He and Carmen were staring, too.

Shoeshine shined his flashlight through the opening, into the shop. "This is it," he said over his shoulder.

As soon as Shoeshine disappeared into the store, Shy and Marcus turned to each other. "Son of a bitch," Marcus said.

"It's that old-man strength," Shy told him. "My pops was the same way."

Carmen moved toward the jagged opening. "I'm not saying nothin' . . . even though that *vato* is like fifty-something years older than you all."

As soon as Shy set foot inside the store he knew they'd hit the jackpot. Shoeshine had hung his flashlight from a sprinkler on the ceiling, to give the room a little light. Some of the tall shelves had collapsed in the earthquake, and equipment lay all over the place, soaking in the puddles of water that covered the floor, but there were a ton of supplies they could still use. Shy went for the rack of shoes first, found some cross-trainers in his size and a pair of socks and put them on. It was like stepping into a couple clouds. He chucked aside his single high-top and sloshed over to the rack of Windbreakers, where Carmen and Marcus were.

Shoeshine tossed them each a small hiking backpack and told them to fill it with clothes and nutrition bars and whatever tools they could find.

"Check this shit out," Marcus called to them, holding up a small satellite radio. "I'm back, baby."

"You got batteries?" Carmen asked.

Marcus started scanning nearby shelves. "This place has gotta have 'em somewhere."

"Till you got batteries," Carmen told him, "you ain't back for shit."

When Shy's backpack was full of socks and T-shirts and an extra pair of jeans and rope and a beanie and a flashlight of his own, he leaned against the back wall and frantically unwrapped one of the protein bars he'd found. He shoved half the thing into his mouth and damn near swallowed it whole.

Carmen and Marcus followed his lead.

Even Shoeshine stopped going through the shelves long enough to down a bar.

For a few long minutes the store went eerily quiet aside from the sound of their chewing.

The silence was broken by the sound of a man clearing his throat. "I got a semiautomatic pistol aimed right at the girl," a voice called out from behind the supply room door. "I'll give you to the count of three to get out of here before I start shooting."

Shy aimed his flashlight at the door. It was slightly ajar, but he couldn't see anything. Shoeshine and Marcus moved their beams across the ceiling and floor while Shy turned his toward the busted door where they'd entered.

Nobody.

The one thing he did notice was a wool blanket halfway covering a small hole near the bottom of the back wall. A hidden second entrance, it looked like. One that led to the alley in back. This was how they'd kept the place to themselves.

"One!" the voice called out.

Shy heard a little kid start crying.

A family lived here.

"Two!" the voice said.

"Come on," Shoeshine said, waving for them to follow him, and the four of them tore out of the sporting goods store the way they'd come in, wearing their new backpacks, aiming their new flashlights at the cluttered sidewalk in front of their quick-moving feet.

Shy ran slightly out in front of everyone, listening for shots that never came. As he veered around the corner, heading east again, he wondered if the man in the store really had a gun or was just bluffing. There was no way everyone out here could have a weapon.

He decided it didn't matter.

They had what they needed.

8
What Can Become of Us

Shy stood in front of the large motor home they'd found, shining his light onto the dripping red circle painted on the door, which he could tell had been jimmied open at some point. The symbol meant something, obviously, and he decided Shoeshine was right about it being different from the fluorescent-green-painted street signs.

The motor home had somehow been shoved up against the wall of a DMV building. Some of the windows were blown out and the trailer's twisted body was leaning at an odd angle, so that the punctured rear tires on one side hovered slightly above the singed lawn.

"Let's just stay here," Marcus said.

"It's as good as anything else we're gonna find in the dark," Shy said, adjusting his new backpack.

"What if someone's already in there?" Carmen asked.

"Not with the door like that." Shoeshine aimed his flashlight at it.

"Like what?" Marcus asked.

"It's not totally closed," Shy told him.

"Oh. Right."

"Someone could be coming back, though," Carmen said. "Maybe that's what those red circles mean."

"If someone was living here," Shoeshine said, "they'd have found a way to seal the door. The circle must be a symbol for Romero Disease."

"Which we can't get," Marcus said, nudging Carmen. "Remember?"

Carmen flipped him off.

Shy pushed himself to his toes to look inside the spidered motor-home window, but the curtains blocked his view. In the window's fragmented reflection he saw two people skulking on the other side of the street. He spun around and shined his light directly at them.

Kids around his age, wearing masks made out of cut-up plastic grocery bags, it looked like. Shower caps on their heads. They ducked down a side road, out of sight.

"You saw those dudes, right?" Shy asked.

"Hell yeah," Marcus said.

"Shoe?" Shy said.

Shoeshine nodded, still staring at the street the kids had turned down.

"This place is giving me bad vibes," Carmen said.

Marcus forced a laugh. "As opposed to all the *good* vibes you got since we landed back in Cali?"

Shy spent a few seconds watching for the kids before turning his light back to the battered DMV building. The roof was caved in and the closest wall had been reduced to charcoal. There was no one staying in there. No one who was still alive, at least.

"You're not even gonna knock?" Carmen said.

Shy turned and saw Shoeshine reaching for the motor home doorknob and slowly pulling open the door. He stuck his head inside and called out: "Anyone there?" When no one answered, he disappeared inside.

Shy glanced across the street. Still no sign of the kids. He looked at Carmen and Marcus and shrugged nervously, then followed Shoeshine into the motor home.

The place smelled awful, like when a rat dies in the wall of your apartment. Shy had to cover his mouth with his shirt as he swept his light around the rest of the cabin. Not a soul inside. Pet hair all over the gray carpet. A few dish shards on the linoleum floor in front of the sink. Two framed photos shattered on the floor and old pizza boxes stacked in a corner.

This was the first time Shy had ever been inside a motor home, and he was surprised by how much room there was. A long couch stretched across the wide cab on one side, next to a cot. A table and bolted-down stools on the other. There was a flat-screen TV mounted on the wall, and lacy curtains covered every window. The sink was full of moldy pasta and crusty dishes—the source of the sour, musky smell, he figured.

Marcus stepped into the motor home next, followed by Carmen, who mumbled through the hand covering her nose and mouth: "Wow, I love what they've done with the place. Makes you feel right at home."

"It's all good if we can air it out some," Marcus said. He buried his face in his shoulder as he opened the closet near the door. Shy saw a few jackets inside, in a range of sizes. Whoever lived here had kids.

"For real, though," Carmen said, still covering her mouth. "This smell's making me gag."

Shy watched Shoeshine move deeper into the motor home, toward the bathroom, where he ducked his head and torso through the door. The man stayed like that for several seconds before pulling himself back out and stuffing something into his back pocket. He closed the door quietly behind him and rejoined the group, saying: "Let's keep moving."

"Wait, really?" Marcus said. "Why?"

"Carmen's right about the smell," Shoeshine answered.

Shy shined his light on Shoeshine's chest so he could see the look in his eyes. "Be straight with us," he told the man. "What's in there?"

Shoeshine only shook his head.

"Come on," Carmen said.

Shoeshine glanced back at the bathroom. "There's a man," he admitted. "Been dead a week or so, maybe more."

"See?" Carmen said to Shy and Marcus.

Marcus cringed, covering his mouth. "*Of course* that's what the smell is. Some dead dude. Why wouldn't it be?"

"We're leaving," Carmen said, moving toward the exit. When no one followed, she stopped near the door and held out her hands. "Please don't tell me you dumbasses still wanna stay in here."

"How'd he die?" Marcus asked. "Was it the disease? Or did someone break in?"

"Who cares how he died?" Carmen called out from the door.

When Shoeshine didn't answer his question, Marcus started toward the bathroom.

Shy wanted to see what was in there, too, and began following Marcus.

"Young fella," Shoeshine called to him.

Shy stopped and turned around.

The man didn't say anything else, but there was an intense look in his eyes, a look Shy didn't know how to interpret.

"Jesus Christ!" Marcus shouted from the bathroom door.

Shy spun back around just as Marcus pushed past him and hurried toward the front door.

"What is it?" Carmen shouted, following Marcus out of the motor home. "Actually, I don't even wanna *know*."

Shoeshine was holding out a small handgun for Shy to see. It was what he must have removed from the bathroom. "Not easy to face what can become of us," the man told Shy. "Remember that." He returned the gun to his back pocket and left the motor home, too.

At first Shy just stood there, stuck, covering his nose and mouth with his shirt. He wanted to follow right behind Shoeshine, get outside where he'd at least be able to breathe. But something wouldn't let him.

He had to know.

Had to see for himself. The worst of it.

Even if he could never take it back.

Shy held his breath as he nudged open the bathroom door with his shoe and stuck his head inside. First thing that hit him was the awful smell of human decay. It was so thick and pungent he could almost taste it through his sealed lips.

His eyes watered as he gagged.

An entire family and their dog crowded together in the tiny bathroom. All dead. Two little girls in matching pajamas, no more than three or four, lying on top of each other in the tiny tub. Twins, maybe. The mom slumped over the toilet, the back half of her head missing. The dad curled up by the door with a grotesque-looking hole in his forehead.

All of them, including the dog, had been shot. That much

was obvious. Shy saw the bullet shells and the blood covering the walls and sink and tub, and he saw the flies buzzing around the girls, especially the one on top, whose eyes were wide-open and bright red from the disease.

Shy's heart was racing, but he couldn't stop looking.

Because this was it. This was the thing he'd been searching for since they made it back to California.

A man had shot his family and his dog to stop their suffering from Romero Disease. And then he'd shot himself.

Shy stood there mesmerized, staring at the bodies and the flies and fingering the diamond ring inside his pocket. He wondered what he'd do if faced with the same set of circumstances. His mom sick. His sister and nephew. No one around who could possibly help.

He'd like to think he'd be strong enough to do the same thing. To pull the trigger. End their pain.

But he knew he wasn't.

9
Sticking Up for a *Blanquita*

"You still think about her sometimes?" Carmen asked.

"Who?" Shy said.

"Don't be stupid, Sancho. You know who I'm talking about."

He did. Addie. The girl he'd been stranded at sea with for several days in a broken lifeboat. "Sometimes, I guess. Why?"

Carmen shrugged. "Just wondering."

They were standing across from each other in the small yard behind the DMV, digging into the earth with the shovels they'd found in the cellar. They both wore their new beanies and Windbreakers. Marcus and Shoeshine were several feet away, digging a second grave. The plan was to bury the bodies they'd just found, then spend the night in the motor home. Shoeshine believed the red circles warned where infected corpses lay. So the motor home was safe for them—everyone else would keep their distance.

Even Carmen, who'd been so anti–motor home earlier, agreed it was best to stay off the streets until morning.

Shy continued digging, occasionally glancing at Carmen. The more he thought about her question, though, the more it pissed him off.

Because he *did* think about Addie.

More than he wanted to admit.

He thought about how they'd started off hating each other on the cruise ship. They were from completely different worlds, living completely different lives. Addie, the rich blond chick from LA who thought she was better than everyone. Shy, the poor barrio kid who'd grown up in the shadow of the Mexican border. But when they were stranded together, something happened. Their desperation forced them to pull off their masks and show each other their fragile hearts. And how many people do you actually do that with over the course of a lifetime?

They started talking, started huddling together for warmth. And by their last night on the broken lifeboat, things had changed to the point that Addie actually meant something to him . . . at least until he found out what her dad had done.

Shy stopped digging and looked up at Carmen, though all he could see in the dark was her slow-moving form. The flashlight he'd placed on the ground only lit up the hole they were digging. And their feet.

Carmen stopped shoveling, too. "Look at you, Sancho. You're thinking about ol' girl right this second."

Shy scoffed. "More like I'm thinking about how her old man's the devil. You know that company's gonna be looking for us, right?"

Carmen didn't say anything.

Just kept staring at him.

When her silence became awkward, Shy hopped into their

hole. It was almost knee-deep now, but Shoeshine wanted it twice that depth so that the bodies would *stay* buried. "Addie's dad is the reason we're digging these graves," he reminded Carmen. "You know that, right?"

"Exactly," Carmen said. "Addie's *dad*. Not Addie herself."

"They're blood, though, Carm." Shy set down his shovel and wiped his sweaty palms on his pants. He could already feel blisters forming. "It's gotta fall on her some, too."

"What if she was just as ignorant about all that shit as me and you? What then?"

"She wasn't, though," Shy said.

"How do *you* know?"

Shy thought back to the Addie he'd grown close to on the lifeboat. Her tangled blond hair falling over the scared look on her face. She had seemed genuinely naive when they sat there brainstorming what her dad's company might have been trying to cover up. But something changed when they got back to the island. She no longer looked at him the same way.

Carmen stood upright outside their ditch. "Yeah, that's what I thought."

Shy could vaguely make out Carmen smoothing strands of hair underneath her beanie. "First of all," she went on, "you don't know shit about girls, all right? I looked in that *heina*'s eyes when I took her to get cleaned up. She didn't know *nothin'*. Trust me. Second of all, I can't believe you got me sticking up for a *blan-quita*."

Shy started digging again.

He hated when Carmen stuck up for Addie. When a girl had zero jealousy it meant she also had zero feelings. Which Shy already sort of knew, but didn't *want* to know. "If you'd heard our last conversation," he told her, "you'd see it differently."

"What conversation?"

"On the island," he said. "Outside the restaurant when she told me bye. She *knew* she was about to go on that helicopter with her dad. And you know what that means, right?"

Carmen didn't say anything.

"She probably knew what those supposed researchers were about to do to us, too." Shy pictured the men pulling out their machine guns on the beach, gunning down all the innocent passengers who were lined up, waiting to be rescued.

Carmen was quiet for a long time. She just stood there in the dark, holding her shovel, staring into their hole.

"You got nothing to say about that part?" Shy finally asked her.

"If that shit's true," she finally said, turning to him, "I swear to God, Shy. I'll find that bitch."

Shy went back to digging.

He could still feel Carmen's eyes on him.

10
Carmen's Man

They'd been digging silently for a good ten, fifteen minutes, when Shy asked: "What about you, Carm? You think about your boy Brad a lot?"

"Brett," Carmen corrected him.

"That's what I said."

"No, you said Brad." She stopped shoveling. "And of course I think about him."

Shy wished he could see her eyes so he'd know how much sadness was there. Words didn't tell you anything compared to someone's eyes.

"We were supposed to get married in, what? Like two months? Now I don't even know if he's alive."

Shy pushed his shovel into the earth, thinking about the crack in Carmen's voice. It seemed important. After a long silence he stopped and looked up at her. "Brett's alive," he heard himself say.

Carmen wiped her face with the sleeve of her jacket. "Don't be a *chingado*, Shy."

"I'm serious," he said.

She was quiet for a few seconds. "And how would *you* know?"

Shy shrugged, though he was pretty sure she couldn't tell in the dark. "I just got this feeling he's okay."

As Shy went back to digging, he made a decision. He would never wish something bad on this guy—Brad or Brett or whatever his name was—because if you tried to land a girl on the back of someone else's misfortune, it made you a punk. And Shy was maybe a lot of things, some good, some bad, but he definitely wasn't no punk.

"Thanks," Carmen told him after a long pause. "Even if it's not true, it means a lot that you'd say that, Shy."

He acted like he was too busy digging to hear her.

11
Burying the Dead

An hour later, the four of them were standing over the ditch Shy and Carmen had dug, staring down at the decomposing bodies of the two young girls they'd just carried awkwardly out of the motor home. The bodies lay side by side now, illuminated by the flashlight Carmen aimed into the grave, her silent tears falling onto them.

Shy's eyes were dry, but something in his brain had snapped. He couldn't stop thinking about what they were doing. Burying two innocent kids who'd been shot by their dad so they no longer had to suffer.

Shy felt sick to his stomach. Because he knew it wasn't just these girls, it was thousands of kids, all across the state. Kids like his nephew, Miguel. All of them dying horrific deaths because of a disease created in a lab. A disease created to make a pharmaceutical company billions of dollars.

And who was the mastermind of it all?

Addie's dad.

Mr. Miller.

Shy made himself a promise as he stared down into the grave. If he ever came face to face with Mr. Miller again, he'd put his ass in a grave, too. After making him suffer. Even if it meant being thrown into prison for the rest of his life. Even if it meant the electric chair. It would be worth it. Someone had to make him pay for what he'd done.

Shy was seething now, as he watched Shoeshine reach down into the grave and take one of the little girl's hands. The man gripped her cold palm between his two big, leathery black mitts and kissed it. He sucked on all of her fingers, one at a time. And then he began to hum.

Shy frowned and turned to Carmen and Marcus, who seemed just as baffled as he was.

The melody wasn't anything Shy recognized, but it was simple and sad and made him think of church hymns—though Shoeshine had told them on the sailboat that he wasn't the least bit religious.

As Shoeshine circled back through the song a second time, Shy found his vision getting blurry. He wiped away a tear on his cheek before anyone could see it. Maybe it was the sadness of the song. Or the sight of the girls piled together. Or the putrid smell coming off them in waves. Maybe it was the accumulation of all this and everything else he'd witnessed since boarding the cruise ship so many weeks ago.

He was seventeen.

Not yet a man because he was too soft. Because he still allowed everything to penetrate his skin. Because he didn't know how to suppress the crazy images circling inside his head.

Soon Shy found himself humming, too. He did so quietly at

first. Blending his voice underneath Shoeshine's so that only he himself could hear it. And he pictured Mr. Miller. And Addie. And the feeling of revenge. But soon he was humming louder.

Carmen turned to look at him.

He didn't meet her eyes thinking she might laugh at him. She didn't laugh, though. She began humming, too.

So did Marcus.

The four of them crouched in the small yard, behind the ruined DMV building, humming down into a homemade grave where two dead girls lay.

Instead of feeling corny, the sound of their collective voices felt calming. Like Shy could breathe again underneath all the darkness.

At the end of the song, Shoeshine scooped both hands into the pile of loose soil Shy and Carmen had left, and dropped a handful onto the two small corpses.

Shy kneeled down beside him and scooped some soil of his own. He paused for a few seconds to glance at Carmen. Then he let the dirt pour through his fingers, into the grave.

12

Reports from the Wreckage

DJ DAN: . . . that we have guests from the other side, but tonight we're fortunate to have a young woman named Cassandra—though she wants to be clear that this is only an alias. She's also speaking into a voice-altering device, isn't that right, Cassandra?

CASSANDRA: No one can ever find out about this. [*Pause.*] You can just call me Cassie.

DJ DAN: Cassie. Good. As most of you already know, this satellite station is scrambled outside of California. Why? Because if the rest of the population learned how horrific conditions are here in California, the negative reaction could be enough to derail the government's current strategy of isolation. But a few people, like Cassie, manage to find us on the Deep Web, an unregulated layer of the Internet. [*Pause.*] Cassie, before you reach out to your friend, I'm hoping you can answer a few questions for us.

CASSANDRA: I can't stay on here very long. [*Pause.*] But okay.

DJ DAN: Great. Because this is a rare opportunity for me and my listeners. [*Pause.*] Now, from what we understand, this newly erected border runs from Mexicali, Mexico, all the way up to Madras, Oregon. Is that right?

CASSANDRA: That's what I heard.

DJ DAN: And it's armed with military personnel?

CASSANDRA: The part where I am is.

DJ DAN: And you're speaking to us from just east of this border, in Avondale, Arizona. Is that correct?

CASSANDRA: Exactly. I'm in Friendship Park, where all the scientists are. [*Pause.*] But I won't be here much longer, actually. I'm planning to cross over with a group that's starting a bus passage.

DJ DAN: So it's true. Some people are crossing over to help. Crossing over illegally, I might add.

CASSANDRA: There are a lot of people doing it. People want to help.

DJ DAN: In spite of the disease.

CASSANDRA: Exactly.

DJ DAN: Well, we can certainly use all the help we can get. We're not getting it from the government, that's for sure. [*Pause.*] Do we know if scientists are getting any closer to a vaccine? Have they replenished the treatment drug yet?

CASSANDRA: They mostly keep that stuff off the news, so I'm not sure. [*Pause.*] But I will say this. A ton of money has been raised for research. I've heard stories about regular people donating their entire life savings.

DJ DAN: We understand little shantytowns have started popping up along the border. Do you know anything about that?

CASSANDRA: They're on both sides. Here it's scientists, like I said. And military people. And some rescue workers. Relief helicopters come and go all through the day. On your side there are tents lined up on the other side of the river. I guess it's people trying to get as far away from the disease as they can.

DJ DAN: The river Cassie's referring to is the Agua Fria. It's usually dry, but the earthquakes caused it to fill again.

Can you confirm for us, Cassie, that all bridges going over the river have been destroyed?

CASSANDRA: I'm pretty sure. [*Pause.*] Is it okay if I say the message for my friend now?

DJ DAN: Yes, of course. I'm just trying to give my listeners a better understanding of what's going on. As I said, it's not often we talk to someone on your side.

CASSANDRA: It's just . . . I can't stay on much longer.

DJ DAN: I understand. Now, please, your message.

CASSANDRA: Okay. [*Pause.*] Also, I have to explain it in a story, so it won't make much sense to anyone else.

DJ DAN: Whatever you need to do.

CASSANDRA: Okay. [*Clears throat.*] So once upon a time there was this boy. And there was this girl. And they went to a beach, separately, and went swimming in the surf. Separately. But while they were out there, the tide forced them together and they started talking. At first they didn't get along at all because of their differences. He was one thing, and she was pretty much the opposite.

The more they talked, though, the more they got to know one another. Eventually it got so they stopped noticing the waves breaking all around them. Or how strong the tide was. Or how much the water temperature had dropped. I'm not saying it was, like, true love or whatever.

I'm just saying something happened between them in those waves. Something important.

The girl knew that once they got back to the beach, the spell would be broken. The boy would rejoin his friends, and the girl would rejoin hers. Because society doesn't allow two people from opposite worlds to exist in the same one. [*Pause.*] Maybe that's the main problem with this country, actually. That two people can end up so separate in the first place. Anyway, they talked for hours and hours, but eventually they were pulled to shore by a man. A sort of lifeguard, you could say. And just as the girl expected, the two were immediately yanked in different directions. Even when they talked, they couldn't really *talk*. And then they ended up so far away from each other that talking became impossible. But the girl never forgot about the boy.

DJ DAN: And she started looking for ways to reconnect, is that right?

CASSANDRA: Actually, no. [*Clears throat.*] She knew that part was impossible. But she needed to warn him about something. [*Pause.*] Have you ever heard of an old brand of shoe polish called Shinola, sir?

DJ DAN: Shinola. I have, actually.

CASSANDRA: Well, back when these two were in the water together, the boy told the girl a story about this shoe polish. At the time, the girl said it was the saddest story she'd ever heard. Which it was. But once she left the beach, she discovered something much worse. A group of people she knew wanted the Shinola brand off the market.

DJ DAN: You've lost me, Cassie, but I trust your friend has understood—

CASSANDRA: There's one last thing, sir. These anti-Shinola people . . . they know about the sailboat. And they know about the letter. It's important for the Shinola company to understand two things: I have the missing page. And not every government helicopter is there to drop off food. . . .

Day 45

13
Protection

Shy woke up on the dog-hair-covered rug, next to Carmen's cot, aware only of a smoky smell and a subtle rocking of the motor-home floor.

His first thought: another earthquake.

Or an aftershock.

He climbed to his feet and looked around. The bright curtains told him it was morning. Nothing from the shelves had fallen. The flat-screen TV was still mounted on the wall. But there was smoke creeping out of the heating vent in the wall.

Shoeshine hurried past him toward the kitchen.

Carmen was still curled up, sleeping. Marcus was passed out against the opposite wall holding his battery-less radio.

When Shy heard something outside the motor home, he

quickly turned toward the window. It sounded like some kind of engine. A *motorcycle* engine.

"Shoe!" he barked. "You hear that?"

Shoeshine continued rifling through the cupboards beneath the kitchen sink, sifting through buckets of cleaning supplies, opening and closing the fridge, the silverware drawer.

"Is it those bikers we heard about?" Shy said, aware of the fear in his voice. He swallowed hard and made a move for the kitchen window, but Shoeshine snatched him by the wrist.

"Keep away from the windows!"

The look in Shoeshine's eyes told Shy they were in deep shit.

Carmen was up now, too, eyes darting all around the motor home. "What is it?" she kept repeating. "What's happening?"

Marcus pressed his palms against the motor home floor. "It's another earthquake!"

"No earthquake," Shoeshine said, shooing Carmen off the cot. "And stay away from the windows, you hear?" He flipped the mattress, ran his hands along the seams, then dropped it back on its frame and broke for the bathroom.

Shy hurried behind him, remembering the two kids in shower caps he'd seen when they first discovered the motor home. They must have told somebody. The Suzuki Gang. And now they were outside.

"What are you looking for?" Shy called out to Shoeshine.

The man ripped open the shower curtain, revealing the bloody tub. The smell. But no bodies. "Gotta be another cartridge somewhere," Shoeshine muttered to himself. "Or some other weapon. He believed in protection."

"Who?" Shy said. "You still have the gun, right?"

Shoeshine gave Shy a blank look. Then he moved toward the medicine cabinet and flung it open and brushed all the small tubes and bottles onto the floor. He stood there, staring at them.

Shy's heart was in his throat.

What if the Suzuki gang came in after them?

The motor home was rocking more dramatically now. Like they were trying to tip it over. And there was smoke creeping along the bathroom ceiling, making it hard to breathe.

Shy now realized what Shoeshine was looking for. If a gun held six bullets, and each dead body they'd found in the bathroom accounted for one shot, including the dog, the gun Shoeshine had was down to one bullet. He was looking for ammo.

A loud blast came from outside.

The sound of glass shattering inside the motor home.

Shy spun toward the main cabin. Someone had shot out one of the windows. He dove to the floor just as he heard a second shot. And he huddled there with Carmen and Shoeshine, the three of them staring at each other wide-eyed.

Marcus appeared in the doorway, out of breath. Frantic. "There's four of 'em. On motorcycles. They got gas masks and a blowtorch."

"I said stay away from the windows!" Shoeshine barked. He grabbed Marcus by the collar and yanked him to the ground. "Best listen to me, boy!"

"They're trying to set us on fire!" Carmen shouted. She grabbed Shy's arm, pulled him toward the bathroom door on her knees. "We can't stay here!"

Shy held his ground, watching Marcus slam his fist into the wall, watching Shoeshine stand and close the cabinet door, then turn suddenly toward the toilet. The man lifted the plastic cover off the tank and tossed it to the floor. "Here!" he shouted, reaching into the tank.

Shoeshine pulled out a dripping-wet metal box and set it on the floor and tried opening the thing, but it was locked. Another shot rang out. Shoeshine stood again, holding on to the sink, and kicked down onto the small metal lock, but all he did was dent the lid.

Someone pounded on the front door. Shy craned his neck so he could see into the smoky main cabin. One of the curtains had caught fire. Even if there were more bullets in the metal box, he didn't see a way out. He turned to tell Shoeshine, but he was too spooked to form words.

Shoeshine brought down two more powerful kicks, deepening the dent. A fourth kick stripped the lock off the front of the box, and he fell to his knees, opening the lid and sifting through the contents.

Shy watched him toss away a loaded money clip, a few pieces of jewelry in ziplock bags. Shoeshine then stood up, clutching an odd-looking black discus.

"That's a Blackhawk knife!" Marcus shouted.

"How's a knife gonna help?" Shy said. "They got guns! I thought you were looking for bullets!"

Carmen scooped up the bag of jewelry and the money clip, then thought better of it and tossed them back down.

Shoeshine hit a button on top of the discus and a thick, curved blade shot out the front. "When I tell you to run, you run!" he shouted, pushing the blade back into its sheath and moving through the bathroom door.

Shy held on to the hall walls, his heart thumping, as the four of them crab-walked back into the smoke-filled main cabin, coughing and trying to breathe. He saw where the windows had been shattered, glass all over the rug, two jagged holes in the opposite wall.

At the closet, they hastily put on their shoes. Their beanies and jackets. They slipped their arms into the straps of their backpacks, Shy eyeing the thick layer of smoke at the ceiling and the flames licking at the drapes.

As Shoeshine carried the duffel bag toward the peephole, Shy closed his eyes for a second, pleading to God, or anyone. This couldn't be it. They'd just gotten back to California. He still needed to see about his family.

Marcus was right, they had to explain what was in the duffel bag. Maybe they could barter the vaccines for their lives.

Shy grabbed Carmen by the elbow, told her: "Stay with me."

She nodded.

"No matter what."

Her terrified eyes gave him a small shot of courage. If he focused on protecting her, he'd worry less about himself. Just like on the sinking ship. Shy pried Carmen's fingers from the closet door and had her hold on to his backpack instead.

"Which way we supposed to run?" Marcus said.

Shoeshine turned to them. "Always east. And don't look back." Then he grabbed Shy by his jaw. "Something happens, you get this where it belongs. That's your priority. Nothing else."

Shy took the duffel bag and tried to nod into Shoeshine's grip.

The man let go of his face and handed him the knife, too. "Toss me this when I tell you."

Shy looked down at the heavy disk, his heart slamming against his chest. Something tremendous would be expected of him. He was sure of it. And what if he failed? Shy glanced at Carmen, who was sucking in short, gulping breaths. Marcus stood against the wall, coughing wildly into the shoulder of his jacket.

Shy spun back to Shoeshine just in time to see him pull out the handgun and kick open the front door.

14
The Suzuki Gang

Shoeshine leaped onto the back of the closest man, both of them tumbling to the dead grass. The man let out a howl as Shoeshine wrestled him onto his stomach, delivered two quick blows to the guy's mask and pressed the muzzle of his gun against the back of the man's skull.

"Back away!" Shoeshine called out to the rest of the bikers. "Or else I'll kill this man dead!"

Shy crowded into the motor home doorway next to Carmen and Marcus, his eyes darting all over. There were four of them, like Marcus had said. Two off their bikes, beside the motor home— one holding a blowtorch, the other near the rear tires, a handgun by his feet. A third man was still sitting on his motorcycle, a rifle resting in his lap.

All of them, including the man Shoeshine had pinned to the lawn, were wearing leather jackets and leather pants and military-style gas masks, the kind that hid their faces.

"Get him off me!" the man underneath Shoeshine shouted, his voice muffled by his mask.

"Jenkins, do something!" the man with the blowtorch called across the yard.

"We're not sick!" Marcus yelled.

Shy had to explain the vaccine. They could hand over four syringes and still have three left. But everything was happening so fast. The man on the motorcycle, Jenkins, suddenly lunged forward on his bike and stopped, trying to intimidate Shoeshine. He raised the barrel of his rifle.

"Drop it!" Shoeshine shouted.

Shy gripped the knife and the duffel bag, scared out of his mind. He knew he should be doing something more, but he felt paralyzed.

When the guy on the bike inched closer, Shoeshine ripped off his hostage's mask and tweaked the man's head so that his veiny brown neck was fully exposed. He pressed the gun against the man's temple, and the man gave a deep, guttural growl.

Marcus and Carmen stood in front of Shy, staring. Their mouths hanging open, chests heaving.

Shy spied the man near the motor home inching toward the gun on the ground.

"You were warned about moving zones!" the motorcycle guy shouted through his mask.

"Everyone was!" the man with the blowtorch added.

"Drop it!" Shoeshine warned. "Or your friend dies!"

"He's *already* dead!" the rifleman answered.

Shy watched in horror as the guy cocked his rifle and shot his own man right in the chest. Blood sprayed Shoeshine's clothes and face as he ducked behind the limp body to avoid a second shot.

Carmen screamed.

Shy grabbed her and they crouched in the doorway, next to Marcus, hardly breathing.

Shoeshine raised his gun above the body in his arms and fired a shot of his own, at the man on the motorcycle. His lone remaining bullet. It burrowed into the rifleman's gas mask, painting it bright red. The weapon fell from the man's hands, and he toppled over the back of his bike, onto the grass.

Shoeshine turned his gun on the two men by the motor home, ordering them not to move.

Shy stood up.

Flames were now leaping off the far side of the motor home. The dead man's motorcycle was still running, though it lay useless on the ground. Shy, Carmen and Marcus cleared out of the hot doorframe, onto the grass, looking at one another in silence. Shoeshine kept his gun aimed at the two remaining men while he slid out from under the body he'd been using as cover.

When Shy saw one of the men make a move for the gun on the grass, he flipped open his knife and charged without thinking. Swiped at the man's arm just as he lunged for the weapon. The knife gashed the man's leather jacket at the forearm, and Shy felt the blade sink into flesh.

The man quickly pulled back, holding his arm and cursing Shy.

"He said don't move!" Shy shouted, kicking the gun away. He reached down to pick it up and tossed it to Shoeshine, shocked by his own actions but pretending confidence, his breaths going in and out and in and out.

Shoeshine held both guns now, though one was out of bullets. He glanced at Shy again, then at the duffel in Shy's hand.

Shy hurried back to Carmen and Marcus and stood there nervously, looking all around. At the flames climbing the side of the motor home, and the dead bodies in the grass, and the blood splattered across Shoeshine's face. The man he'd just gouged who was holding his arm. Shy clutched the duffel. It was up to him to get the vaccine out safely.

"We're here to protect you," one of the men mumbled through his mask. "Can't you *understand* that?"

"Not everyone wants your kind of protection," Shoeshine answered.

The other man lifted his mask and cried, "Look at Jenkins, man! He shot Jenkins in the face!"

"We're not even sick!" Marcus shouted again.

"You don't know that," the first man answered. "It's everywhere now. Our only hope is if everyone remains in their zones."

Shoeshine turned to Shy, Carmen and Marcus and said: "Go now. Stay together."

"What about you?" Carmen said.

"I'll catch up."

"Why can't you just come with us?" Marcus wanted to know.

"I said go!" Shoeshine shouted.

Shy slung the duffel bag over his shoulder, and the three of them hurried away from the motor home.

Before they rounded the half-collapsed DMV building, Shy turned to get one last look at the surreal scene. Two bodies on the ground, dead. The motor home in flames. Shoeshine holding a gun in each hand, both aimed at the remaining men whose faces were hidden by gas masks.

And then they were past it. Running east. Fast as they could down a narrow, buckled street.

Toward the rising sun.

15
Someplace Safe

Shy, Carmen and Marcus raced through the maze of destruction they found in the first major intersection. Deserted cars. A wrecked big rig jackknifed in the center divide. A flipped-over FedEx truck with all its doors flung wide open and a grotesquely bloated face framed in the windshield.

Shoeshine knew what he was doing, Shy told himself as they rounded the big rig. He wanted Shy to get the duffel bag as far away from those Suzuki guys as possible. To be safe. Then he'd catch up. It was all part of his plan.

Still.

Shy had a sick feeling as they cut down the narrow road on the other side of the intersection. How could they leave Shoeshine behind? He'd saved their lives on the island. And he'd sailed them all the way back to California on a boat he'd fixed himself.

You don't leave people like that.

But what if they *order* you to?

Just put it out of your head, he told himself.

And run.

The early morning was quiet aside from the subtle hum of a few distant helicopters. And their shoes hitting the pavement. And their furious breathing. But then Shy heard something else.

Another motorcycle.

He looked back, still running, watching the thick smoke rising off the burning motor home. Watching a helicopter several blocks away just hovering there as a man pushed out supplies attached to a rope. Based on sound alone, he worried the bikes were headed toward the DMV. And Shoeshine.

Shy spun back around to tell Carmen and Marcus they had to go back, but just then a man in a suit and no mask stepped right into their path. He held up his hands and called for them to stop.

They tried to sprint right past him, but at the last second the man reached out and grabbed Carmen by the arm, jerking her back. "You have to come with me!" he shouted. "I can help!"

"Yo, get off her!" Shy shouted, marching back toward the man.

Carmen ripped her arm free just as Shy lunged at the man, cracking him in the side of the face, the impact jarring Shy all the way to the bone.

The man hit the deck. Hard.

Shy stood over him, fists still clenched, daring him to move.

Carmen pushed past Shy and kicked the man in the legs.

"What are you doing!" Marcus shouted, pulling Carmen away. "He's a priest!"

The man looked up at them, cowering slightly and holding the side of his face.

Shy refused to budge. No way was he going to let someone put his hands on Carmen. He didn't care *who* it was. But he also saw what the man was wearing. Black suit jacket over a clerical collar. Nicked-up briefcase on the pavement beside his feet.

"Please, I can help," the man said. "Those men have been terrorizing anyone they see on the road for weeks. It's not right."

"You really a priest?" Shy asked.

The man nodded and sat up. "I'm the pastor at Saint Augustine's," he said. "Or I was, anyway. My church burned down after the earthquake."

Marcus helped the man to his feet, apologizing.

Shy and Carmen apologized, too, though Shy still didn't trust him. He didn't trust *anyone*. Not all the way. Even if the guy did seem like a legit church person.

"I can take you someplace safe," the pastor told them.

"Where?" Carmen asked.

"A psychiatric clinic across from the hospital." The man picked up his briefcase. "I've got several people staying with me already. No one's sick, I promise."

Shy eyed the man, skeptically. "Why? What's in it for you?"

"He's a priest, dumbass," Marcus said. "He's *supposed* to help people."

"What about Shoe?" Carmen said.

Shy peered back down the street. What would happen when that new motorcycle guy found two of his own men dead? Shoe-shine couldn't hold off *everyone*.

Marcus nudged Shy to get his attention. "We gotta go with the pastor. To regroup and shit."

"How would Shoe find us?" Carmen said. "We can't just leave him."

"Aren't we splitting up anyway?" Marcus asked.

"Not before he gets *this* back," Shy said, holding up the duffel. "Or else it's on us."

"You ever think maybe that was his plan all along?" Marcus raised his eyebrows at Shy. "To pin that shit on us?"

Shy shook his head. "Shoe's not like that."

Marcus glanced up at a helicopter flying overhead and then turned and spit on the pavement. "That shit back there," he said, rubbing his eyes. "It's got me all messed up, man."

Shy watched the pastor pull three hospital masks out of his briefcase. "How far'd you say this place was?" he asked.

"Just over the freeway," the pastor answered, holding out the masks. They were still wrapped in plastic. "Put these on. They'll protect you from the disease."

Carmen and Marcus waved him off, but Shy took one, figuring it would help him deal with the smoke near the motor home.

"Why aren't *you* wearing one?" Carmen asked the pastor.

"I have my faith."

"Let's go with him," Marcus said again. "Get off the street for a minute. Me and Shy can go out looking for Shoe later."

Carmen turned to Shy.

He shrugged, thinking he should at least stay with them part of the way. "Let's go, then."

They followed the pastor east, around fallen power lines and wrecked cars, past cracks in the pavement so wide they had to leap across them. But Shy couldn't shake the sick feeling in his stomach. Before they even reached the end of the block he asked the pastor: "So *where's* this place again?"

"A few more blocks east," the man answered as the four of them continued moving at a brisk pace.

"I know," Shy said. "But what's the address?"

The pastor pointed ahead. "See what's left of the freeway up there? We're on the other side, right across from the Brotman Medical Center."

Shy could now see that the freeway overpass had collapsed in the earthquake, leaving a mountain of rubble. He stopped in his tracks and called out to Carmen and Marcus: "You guys go. I'll meet you there."

Before anyone could argue, Shy spun around and took off back the other way. He heard them shouting things at his back, especially Carmen, but the sound of the wind whipping past his ears made it impossible to make out what she was saying.

16
Rules Don't Apply

Shy cowered when he heard a loud explosion.

He ducked behind an empty SUV, less than a block away from the DMV building, and stayed hidden there for several seconds, listening to the crackling fire and trying to think. It had sounded like a bomb, which made him flash back to when the LasoTech ship had launched a flurry of napalm missiles at Jones Island. But this couldn't have been an actual bomb.

He stuck his head out to study the dark plume of smoke lifting into the blue sky. The motor home gas tank must have blown. And last he'd seen, Shoeshine was right in front of the thing. Shy secured the hospital mask over his nose and mouth and took off running.

He'd only made it halfway around the DMV building when he was nearly run over by two gas-masked men racing away from the blast on a single motorcycle. One appeared to be badly injured. The driver looked directly at Shy through his gas mask but didn't stop.

Shy watched them speed away, then hurried around the building, toward the smoke and heat, where he saw Shoeshine and two bikers in a standoff. They were fifteen yards apart, the motor home behind them engulfed in flames. A handgun and rifle were aimed at Shoeshine, and Shoeshine moved a single handgun back and forth between the two gas-masked men.

"Put it down!" one of them demanded. "There's no way out!"

Shoeshine didn't answer. His hair had been singed in the explosion. His clothes, too. Shy saw that the jacket material up and down the man's left arm was glistening in the light of the fire.

Blood.

"Drop it!" the other man shouted in a familiar-sounding accent. He was Mexican. And Shy could tell he'd shown up later, because his gas mask was green instead of black. His leather jacket was torn at the right shoulder, like he'd been shot, too, though he was still using that arm to hold his gun. "Drop it or you're a dead man!"

"Which one will I take with me?" Shoeshine called out over the raging fire.

Shy searched the ground for a weapon.

There was another handgun lying in the grass, but it was too far away. He'd be spotted. And what if it was the one without bullets? Instead he lifted a chunk of cement from the crumbling base of the DMV and crouched there, sucking in breaths through his mask, sweat dripping in his eyes from the intense heat.

"You don't get it, do you?" the first biker shouted. "We're the only ones doing anything! No one on the other side cares if we live or die!"

Shoeshine moved the gun between the men in silence.

Shy cursed himself when he remembered he still had the duffel bag. The vaccine. He should've left it with Carmen and Marcus. He set down the chunk of cement, his whole body shaking, and pulled off the duffel and his backpack. He hid them behind the scorched bush he was using for cover.

He hadn't looked away for more than a second when he heard the guns suddenly go off in a chorus of loud pops. He looked up in time to see two bodies drop to the dead grass.

One of them was Shoeshine.

"Shoe!" he shouted.

The biker who remained standing glanced over his shoulder at Shy, beady eyes framed in his green mask, then set off toward Shoeshine, raising the barrel of his rifle.

Shy lifted his cement chunk and ran at the man, heaving it with every ounce of strength he had left. The cement spun in the air several times before cracking the man right in the back, just as his rifle discharged. The shot burrowed into the earth as the man stumbled to his knees.

Shy fell, too, tripping over a fallen motorcycle.

He gathered himself as quickly as he could and looked up. The biker was already on his feet again, marching toward Shy now, aiming his rifle.

Shy scanned the grass around him frantically, looking for some other form of defense. But there was nothing. He looked up into the barrel of the rifle and froze. Eyes bugged. Fear slicing cold through his veins.

He didn't want to die.

Not like this.

Not before he'd made it home to his family and given the ring in his pocket to Carmen.

The biker cocked the rifle, said: "You think the rules don't apply just 'cause you're a kid?" He was standing directly over Shy now, finger on the trigger, breathing loudly into his mask. "Huh? Answer me, boy!"

All Shy could do was shake his head no.

He glanced at Shoeshine, still on the ground behind him, cupping a hand over his upper thigh. Blood shining bright through his fingers. With his other hand he was reaching for the gun he'd just fired, but it was out of reach.

No one was going to save Shy this time.

The biker pushed down Shy's hospital mask with the barrel of his rifle, and Shy squeezed his eyes tight and held his breath, waiting for the sound that would end his life.

But all he heard was the crackling of fire . . .

And the whir of distant helicopters . . .

After a few long seconds Shy slowly opened his eyes and looked up.

The man was standing there wide-eyed, like he'd just seen a ghost. Shy watched him lower his rifle until it slipped from his grip and fell to the grass.

At first Shy thought maybe he *had* been shot.

Maybe this was death. You didn't even know it right away. But then he reached a hand up to his chest and found that he was still breathing.

The biker mumbled something through his mask and picked up his rifle and let off several rounds straight up into the sky, cursing in Spanish.

A sense of relief slowly came over Shy.

The man couldn't kill a kid.

It was too much for his conscience.

"Get up!" the man shouted.

Shy got up.

"Are you sick?"

"No."

"You been around anyone who was?"

Shy thought about Rodney and all the other sick people on the island. "No."

The biker glanced at his men on the ground, unmoving, then barked at Shy: "You're going to the Sony lots, you hear me? Ask for Gregory Martinez."

Shy glanced at Shoeshine. Still lying there, holding his thigh. Watching.

"That's where you're gonna stay until this thing's over," the biker said. "Understand?"

Shy nodded, though he didn't understand anything at all. Except that his life had been spared. Which was all that mattered right now.

The biker scooped up the duffel bag from behind the bush, carried it toward the one motorcycle still standing.

"There's nothing in there!" Shy shouted.

He glanced at Shoeshine again, then lunged for the duffel. But the biker shoved him away easily and unzipped one of the pouches near the seat on his bike. Instead of stuffing the duffel inside the pouch, though, like Shy was expecting him to, he took a thick manila envelope out of the pouch and slipped it into the duffel. Then he zipped up both bags and tossed the duffel back to Shy.

Shy held it to his chest, watching the biker check the pulse of the man Shoeshine had just shot, then climb back on his bike and start the engine. He revved it a few times, staring down Shoeshine. "You were lucky this time."

Shoeshine just sat there, staring back at him.

After a few uncomfortable seconds the biker turned to Shy and called out over the growl of his engine: "Who you asking for at the lots?"

Shy's mind was a blank.

"Gregory Martinez," the biker told him again. "You gonna remember that?"

Shy nodded.

"Once you're inside, you stay there till it's over." He touched around the rip in his shoulder, staring at Shy, then kicked his bike into gear and darted away.

Shy waited until the motorcycle was completely out of view before hurrying to Shoeshine. He dragged the man as far away from the enflamed motor home as he could, asking: "You hurt bad?"

Shoeshine shook his head.

The blood on his arm wasn't his. Shy could tell because there was no bullet hole. The blood seeping out of the man's thigh wound, though, was pulsing through his fingers. "Tell me what to do," Shy pleaded. He sounded like a scared little kid. Because that's what he was. A boy. It's why he was still alive. "Can you make it to a hospital?"

Shoeshine grabbed Shy by his face and pulled him down so that their eyes were only inches apart. "What'd I tell you to do?"

"Me?" Shy's mind went blank again. "Lemme go, Shoe."

"I said take the duffel and leave," Shoeshine barked. "Don't look back."

"Yeah, but—"

"And here you are," Shoeshine said, pushing Shy's face away.

Shy retrieved the duffel bag and his backpack. He was still terrified from having a gun in his face. But now he was confused, too. He'd just saved Shoeshine's life. That had to count for something. But all the man seemed to care about was the stupid vaccine.

"Shit doesn't make any sense," Shy said, keeping a few feet away from Shoeshine this time. He held up the duffel. "Why you willing to risk your life for this? You don't even like people."

"Doesn't matter what I like or don't like," the man a
Some of the anger seemed to drain from his face.

"For once in your life," Shy said, "could you just give
straight answer? Seriously, why do you care so much?"

Shoeshine shook his head, his eyes burrowing into Shy's
"There *are* no answers, young fella. Let alone straight ones." He
took a breath and let it out slowly, his eyes still on Shy's. "This
is the path I've found myself on, that's all. And I aim to see it
through."

17
Behind the Curtain

It took Shy a few seconds to figure out he could use the hood of the minivan beneath him as leverage to boost Shoeshine. He glanced down at the steep stretch of freeway rubble once more, then squatted, positioning his right shoulder underneath the man's good leg. "Ready?"

Shoeshine gripped a thick metal stake protruding out of the concrete, and Shy came out of his crouch, lifting the man an inch at a time, up to the jagged ridge above them. It was their final hurdle in a long and torturous climb, though, and Shy had nothing left. His strength was tapped. And soon Shoeshine's weight was coming back down on him.

"Shit, hang on." Shy paused in an awkward squatting position, staring down at the van, wondering how the hell he got here. Just weeks ago he was living a normal life, in a normal city, surrounded by normal people. Now he was carrying a mysterious old black man on his back over a fallen freeway.

Through the cracked windshield he could see the top of a woman's head. Long gray hair crusted with dried blood. He and Shoeshine had come across at least a dozen such corpses during the climb. Bodies twisted in the rubble. Bodies trapped in cars. Bodies flattened between massive chunks of concrete. All of them giving off the same nauseating smell of decay. He wasn't sure how much more he could take.

Shy took a deep breath and drove with his legs again, boosting Shoeshine back up near the lip of the ridge. This time the man was able to roll over the side, onto the flat, wide stretch they'd been working toward for more than an hour.

Shoeshine reached down for Shy's hand.

Shy pushed off a warped guardrail, slowly pulling himself up. He managed to hook a leg onto the ridge and hoist himself over the edge, where he rolled onto his back and lay still for several seconds, pulling in deep breaths, the duffel bag safe by his side.

He closed his eyes, picturing the scene back at the motor home again. It still didn't make any sense. Why had he and Shoeshine been spared? Was it simply that the man in the green gas mask had a conscience? That he took pity on them? Because Shy couldn't come up with anything else.

He sat up, adjusting the hospital mask around his neck.

They were surrounded by dozens of empty cars, some with the driver's-side doors left wide open. Shy looked out over the fallen city from above. A surreal sight of collapsed buildings, far as the eye could see. Cars flipped on their hoods or crushed by debris. Wide chasms where the earth had been ripped open at the seams. Entire neighborhoods torched by fire.

In the bright blue sky, two birds chased each other playfully, seemingly unaware of the destruction. Shy watched them, understanding that the life he'd once known was gone for good. All those mellow days at school. The pretty girls moving through the halls, sometimes stopping at his locker to flirt. All those never-ending Sunday hoop sessions at the Otay Mesa Y with his boys. And when he got back to his apartment, how he'd find his mom sitting at the kitchen table doing bills, her news program playing quietly on the radio behind her.

All that was in the past.

It didn't exist anymore.

"You see it, don't you, young fella?"

Shy turned to Shoeshine, surprised to find him sitting up with a slight grin on his face. The man had been in bad shape during the climb. He'd lost all his "old-man strength," and his partially burned clothes were soaked with blood and sweat.

"See what?" Shy asked.

Shoeshine thrust his strangely untouched chin beard out toward the view. "Cities like this are built so that we can pretend to understand the logic of things. So we can pretend meaning and order and authority. But it's all a fiction."

Shy looked out over the city again, confused. Shoeshine rarely gave opinions, and when he did, they came out in riddles that made Shy feel ignorant, like he needed to read more books.

Shoeshine wiped sweat from his forehead with the back of his wrist and went on. "But sometimes we're given a glimpse behind the curtain. Like now. Here is your inconsequence, she is telling us. Here is your eternal solitude."

Shy nodded, thinking how this wasn't the best time for some deep philosophical discussion about natural disasters. They still had to get back down the other side. And Shy was the one who'd have to do all the work.

"Let me ask you, though," Shoeshine said. "What happens when the ground you stand on begins to shift?" He waved a hand at the view. "Who will open their eyes to it? Who is humble enough to look beyond his own flesh?"

Shy shook his head, starting to feel a little weirded out. Shoeshine sounded like he was high or something. And his eyes were locked on Shy's with an intensity Shy had never experienced, like the man was searching for something important, something pure. And now that Shy thought about it, hadn't Shoeshine *always* paid special attention to him?

But why?

He was just a regular kid.

Shy wished he could tell the man to quit wasting his time. But he didn't know how to put it. And what if he was wrong? What if Shoeshine searched everyone he met in this same way?

Instead, Shy turned away, telling the man: "I don't even know what you're saying anymore."

"Not in here, maybe," Shoeshine said, tapping the side of Shy's head. "But in *here* you do." He jabbed a finger into Shy's chest. "There are two kinds of people in this world, young fella. Those who can sit in the loneliness of existence and those who turn away. Long before that first wave hit our ship, I knew which you were. I've been watching all along, son."

Shy shook his head, dismissing him. What did Shoeshine mean about sitting in loneliness? It didn't even make sense. And why had he called Shy "son"? Nah, they were both just tired and hungry. That was all. And they were scared. Or maybe this was the kind of crap people always wanted to talk about after getting shot in the leg.

But soon Shy found himself picturing something. Back when he was floating alone in the middle of the ocean. Minutes after their cruise ship went down. He remembered the feeling of nausea he'd had staring out over the immensity of what he could see. Nothing but water and more water. And how it whispered to him as he floated there, lost. No idea what swam beneath his feet or how he might survive.

Maybe that was what Shoeshine meant.

The nausea.

How overwhelming the world could seem when you were thrust into the guts of it. How little power you realized human beings actually had compared with the earth.

"Come on," Shy said, climbing to his feet and slinging the duffel over his shoulder. He held out his hand and helped the man up. "We gotta find someone who can help with that leg."

Shoeshine shook his head. "Just get me some supplies. I can take care of it myself."

Shy glanced down at the man's blood-caked pant leg. "We'll see," he said, knowing Shoeshine needed an actual doctor.

Before they started toward the other side, Shy studied the view of the ruined city one last time, trying to see it like Shoeshine. As something more than what it was. A part of him genuinely wanted to be the person Shoeshine believed him to be. But all Shy saw was an endless stretch of unfathomable damage, same as before.

18
Reunion

It took even longer to climb down the other side of the collapsed freeway, but as Shy half carried Shoeshine through the first major intersection, he spotted the hospital. The pastor was telling the truth. Shy felt relieved. And he was anxious to link back up with Carmen and Marcus. This was the longest they'd been apart in over a month.

His first thought was to go directly to the hospital and look for a doctor. Shoeshine was in even worse shape now. He could barely keep his head up. And he no longer answered when Shy tried to get him talking. But then Shy noticed the psych ward across the street. And he remembered the pastor saying he was using it as a safe haven. Maybe someone inside would know what to do.

Shy struggled to get Shoeshine across the wide, vacant street and then sat him down against the side of the building. "You're gonna be okay," he said, trying to catch his breath. He cupped his hands against the glass doors and peered inside. The reception area was empty, and both doors were locked. He pounded the glass, calling Carmen's name, then stood there waiting, his left hand wrapped tightly into the duffel bag straps.

They were on an industrial street, where the damage didn't seem quite as bad. The psych ward had suffered only a few busted windows on the upper floors. The hospital across the street looked okay, too. Only the far right side had caved. Then Shy noticed all the red circles spray-painted on the outer walls of the first floor. There were sick people inside.

Shy pounded the glass again. "Carm, come on! It's me!"

A few seconds later, he saw her through the glass, coming toward him. His chest swelled.

She paused to undo the lock, then flung open the door and hugged him. He was about to ask if everything was okay when Carmen pushed away and slapped him across the face. Hard.

Shy reached for his tingling cheek. "What the hell?"

"Don't you ever bail on me like that again, *pocho*," she said, waving a finger in his face. "I'm not playing."

"Jesus," Shy said.

"That's *pura miedra*, and you know it."

"Fine," he said. "But you don't gotta slap me."

"That's the thing, I *do*." Carmen pulled Shy toward her for another short, firm hug, before shoving him away again. "Or else your dumb ass won't listen."

"I had to help Shoe," he said.

They both looked just as the man began sliding down the wall, onto his side. Shy reached out quickly and grabbed Shoeshine's head before it cracked against the sidewalk.

Carmen covered her mouth. "What happened?"

Shy sat Shoeshine back up and held him there. "He got shot."

"Shot?" Carmen kneeled down in front of the man, trying to balance his head straight against the wall. "Shoe, can you hear me?" She shook him by the shoulders, then gave him a little slap on the cheek.

Nothing.

"Why you keep slapping everyone?" Shy said.

"I'm trying to wake him up, asshole."

"I'm saying, there's better ways to approach shit."

Shoeshine's eyes had rolled back in his head. His hand had fallen away from his thigh, too, and through the rip in the blood-caked jeans, Shy could see the nasty bullet wound, the jagged flesh around it clotted with dark blood. He reached down quickly to cover it up, but he could tell by the look on Carmen's face.

She'd already seen it.

19
A Scientific Prediction

After stashing the duffel, Shy paced back and forth in the crowded conference room, studying the group of random strangers hovering over Shoeshine. Some were from the other side. Do-gooders who'd crossed over to try to help Californians. The others were people the pastor had "rescued" after finding them wandering the streets without an established zone.

The pastor claimed they were treating Shoeshine's wounds to prevent infection, before removing the bullet from his leg. But Shy didn't feel very confident. Of the eight people spread out around Shoeshine, none were actual doctors. The closest was the large bearded man who claimed to have been a vet assistant back in Colorado.

Shy stopped pacing long enough to look over the bearded man's shoulder. He was now pushing a needle into a small vial.

"What's *that?*" Shy demanded. "I thought you were getting the bullet out."

An older Asian woman turned around. "He has to numb the leg first."

"Everything we're using comes straight out of a package," the pastor tried to reassure Shy. "There's no threat of Romero Disease. It's all perfectly sterile."

Carmen tugged at Shy's arm. "Come on. There's nothing you can do."

But Shy didn't want to leave until he knew Shoeshine was going to be okay. The man looked so vulnerable lying there on the long wooden conference table. His wild hair partially burned. Eyes rolled back. Shoeshine had been their rock, the one they'd looked to since back on the island. What if he didn't make it?

Then a more selfish thought occurred to Shy.

Who would take the vaccine to Arizona?

The pastor held Shoeshine's legs as the fake vet drove the long needle into the man's dark skin, just above the knee. "Jesus," Shy said, turning away.

Carmen tugged on his arm harder now, guiding him away from the crowd. "I'm taking you out of here," she told him.

Shy looked back at Shoeshine one last time before allowing himself to be led out of the room.

In the small office kitchen Shy wolfed down pretzels and cookies out of huge Costco bags, washing each mouthful down with long gulps of bottled water. He felt guilty feeding his face while Shoeshine was laid up with some vet assistant digging around in his wound, but he couldn't stop. It felt too good to eat and drink as much as he wanted.

"They know the disease is spreading through water now," Carmen said. "But here's the freakiest part. According to what we just heard on Marcus's radio, scientists think it could eventually go airborne. And if that happens . . . *everyone* could get it. Even people outside of California. We'd be the only ones left."

Shy pictured a strong wind blowing the disease across his street back home, into his building, into his mom's lungs.

"Marcus is in the tech room," Carmen said. "He finally got batteries. They're all sitting around his radio, listening to some DJ."

Shy nodded.

"It all comes down to the vaccine, Shy."

Shy pushed away the pretzels. "We're still going home, Carm."

"I know, but how?"

Shy shook his head, thinking about the vaccine. And the letter. Shoeshine. "Those people working on Shoe," he said. "They're here to help, right?"

Carmen nodded.

"'Cause here's what I'm thinking. If Shoe can't go on—"

"It doesn't automatically have to fall on us," Carmen interrupted. "Right?"

"Exactly." Shy took a last sip of water and re-capped the bottle. He didn't want to acknowledge that Shoeshine might not be able to continue. But he'd also seen the man's wound up close. And it's not like he was being worked on by a real doctor. "If a group of them agrees to do it, we're free to start heading for SD. No matter how long it takes."

Carmen nodded, but she looked concerned.

"What?" Shy said.

She shook her head. "When you went over the freeway, you saw the city, right?"

Shy uncapped the water again but didn't drink. "It's bad, I know."

"What if it's like that back home, too?" Carmen said, her eyes glassy. "What if everything's gone?"

Shy pictured a massive pile of rubble where his building used to be. He knew there was a possibility the whole trip was pointless. That there was nothing left. But he couldn't think that way.

Just then he heard shouting coming from down the hall. He slid off the table and pushed open the door to listen.

"Get off me!" a man shouted.

Shy spun back to Carmen. "That's Shoe! Come on!"

20
No Return

Shy cringed watching Shoeshine bite down on a thick leather strap and reach a pair of metal tongs into his own bloody thigh. The man growled in pain as he dug around for the bullet, the veins in his neck bulging, spit bubbling between his lips.

"Why's *he* doing it?" Carmen shouted.

The bearded vet assistant spun around, pointing at the bloody gauze shoved up both his nostrils. "This is what I got for trying to help."

"He just slugged Bill," someone else said.

Shy pushed through the crowd and went to Shoeshine. "What are you *doing*, man? They're trying to help." When Shoeshine didn't acknowledge him, Shy turned to the pastor. "I thought you numbed his leg."

"All we had was Novocaine," the pastor said. He squirmed,

watching Shoeshine continue digging. "And that's a bullet wound."

"Yo, he needs a *real* doctor!" Marcus was now in the conference room, too, holding his radio. He went and stood near Carmen.

"They're all at the Sony lots," a blond woman said. "But they're not letting anyone else in."

"Unless you have a lot of money," someone called out.

"What about the hospital?" Carmen asked.

"The last doctor fled *weeks* ago," the pastor answered.

As people continued talking over each other, Shy turned back to Shoeshine, who was in so much pain sweat was pouring down his face. But Shy was also thinking about the Sony lots. If he was remembering right, that was where the biker had told him to go.

"Someone do something!" Carmen shouted over Shoeshine's growling.

"He won't let us near him," the pastor said.

And Shy remembered the biker slipping a manila envelope inside the duffel bag. He moved over to where he'd stashed it, kneeled down, unzipped the top and pulled out the envelope. He looked up, saw Carmen was watching him.

Shy unfolded the top of the envelope and peered inside.

His eyes widened.

Thick stacks of twenty-dollar bills. The biker gave him *money*? Why?

Shoeshine was shouting even louder now. Shy spun back in time to see the man lift a bloody bullet out of his thigh with the thin, pointy tongs, then drop it into a metal pan on the table beside him. Everyone cringed and turned away, including Carmen and Marcus.

Shoeshine spit out the leather strap, panting, and grabbed a stack of gauze. He shoved it against his open wound, slid off the table and started pushing people out of his way.

"Shoe, hold up!" Shy shouted, stuffing the envelope back into the duffel and hurrying toward the door. He positioned himself between Shoeshine and the exit. The guy looked awful. "What the hell you doing? You need rest."

Shoeshine shook his head. "No, I need to sew myself up."

Shy spun to the group. "Can someone at least help him do *that*?"

They all looked at each other. "We don't have sutures here," the pastor said. "And the wound is too deep for the Dermabond we *do* have."

"Everything we'd need is across the street," someone said.

"Why isn't it here?" Carmen demanded.

Nobody answered.

Shoeshine tried to push past Shy, saying: "I know what I'm looking for." But he was weak from all the pain, and Shy easily blocked him.

Marcus was there now, too, pushing back Shoeshine by his arms. "Tell us what you need and *we'll* go." He turned to the pastor, asked: "How do we get inside?"

"It's not locked," the pastor answered. "But you don't want to go in there."

"Why not?" Shy said.

"The hospital's out of the question!" the bearded man shouted. "It's a breeding ground!"

"You'll be infected for sure," someone said.

"Nah, man," Marcus said. "That shit can't touch us."

The bearded man stepped forward. "Fine. Go, then. He needs a suture kit and more Betadine. And gauze. Your best bet is ER."

Someone tossed Marcus a hospital mask.

"But understand," the bearded man added, "we can't allow you to return."

Shy shrugged.

Marcus grabbed him by the arm. "Let's go."

Shy tossed the duffel to Carmen. "Look in there when we're gone." He pulled up his mask. "We'll pound the door when we're back. And you and Shoe can meet us outside."

Carmen set down the bag. "I'm going with you."

"We got this," Marcus told her.

"Why, *pendejo*? 'Cause I'm a girl?" She made a move for the door, but Shy cut her off.

"We need someone to stay with Shoe," he insisted.

Carmen scowled but didn't argue.

"Look in the bag," Shy told her again. Marcus pulled at his arm.

Shy readjusted his hospital mask as the two of them raced through the hall. They cut through the reception area, kicked open the front doors, and Shy found himself moving back out onto the street.

21
Breeding Ground

The smell inside the hospital stopped Shy in his tracks. It was a violent mix of cleaning chemicals and rot. Shy held his hand over his mask and tried breathing through his mouth for a few seconds, but that didn't work either—the smell was so strong he could taste it.

He knew there'd be bodies inside. The sloppy red circles spray-painted all over the front of the building told him as much. But this was different. The smell was a hundred times more intense than the motor home.

How many people had died in here?

How long had they been dead?

It was pitch-black, too. Shy couldn't see two inches in front of his face. He reached into his backpack for his flashlight, clicked it on and moved his thin beam of light around what looked to be a large admission area. Someone had covered all the windows with newspapers, which explained why it was so dark.

Shy turned to Marcus, who was gagging behind his mask. "Ready?"

Marcus nodded, pulling out his flashlight, too. "Get this shit over with," he mumbled.

They shined their beams of light along the walls and floor and ceiling as they slowly moved deeper into the hospital, past the main admissions desk, into a large open area where the smell grew even stronger. Shy suffered a coughing fit so violent he was afraid it might end with his lungs spilling out onto the floor. He was only able to calm his stomach by taking long, even breaths, in spite of the smell.

There were four hallways to choose from, and he and Marcus shined their lights on all the signs until they found the ER. As they started in that direction, Shy began noticing large, random shapes. They were all around him, in the middle of the tile floor and half hidden under desks and crowding the entrance of the hall he and Marcus were moving toward.

Bodies covered with sheets, he realized.

The dead.

They stepped over a blockade of them and continued down the hall, toward the ER, but curiosity got the better of Shy and he stopped near one of the bodies. He kicked off the sheet and shined his flashlight onto the bloated and rotting face of a young woman. A nurse, judging by the green scrubs she was wearing. Dark red eyes. Big chunks of her cheeks torn away. A pointless silver cross still hanging around her decaying neck.

Shy thought he heard something back in the main lobby, a loud thumping sound, and he spun around, listening. When he didn't hear it again he turned to the nurse and tried to kick the sheet back over her face with his foot. But he couldn't do it. He had to reach down, trying not to gag, and use his hand.

He stood up, wiping his palm on his jeans, and breathed slowly into his mask. "You heard that back there?" he asked Marcus.

Marcus nodded. "Let's grab what we need and get the fuck outta here."

They had to climb over a small pile of bodies near cardiology. Shy's head was spinning. He kept thinking of what Shoeshine said about the loneliness of life. Maybe he was right. Every corpse here was wrapped in its own sheet. Completely alone. And in real life it wasn't much better. They stuck you in a coffin and buried you in the ground. Or they cremated your ass and stored you in a jar.

When they passed pediatrics, Shy couldn't help himself. He stopped. Because this was different. He pushed open the door that led to the kids' part of the hospital and peeked inside.

"Bro, come on!" Marcus barked.

Shy ignored him, shining his light around the room, illuminating smaller bodies, stacked on top of each other, in every corner of the large reception area. Each one covered by a single white sheet. The smell so intense he felt wobbly. He held on to the doorframe to keep his feet, his stomach dropping out completely, like the one time he'd ridden a roller coaster.

All these little kids, dead.

From Romero Disease.

Which meant LasoTech.

Shy saw a glass wall across the room, and he knew instantly what it was.

The newborn room.

Babies.

A surge of energy bubbled inside of him. He threw open the

heavy door and started slamming his shoulder into it, battering the thing against the cinder-block wall, again and again, until the door began to sag to one side because he'd busted the top hinge.

He ripped off his mask and leaned over and vomited onto the black-and-white tile floor. He heaved and spit and heaved some more, then wiped his mouth with the mask and chucked it away and grabbed his aching shoulder.

When he turned back to Marcus, blurry-eyed and still on his knees, he was surprised to see Carmen standing there, too, wearing a hospital mask and gripping the duffel bag. She must have made the sound he'd heard earlier.

She hadn't listened to him.

Because Carmen didn't listen to *anyone*.

"We can't go home," Shy told her.

"I know," she answered.

He watched tears start coming down her cheeks. "No, I mean we have to go to Arizona," he said.

Carmen nodded and held out her hand to help him to his feet. He stood and turned to look at the glass wall once more. Where they kept sick babies.

"Shy, let's get out of here," Marcus mumbled through his mask.

"Shoe gave me five minutes to come get you," Carmen said, pulling Shy toward the broken door by his wrist.

They were right. The sooner they found Shoeshine's suture kit, the sooner they'd be done with this place. And then they could start east. Get the vaccine to these supposed scientists in Arizona. Shoeshine had been right all along. It was what had to be done. It was the journey they'd found themselves on.

Home would have to wait.

Shy took the duffel from Carmen. But instead of leaving, like he wanted to, he found himself moving deeper into the room.

Toward the glass wall.

Toward the babies.

Carmen was behind him, shouting his name. Grabbing for his arm. Marcus was shouting, too. But Shy couldn't stop.

He had to see behind this curtain, too.

He had to know the worst of what LasoTech had done.

22
Reports from the Wreckage

DJ DAN: . . . Ben Vasquez, a photojournalist joining us from Blythe, California, near Arizona. Ben, you crossed into California several weeks ago to do one story, but you soon became consumed by another, is that right?

BEN: Two others, actually. And they overlap. [*Pause.*] A few days after the earthquakes, the *New York Times* asked me and a small crew to do a story on the damage and the early recovery efforts. We spent five days compiling video footage in places like Orange County and downtown LA and San Bernardino, but when my crew and I tried to arrange for a refuel, so we could helicopter out, we were told that was no longer an option. Anyone who'd set foot on California soil since the earthquakes had to stay put until a vaccine was distributed. And we were told about the border going up.

We were furious, of course. And devastated. Our families were back home, waiting for us. Not knowing what else to do, we continued working. But our focus soon shifted, like you said. We kept meeting different groups of people who'd crossed the border, into California, to try to help. The media has been referring to them as "crusaders." And it's these crusaders who've helped us track the other story we're drawn to: the progress of scientists working on a treatment.

DJ DAN: And what are you hearing?

BEN: Nothing to report in terms of a vaccine, I'm afraid. But there's been a lot of talk lately about a viable treatment drug. Multiple pharmaceutical companies claim to be experimenting with a pill that will not just mask the symptoms of Romero Disease but eliminate the disease altogether. Over the course of time.

DJ DAN: This is very exciting news. And you believe they're close?

BEN: That's what we keep hearing. Of course, even after the drug exists, it still has to be approved and distributed. And like I said, we're talking about a treatment, not a vaccine.

DJ DAN: It's still very exciting. Now, why don't you describe these crusaders for my audience?

BEN: Sure. The initial wave arrived directly after the earthquakes. They mostly consisted of government groups like the Red Cross and FEMA and the National Guard, as well as a number of media groups, like my crew and me. We were responding to the earthquakes and were totally unprepared for the rapidly spreading disease. We're estimating that nearly a third of my wave has died from the disease.

The second wave was mostly organized, too, but they were no longer affiliated with the American government. Not directly, anyway. These crusaders snuck into California illegally, fully aware that they wouldn't be allowed back. They've proven incredibly helpful, as you know, bringing in food and medical supplies and radio equipment—they've even smuggled in weapons for people to use as protection. We recently met with one group that's started up a bus route in the middle of the desert. They assist anyone wanting to travel to and from the border. Another group helps organize self-sustaining communities just west of the border in Avondale.

A third wave began emerging a couple weeks ago. These groups are much more politically motivated. They're horrified by the government's decision to cut off California and parts of Oregon from the rest of the country, and their sole focus is protest. The majority of their demonstrations take place east of the border, but a few have actually crossed over to protest from the California side. They've done an amazing job creating awareness.

DJ DAN: But not all of these groups are here to help, is that right?

BEN: Unfortunately, a much smaller fourth wave has emerged. These people don't believe a vaccine will be enough to stop the spread of the disease. Especially if it goes airborne like a few kooky scientists are predicting. These guys enter California and parts of Oregon in four-wheel-drive vehicles carrying an arsenal of weapons, wearing full dry suits, sometimes breathing through oxygen tanks. Their objective is to raze everything within twenty miles of the border, including camps full of people. Most of these groups are still in the desert, near the border. But we're afraid some may start moving west.

DJ DAN: The point is, not all crusaders are here to help.

BEN: Oh, no. Some have come to kill. . . .

Day 46

23
Good News, Bad News

Shy stood near the far window, stripped down to his *chones*, peering across the empty trailer at Carmen and cursing himself. It was about the least appropriate time to be drooling over a female, but that's exactly what he was doing.

Asshole!

She sat on a plastic folding chair, wearing nothing but the bra and panties she'd swiped from the sporting goods store. She was trying to cover herself with her arms and her long, wavy hair, but she could only hide so much. Little stretches of her beautiful brown stomach were still visible, including the patch of words tattooed just below her belly button. Shy was too far away to actually read the tattoo, but he imagined it was something deep. Some philosophical saying or passage from a poem that he'd understand on a *way* deeper level than some punk-ass, prelaw fiancé.

Shy glanced at the armed guard beside him, who was wearing a full-on dry suit and gas mask.

After Shy, Carmen and Marcus left the hospital the previous night, where the only suture kits they found in the ER were empty, the pastor had tossed Shy keys to a storage facility a few blocks away, and that was where they'd spent the night. In a large, roach-infested concrete cubicle, surrounded by some random person's boxed-up belongings.

They passed the long, sleepless night mostly in silence. Shoeshine sweating bullets and holding his wounded leg. Shy picking away at one of the extra pockets Shoeshine had sewn into the gut of the duffel bag, then pulling out the comb-over man's letter and rereading it another fifteen, twenty times, concentrating on the missing page that he was sure had the rest of the vaccine formula. Carmen and Marcus listening to some DJ reporting on the types of crusaders who'd come into California.

When they'd stumbled into the Sony lots in the morning, Shy asked the men in the security shed for Gregory Martinez, like he was told to, and he handed over the envelope of cash. A few minutes later, Marcus and Shoeshine were led to an emergency tent, and Shy was stripped down to his boxers, across the trailer from Carmen, with some doctor taking a blood sample to test for Romero Disease.

It was over an hour before the head security guy finally came back into the trailer, this time without his gas mask on. He had a shaved head and wore thick-lensed glasses. He was Mexican, and Shy assumed the rest of the security guards were too, based on their accents. "I have some good news and some bad news," the man said, looking mostly at Shy. "Why don't we start with the good. None of you tested positive for Romero Disease."

Shy and Carmen glanced at each other, Shy trying to keep his eyes above her neckline. "What about the bad?" he asked.

The man crossed his arms and leaned against the wall near the door. "Here's the deal: we're already over capacity. And Gregory says the medical attention your friend requires would be an additional charge. After he's stitched up, I'm afraid we're gonna have to let you go."

"Are you serious?" Carmen barked, still covering herself. "We just gave you almost five grand."

"That's all we got," Shy pleaded. They needed to get inside. Their plan was to try and get on the radio show they'd discovered the night before and tell their families where they were. It would also give Shoeshine a full day to recover after getting fixed up.

"I'm sorry," the man said, pushing off the wall.

Carmen scoffed and turned to Shy. "Wasn't it one of those Suzuki guys who told us to come here in the first place?"

"Exactly." Shy turned to the man. "How do you think I knew to ask for Gregory Martinez?"

"See, you got that part wrong," he answered. "The lots aren't run by the Suzuki Gang. We're our own operation."

"The three of us only wanna be in there for *one* day," Carmen said.

The man smiled. "Once you got inside, you'd want to stay. Believe me."

Carmen shook her head. "One day. Swear to God."

Shy glanced down at the duffel by his feet, another idea suddenly coming to mind.

A second security guard came to the door with a large towel. The man in the glasses took the towel and tossed it over to Carmen. "To cover yourself," he said.

"What about trades?" Shy asked.

The guard turned to look at him. "Trades?"

"Like, what if I have something that's worth a lot of money? Would you take that instead of cash?"

The man stood there, thinking.

It was a steep price to pay for just one day, but they didn't have a choice. The radio DJ was supposedly inside these gates. And they needed to make sure Shoeshine was healthy enough to keep going. And maybe they could fill their backpacks with food and water before starting their long journey.

"I'd have to ask Gregory," the man said. "But if you have something of legitimate value . . . I don't see why not."

Shy kneeled to unzip the duffel. He grabbed the sparkling diamond ring and held it up for the man to see. "This is the real thing, man. Look at all these carats. It's probably worth ten, fifteen grand at least."

The guard walked over and took the ring from Shy. "How do we know it's not a fake?" he asked, checking it out.

"Used to belong to this superrich oil guy," Shy said. "Trust me, he wasn't buying no fakes." He glanced at Carmen, who was staring at the ring, too.

The guard seemed impressed. "Tell you what, I'll check with Gregory. If he likes what he sees, you're in. If he doesn't, I'll come back with your clothes and we can agree to part ways."

"He'll like what he sees," Shy assured the man.

He and Carmen watched the guard leave the trailer. Carmen then turned to Shy and said: "Was that what I think—?"

"I didn't steal it," he said, cutting her off. "Swear to God, Carm. He gave it to me right before he went overboard. I don't even know why."

Carmen had been with Shy when he saw the ring for the first time on the cruise ship. The oilman was showing it off on the Lido Deck, bragging to everyone who would listen about how many carats it was and how he was going to spring it on his girl at dinner. Except he never got the chance. Later that night the tsunami hit. And the ship went down. And the oilman somehow ended up on the same broken lifeboat as Shy and Addie.

"Why didn't you tell me?" Carmen asked.

Shy shrugged. "Never really thought about it, I guess."

"You never *thought* about it?"

Shy shrugged. It was a straight-up lie, of course. He'd thought about it a *million* times. But in his head it was always some big storybook moment. Them making it home and finding everything still perfectly intact. Everyone hugging each other and their moms crying. And in the celebration he'd kneel down and slip the ring onto Carmen's finger, and everyone would cheer and do a toast and say it was a perfect match.

Carmen adjusted her towel, shaking her head.

Shy's heart sagged. He didn't even know why. "I just hope it's enough to get us in," he mumbled.

The guard returned a few minutes later with four tied-up plastic grocery bags. "More good news," he announced with a grin. He tossed the first bag to Carmen, then the other one to Shy. "Gregory has agreed to the trade. Get dressed. You guys are in."

Shy gave a thumbs-up to Carmen as they both untied their bags and reached in for the jeans and white T-shirts they'd been given. But he was pretty bummed at the same time. Not only had he given away his good-luck charm, he'd given away the only thing of value he would ever be able to offer Carmen.

24
The Sony Lots

Shy followed Carmen, Marcus and the guards through a tall brick tunnel into the mouth of the property, where they were met by another group of people, including a man named Darius, who introduced himself as their guide. Darius wore a slightly soiled suit and tie, and a fedora. "Whatever you need during your time here," the slender man told them, "I'm your guy."

He then led them through a tour of the massive grounds.

Shy was blown away by what he saw. There was a large, open grassy area, only partially burned, where at least a hundred people sat around on plastic folding chairs, watching a group of kids chase around a soccer ball. On one side of the grassy area were several three-story office buildings covered in yellow caution tape. The buildings sagged, and many of their windows had been blown out. But on the other side of the field there were two large trailers pushed together and perfectly intact. This was the cafeteria, Darius explained.

As they moved deeper into the property, Darius told them how the Sony lots had functioned before the earthquakes. Scenes from movies and TV shows were shot here. The property was split up into a number of different lots, all operating independently, under the Sony umbrella. And each lot had a vastly different look and feel depending on what was being shot.

Shy stared into what Darius called the Wild West lot. It had an actual barn and stables and tumbleweeds and scorched bales of hay. He couldn't believe how elaborate each detail was. The Las Vegas lot was the same way. The front half was a fancy casino with slot machines and gaudy sculptures and bars with fake bottles of alcohol stacked in pyramids. Inside there were rooms with heart-shaped hot tubs and mirrored walls and ceilings.

The entire property was dedicated to little make-believe worlds—even now that the cameras were turned off and everyone else in California was living like squatters. Shy recalled what Shoeshine had said about people hiding from reality. This was a perfect example. Maybe that's all TV was, a place to hide.

Darius showed them the rest of the East Wing, which included the Coffeehouse lot, the Bowling Alley lot, the Cruise Ship lot, two different Police Station lots and the Haunted Swamp lot. Three lots had been destroyed in the earthquakes and were marked off with caution tape, but the rest had suffered only minor damage and, according to Darius, were open to all residents.

Eventually the man led them to a large collection of trailers lined up behind the cafeteria. They were the kind movie stars hung out in while they waited for their scene. Darius keyed open one of the trailers in the back row and said it was where the four of them would be staying.

"Just a couple simple rules," he said, standing in front of the door. "One: basic foods and bottled water are distributed twice a day in the cafeteria. There are three different rotations to cut down on crowds. You'll be part of the B rotation. Because we have generators, a couple times a week there will be a hot meal. We have to conserve like everywhere else, but we do our best to make residents feel comfortable."

A *hot meal?* Carmen mouthed to Shy.

He shrugged, trying not to get too excited. They would only be here for a day, and he was pretty sure there wouldn't be any hot meals in the desert.

"Two," Darius continued, "residents are free to explore any of the various lots unless we've either cautioned them off or we're using them for our children's programming."

"Children's programming?" Marcus asked. "You got these kids out here playing Twister?"

"You'd be surprised," Darius said, grinning. "The parents here, they don't want their little ones to know how bad things are. The more this place feels like summer camp, the better."

"So what do *you* get out of all this?" Shy asked.

Darius turned to him. "Well, for one thing I'm a whole lot safer. That disease out there is a bastard, man. And we got doctors who test every single person who sets foot inside this place. We're about as close to untouchable as you can get."

The hospital's pediatric ward flashed through Shy's head again. He couldn't shake it.

"But it's an investment, too," Darius said. "Me and all the staff, we were working here when the earthquakes hit. The bigwigs—the actors and producers and business-type people—they all took off, but a bunch of us security guards saw it as a business opportunity. So we stayed and fixed the place up, best we could. At first we charged a small amount to people who'd lost their homes. But when the disease started spreading . . . that's when *everyone* wanted to stay here. And we upped the price. And let doctors in for free if they agreed to practice their medicine in here."

"But what good is money now?" Carmen asked.

Darius paused for a few seconds. "Look, eventually this thing's gonna come to an end. It *has* to. And when that happens, we'll be sitting pretty. And if it doesn't . . . shit, I'll be dead anyway, right?"

"Speak for yourself," Marcus said. "I plan on *survivin'*, bro. No matter what kind of shit gets in my way."

Shy looked around the rows of trailers. He knew they were lucky to get a day inside these walls, where they were safe. But he still felt weird about giving up his ring. What would happen if things really *did* go back to normal? Would it end up in a pawn-shop somewhere? Would one of these security guys give it to *his* girl?

Shy met eyes with Carmen for a sec before turning away.

"One last thing," Darius said. "Try and stay away from the perimeter. We've had a little trouble with outsiders recently."

"What kind of trouble?" Shy asked.

"They've thrown over a few glass bottles," Darius said. "And a brick. Stuff like that. One guy shot out a camera lens in one of the lots. Just keep your eyes open is all I'm saying."

Shy wasn't surprised. While the people in here were pretending it was summer camp, everyone on the outside was struggling just to survive. *Of course* they hated the Sony lots.

"Anyway," Darius said, clapping his hands together, "my guys left you a small welcome gift inside. And you'll find four pads with pillows and blankets—"

"One more question," Shy interrupted. "Where's that DJ guy's studio? We heard you can go on his show and tell your family where you are."

"You mean DJ Dan," Darius said.

Shy nodded.

"See, a lot of people get that mixed up," Darius said. "DJ Dan broadcasts his show out of the Sony Records building, which is a couple blocks north of here."

Shy's heart dropped. Aside from getting Shoeshine medical attention, DJ Dan was the main reason they'd come here.

Darius motioned toward Marcus's radio. "I'm glad you mentioned that, actually. We ask that residents not listen to that show out in the open. A lot of folks . . . Like I said, they don't want to think about what's actually happening out there."

Shy felt like collapsing onto the ground. Giving up. Nothing had gone right from the second they'd landed in California. And now he'd handed over his ring for *nothing*.

But he didn't collapse. Even collapsing would take too much effort. Instead he reluctantly followed Carmen and Marcus up the three steps that led to the trailer door Darius was holding open.

"Smells *amazing*," Carmen said.

The scent hit Shy as soon as he stepped inside. He looked around the narrow trailer. It was empty aside from four thin pads lying on the floor, four sets of bedding and four steaming bowls of chili.

"Your welcome gift," Darius said, wearing a big smile.

"Are you shittin' me?" Carmen said, looking to Shy.

He shrugged, still stuck on the DJ and his ring.

"Enjoy," Darius said, stepping out of the trailer.

Before the door clicked shut behind the man, Carmen and Marcus were squatting over their bowls, shoveling spoonfuls of chili down their throats.

Shy watched them for a few seconds, trying to think up a new plan to find the DJ. But his hunger cramps got the best of him, and he went to his chili, too.

25
Man Behind the Mask

Shy cracked open his eyes, wiping the drool from the side of his mouth. He sat up and looked around, surprised he'd actually fallen asleep. Carmen and Marcus were *still* out cold. Shoeshine was in the trailer now, too, sitting against the far wall, writing in his journal. The duffel bag, which Shy had carried in with him, now lay open by the man's feet.

The sun was already setting. Shy didn't see how that was possible. It wasn't even noon when they'd arrived at the trailer. The post-chili plan had been to go outside and talk to people, gather information, find out about the other Sony building and if there were any trains running east. It wasn't to fall asleep.

Shy went over to Shoeshine. "They fix you up okay?" he asked in a low voice.

The man lifted his pen from the page and looked up. "One night of rest, young fella, and I'm good."

"That's what the doctors told you?"

"That's what I told the doctors." The man went back to writing.

Shy shook his head and glanced at Carmen and Marcus. He'd have to explore on his own. "If they ever come out of their comas," he told Shoeshine, "tell 'em I'll be right back."

Shoeshine nodded without looking up.

Shy spoke to a few people on the fringe of the crowded lawn, but nobody knew much about the outside world. Some even asked *him* questions. Were people still dying? Were there really marked zones now and people on motorcycles patrolling the streets? The only useful bit of information Shy got was from a middle-aged man dressed in fluorescent-green swim trunks. Last he'd heard, one train a day still left out of Union Station downtown. Whether it ran east or not, he couldn't say. And he didn't know anything about the DJ.

Shy wandered around a few of the lots, brainstorming what he'd say on the radio. Shoeshine thought the whole thing was a bad idea, of course. But he didn't understand. If Shy wasn't going straight home, he had to at least reach out to his mom.

He explored a few of the lots, tripping out on the elaborate set pieces and camera cranes. It was amazing that a place like this even existed. On the long sailboat ride back to California, he never imagined ending up in a place where people shot movies and TV shows.

Eventually Shy found himself standing in front of the large Cruise Ship set, which sat right up against a tall barbed-wire fence that separated the lots from the outside world. There was no bottom to the ship, and the main deck was quite a bit smaller than what you'd find on a Paradise Cruise liner, but the flood of images it brought back was overwhelming.

He remembered leaning over the side of the Honeymoon Deck, losing his grip on the comb-over man's shirt, watching him disappear into the dark sea below. He remembered the man in the black suit following him around the ship, drilling him with questions. He remembered Rodney. And Kevin. Supervisor Franco. He remembered wandering past Carmen's cabin in the middle of the night, standing in front of her door, unable to knock—and then when he'd turned to leave, she opened the door and called his name.

And then he remembered the end.

Him standing there frozen in front of that Normandie Theater window, staring at the first tsunami wave as it rose and rose, right before his eyes, till it was twice the height of their ship at least, and how the air was sucked right out of his chest when the wave exploded into them, shattering windows and caving walls and sending passengers flying through the air in slow motion, and how he couldn't hear a thing.

Shy turned away from the make-believe ship, suddenly nauseated and short of breath. He kneeled down and put his hands on the concrete to try and ground himself. He was still in this position, staring at a trail of ants marching in a crooked line, when he heard a familiar-sounding whistle.

He stood and looked around.

He recognized the melody of the whistle from back home. The sound rose and fell, twice. A Mexican thing. But he didn't see anyone.

A few seconds later, he heard the whistle a second time. It was coming from behind the barbed-wire fence, he realized, and he took a few steps forward to get a better look. Trees and thick bushes mostly blocked the tall fence, but a few sections of bush had been thinned by fire and in the fading daylight Shy spotted the figure of a man sitting on a motorcycle.

His heartbeat quickened.

What if it was someone from the Suzuki Gang?

But they were separated by a fence. And it shouldn't matter anyway—it was a guy from the Suzuki Gang who'd sent him here in the first place.

"Hey, *cabrón*!" the man called to Shy in a muffled voice. "Come over here a sec! I got something for you!"

Shy's first instinct was to bail. To go back to the trailer so he could grab food with Carmen, Marcus and Shoeshine. But he took another couple steps forward instead. He noticed the guy's gas mask was green. There was a tear in the arm of his jacket, too. It was the man who'd told them about the Sony lots. The man who'd given him the fat envelope full of cash.

Shy glanced over his shoulder.

No one else around.

A tree had fallen into the barbed wire at the top of the tall chain-link fence, and Shy wondered if anyone had ever tried sneaking in that way.

"What's going on?" Shy called to the man.

The biker kicked out his stand and swung himself off the motorcycle. "I'm shocked," he said through his mask. "You actually listened for once." He went right up to the fence and linked his fingers in the chain link.

"What are you talking about?"

"You came like I said."

Shy shrugged.

So *that* was it. The guy felt like a hero for giving a kid a safe place to wait out the disease. Little did he know Shy would be back on the road in less than twenty-four hours.

"I got something you might want," the biker said, pulling off his leather gloves and reaching into his pocket. He held a balled fist toward the fence, saying: "Go on. Take it."

"What is it?" Shy was curious now, though he still wasn't sure he could trust the man.

"Come here."

"Nah, I'm good," Shy told him.

The man pushed away from the fence. "Guess I'll just keep it, then." He tossed whatever it was up in the air, caught it and held it out between his thumb and forefinger.

Shy couldn't believe it.

His ring.

He went right up to the fence. "Yo, where'd you get that?" The words came out before he even realized it.

The biker gave a muffled laugh through his mask. "I don't even wanna *know* who you boosted this off of." He lofted the ring over the tall fence.

Shy snatched it out of midair and looked over the diamond and its silver setting. It was definitely his ring. His good-luck charm. He flashed on Carmen's face as he shoved it in his pocket. Then he turned back to the man, confused as hell.

"Don't say I never did nothing for you."

"How'd you get it?" Shy asked.

The man shook his head. "I told Gregory it was bullshit asking for extra. The money I gave you was more than enough." The biker then pulled off his green gas mask.

Shy's entire body went cold.

Half the man's face had been badly burned, the skin pink and raw and scabbed. His usual bushy, Brillo-pad hair had been shaved down to the scalp, and his scruffy beard was peppered with gray.

Still.

Shy recognized him instantly.

His old man.

He took a step back, unable to wrap his head around it.

He hadn't seen his dad in over a year.

"I surprise you, boy?"

"How'd you . . . ? What are you *doing* here?" Shy's heart was hammering away at his insides. All of a sudden he was that stupid little kid again, the one who was always nervous around his own dad. Even when he had no reason to be nervous. "You shot my friend," he managed to say, rattling the fence a little.

"I shot a man who was shooting at me. Shot him in the leg, too, when I could've aimed for his chest." His dad clutched Shy's fingers through the chain link. "I've been looking for you, boy. Ever since the earthquakes hit. I even went on the radio a couple times."

Shy tried to free his fingers, but his dad's grip was too tight.

"Imagine how I felt when I lifted your mask," his dad said. "Almost shit my pants. But when I was riding away, I told myself nothing else matters now. I got my son back."

Shy looked away from his dad's intense gaze.

"Your mom told me you worked on a ship." The man shook his head. "I prayed you weren't out there when it happened. Then I thought maybe I should pray you *were*."

"I was out there."

"Well, you're here now," his dad said. "And I swear to God, Shy, I'm changed. You'll see." He looked over his shoulder at the street behind him growing darker by the minute. "I'm gonna keep you in here till this shit's over, understand? Where it's safe. Then we're gonna be together."

Shy didn't answer.

He didn't know what to do or think. He was looking into the eyes of his *dad*. His *family*. But at the same time, they were the eyes of a complete stranger. Shy had spent the past year and a half pushing these eyes out of his head. Out of his *life*. He'd stopped returning his dad's phone calls. Blocked his emails. Claimed he was busy any time his dad asked about a visit—which wasn't often.

"I'd stay in there with you," his dad continued, "but I got a few more things to do. You'd be proud of me, boy. We're out there helping people."

Shy finally pulled his hands free and took a step back. "What do you mean you're helping people?" he said, feeling a sudden surge of courage. Because *he* was different now, *too*. He'd been through the worst shit imaginable and come out the other side. "You shoot people. You try and set 'em on fire while they sleep." He sucked in a deep breath, trying to think. "You got it all wrong, man. When this shit's over, I'm going *home*."

"Home?" His dad shook his head. "Home doesn't exist no more, Shy. There's nothing left down there."

"You think you can just suddenly be my dad again?" Shy shouted. Anger was spreading all through his veins now. He kicked the fence as hard as he could, the entire length of it rattling loudly. He ignored whatever his dad was trying to imply about Otay Mesa.

"Watch your mouth, boy," the man said in his low, teeth-clenched growl, the one that meant he was close to exploding. Shy had heard this voice over and over during the year he'd spent with his dad in LA. But it didn't scare him like it had back then.

"No, you watch *your* mouth!" Shy shouted. "You ain't my dad, man. You never taught me shit. Not one fucking thing!"

His old man grabbed the fence with such force Shy thought it might come down. He looked up again, at the tree leaning against the barbed wire, worried his dad might notice it, too. But his dad was too busy trying to scare Shy into obedience. Like he always did.

"Shy?" he heard someone call out behind him. "Shy? Everything okay?"

He didn't have to turn around to know who it was.

Carmen.

"You still don't know shit from Shinola," his dad growled. "Do you, boy?"

"I know this," Shy said in a clenched-teeth growl of his own. "You don't get to tell me what to do no more." Then he turned and walked off, toward Carmen, leaving his old man standing there outside the fence, calling his name.

26
The LA Days

"But you never even *mentioned* him before," Carmen said in a quiet voice as Shy led her and Marcus along the dark path that would take him back to the Cruise Ship lot.

"Maybe he's not worth mentioning," Shy answered.

"What are the chances, dawg?" Marcus said. "Finding out your pop is part of the exact group we're trying to avoid?"

"That's what *I* told him," Carmen said.

Shy shrugged, thinking if he kept ducking their questions they'd eventually leave it alone. He wasn't in the mood to talk about his dad. Getting the vaccine to Arizona was the only thing on his mind now. That and reaching out to his *real* family through the radio show, which was where they were headed now.

At dinner they'd met a woman who'd been to Sony Records. She'd even been on the DJ's show. When Carmen asked for directions, the woman excitedly wrote them down and wished them luck. They decided to sneak in and out of the lots because, according to the lady, every time you entered through the front gates, security made you go through the same elaborate Romero Disease testing. And they didn't have time for all that.

Near the Cruise Ship lot, Shy pointed toward the tall fence. "See how that tree's leaning against the barbed wire?"

"You think we can all climb it?" Marcus asked, glancing at Carmen.

"What, you think I can't?" she barked a little too loudly. "You got serious gender issues, *ese*. Who raised your ass?"

"Chill," Marcus said, looking over his shoulder. "Damn. You want everyone to know we're sneaking out?"

"For real, Carm," Shy said.

Carmen rolled her eyes and moved toward the fence first, Shy and Marcus following close behind.

As Shy pulled himself up the rattling chain link after Carmen, he told himself to concentrate on what he was going to say on the radio show. That had to be his focus for now. Nothing else. But it wasn't long before he slipped up, started picturing his old man's burned face. How'd it happen? he wondered. And what had his old man been trying to insinuate about back home?

At the top of the fence Shy wrapped his arms around the thick tree trunk and swung his legs carefully over the barbed wire, joining Carmen on the other side. After Marcus made it over, the three of them climbed down the other side of the fence, hopped onto the asphalt and looked around.

"What now?" Marcus asked.

Shy pulled the directions out of his back pocket and studied the street names under his flashlight. "Follow me," he said, crossing the dark street.

They walked in silence, constantly checking their backs. Soon

Shy's thoughts drifted off to a particular night during his freshman year. His old man had come home drunk from the recycling plant with a smudge of lipstick on the collar of his uniform. It was obvious he'd stopped by the bar again. Probably messed with some chick. Again. Shy's mom noticed at the dinner table and knocked her water glass off the table, and it shattered on the tile floor.

The argument quickly escalated and soon they were shouting at each other. His old man pushed out of his chair, sending it to the floor. His mom screamed that this was the last time, she was done playing the fool. "Pack your shit and leave!" she shouted, shoving a finger right in Shy's dad's face.

Only this time his dad didn't make up any stories. He slapped her hand away so hard she lost her balance and fell to her knees. She looked up, tears coming down her cheeks.

Shy sat there paralyzed. Watching.

His dad shouted: "You want me to leave? Fine! I'm gone! I'm done pretending to love you!"

Shy's mom got up and the two of them stood toe to toe for several seconds, shouting each other down, Miguel bawling back in his room, Shy's sister hurrying to check on him. Shy's dad said he wasn't going anywhere, though, unless his son came with him. He turned to Shy.

So did his mom.

The only reason Shy didn't put up a fight was to protect her. If he went with his dad, maybe that would be the end of it, maybe there'd be no more fighting.

Two days later, he and his dad were handed keys to a tiny two-bedroom apartment in Mar Vista, and Shy found himself carrying boxes up unfamiliar steps, dropping them onto the stained rug of an unfamiliar living room.

It wasn't long, though, before his old man realized he didn't have time to take care of a kid. He already had a girlfriend in LA, it turned out, and he spent most nights at her place. Shy had to figure out everything on his own. What high school to attend and how to enroll and where to get groceries and how to cook enough so he wouldn't starve.

Eight months later, when his dad landed a cushy office job with the Culver City Maintenance Department, he broke the news. He was sorry, but it just wasn't working out. He was taking Shy back to Otay Mesa to live with his mom.

Shy remembered trying to act like he was disappointed.

It wasn't until he set foot back inside his old apartment, and took a whiff of the food cooking, that he realized how homesick he'd been. His grandma, who was now living there, too, gave him a hug. So did his mom and sis. Even little Miguel. They led him into the kitchen where his all-time favorite meal was sitting on the stove, waiting for him. Chile Colorado with rice and beans. A steaming stack of homemade tortillas. His grandma's famous sweet tamales for desert.

"What now?" Carmen said, snapping Shy right out of his memory.

They were standing in front of a chained glass door that said SONY RECORDS. This was it, their chance to reach out to their families. To tell them where they were.

"We just knock, right?" Marcus said.

"I guess so," Shy told him.

Carmen cupped her hands up to the glass door and peered inside. She turned and looked at Shy and Marcus, shrugging, then knocked.

Shy took a step back, waiting to see if DJ Dan would come get them.

27
Reports from the Wreckage

DJ DAN: . . . actually leaving the Sony lots by choice. Most people would give anything to be there right now. It might be the safest place in California.

CARMEN: We don't have a choice, mister. We have something important we need to do.

DJ DAN: What could be so important you'd risk your lives?

[*Pause.*]

MARCUS: We can't say.

DJ DAN: Well, I'll tell you. I have a number of listeners who'd give anything to switch places with you. [*Pause.*] But I've made my point. You've come here tonight to reach out to your families, is that right?

CARMEN: Exactly.

SHY: Thanks for letting us do this, by the way.

MARCUS: I'll go first. [*Pause.*] Oh yeah, and we decided not to use our names. But my mom knows who this is. This message goes out to her. And my baby sis, Joslin. And Auntie Dee and Vincent and Nigel and everyone else on the East Cypress block of Compton. I survived some crazy shit, y'all—Wait, can I say that?

CARMEN: Like someone's gonna bust in here and arrest you. Think about it.

DJ DAN: Go on.

MARCUS: Anyways. [*Laughing.*] Like I was saying, out of some kinda miracle I'm still here. But I wanted to let y'all know . . . I'll be home soon. Soon as we get done what we gotta do. [*Pause.*] Shit, I already been through the worst of it. You'll see my ass soon.

CARMEN: For me, it's my mom, Netty, and my two brothers, Marcos and Raul. And my fiancé, Brett. I love all you guys . . . so much. And I pray you're okay. [*Pause.*] Brett, if you're listening to this, please take care of everyone for me. Make sure they're safe. I'll be back home just as soon as I can.

SHY: I'm trying to reach out to my mom, Lucia, and my sis and nephew. [*Pause.*] We wanted to come straight home, but we can't. This thing we gotta do . . . it's real important. I'll explain later. For now, though, I just wanted to say I think about you. All the time. [*Pause.*] And I love you. And the only thing that matters is that we're all together again.

DJ DAN: Okay. Good. Now, before I let you go . . . I just need to make sure you kids understand the situation. And I'm doing this for anyone else out there who's thinking of taking to the road, too. [*Pause.*] Are you aware that a group known as the Suzuki Gang has banned all travel?

SHY, CARMEN and MARCUS: Yes.

DJ DAN: And you know that they've threatened to shoot anyone they catch moving from zone to zone?

SHY, CARMEN and MARCUS: Yes.

DJ DAN: Gas is extremely limited and unregulated. Chances are you'll be making this trip by foot. You understand this?

SHY, CARMEN and MARCUS: Yes.

DJ DAN: Not to mention that it's extremely difficult to get access to government drops when you're not in an established zone. It's very possible you'll run out of food and water somewhere along the way. [*Pause*.] And knowing all this, you're still willing to make this trip east?

CARMEN and MARCUS: Yes.

SHY: You don't understand, mister. We don't have a choice.

Day 47

28
How to Ride

"I guess all we can do now is hope they were listening, right?" Carmen said.

Shy nodded. "Or at least somebody told them about it."

"If they're even still alive, that is." Carmen ate a slice of her orange, staring at one of the fake lifeboats that were attached to the side of the fake cruise ship. The sun behind the fake atrium was just beginning to peek its head out.

Shy shrugged and rested his Styrofoam bowl in his lap while he took a sip from his water bottle.

"All those things DJ Dan told us last night," Carmen said, "did they freak you out?"

Shy nodded. "But it's not like he told us anything new."

"I guess."

Shy spooned the last bit of grainy gray mush into his mouth

and set the bowl on the ground beside him. The Sony lots' cold oatmeal tasted like ass, but he knew he needed the nutrients. As soon as the sun went back down, the four of them were leaving the lots for good and heading for Arizona. Who knew how long the supplies they'd stuffed inside their backpacks would have to last.

As Shy watched Carmen look up at a helicopter passing overhead, he fingered the ring in his pocket. It was the reason he'd asked her to follow him out to the Cruise Ship lot after they woke up. He was going to give it to her now, in case anything happened. And it wasn't some big romantic, marriage kind of gesture either. He just wanted her to have it. As friends.

Now if he could just figure out the right way to explain it.

"Uh, Shy?" Carmen said, jarring him out of his head.

"Yeah?" He shoved the ring back in his pocket.

"Is that who I think it is?" Carmen pointed down the narrow main path that ran between the various lots.

Shy stood up.

He wasn't surprised to see his old man again. Only he wasn't on the other side of the fence this time. He was *inside* the property. And instead of wearing his leather Suzuki gear and green gas mask, he was rocking a plain old Raiders T-shirt and jeans, and he was walking his motorcycle up the narrow path, toward them.

The man stopped about twenty yards away and called out: "Shy! Come over here, boy! I wanna talk to you!"

Carmen stood up, too, shouting: "That's too bad, *vato*, 'cause Shy doesn't wanna talk to *you!*"

"It's fine," Shy told her in a quiet voice.

She gave him a dirty look. "You sure?"

He nodded. Before falling asleep the night before, he'd made a decision. He needed to find out what his dad knew about back home. No matter what it was. "Lemme get this over with, and I'll come find you."

"That's really what you want?"

Shy nodded.

Carmen looked at his dad again, telling Shy: "I'll be on the main lawn if you need me."

Another helicopter flew overhead as Shy watched Carmen start back down the path carrying orange peels and Shy's half-empty bowl. She slowed a bit to glare at his old man before brushing past his bike, nearly knocking the thing over.

Shy's dad waited until Carmen was at the bottom of the path before turning back to Shy. "Just like your old man," he said with a grin. "You dig the ones with attitude." He motioned toward the Wild West lot. "Follow me."

"I'm not like you at *all*," Shy mumbled as he followed his dad.

"So, I heard you on the radio last night," his dad said, leaning his bike on its stand inside the fenced-off horse run. Behind them was a row of enclosed stables that looked too small to house an actual horse. "You aren't really thinking of leaving, are you?"

Shy shrugged. "Why you wearing regular clothes?"

"They make us check everything at the front before we come in. And then they put us through the same tests as everyone else." Shy's old man peeked inside one of the empty stables. "I can't let you leave here, Shy. It's too dangerous. And this is my second chance."

"Second chance for what?" Shy said.

"To be your dad." He turned and looked right into Shy's eyes. "Like I told you yesterday, son. Those earthquakes changed me."

Shy looked away. He focused on the inside of the stables. He'd followed his dad out here to ask about his family back home. His *real* family. Not to listen to the same empty promises his dad had been feeding him since Shy could remember.

"I've been thinking about something you said yesterday." His dad cleared his throat. "About me never teaching you anything."

"It doesn't matter anymore—"

"No, you were right," his dad said, cutting him off. "Lemme ask you this. Ever ridden a motorcycle before?"

Shy shook his head. Even though he'd rehearsed it in his head, he was nervous to ask about back home. What if his dad really knew something and it was really bad? Would he be able to deal?

"I'm gonna teach you how to ride." His dad patted the seat of his motorcycle for Shy to get on.

"Look, I followed you out here for one reason," Shy said. He cleared his throat. "What do you know about back home? Honestly, did something happen to Mom?"

His dad ignored him. "You don't wanna get on, that's fine. I'll just talk you through it instead." The man climbed on the bike and held up the key. Then he slipped it into the ignition. "First you turn the key like this. See how that red light just came on? That means it's ready to start. Gears work like this." He pointed to the thin round pedal underneath his right foot. "Down is first. Up one from that is neutral. Up from that is second and so on."

"Come on, Pop," Shy said, getting pissed.

"Hang on," his dad said. "Let me show you this first. Then I'll answer whatever questions you got."

Shy heard another engine in the distance. It sounded different than a motorcycle, though. Bigger. His dad turned toward it, too. When the sound faded, Shy said: "Let's just get this over with then."

"Being able to ride is important out here, boy. You've seen the roads." When Shy didn't say anything back, his dad added: "You don't have to decide right this second, but I've been thinking . . .

if you really don't wanna stay here, maybe you could ride with me and the guys. The shit we're doing is important, son."

Shy almost laughed in his dad's face. Did he really think Shy was gonna ditch Carmen, Marcus and Shoeshine to ride with the group of thugs that tried to set his motor home on fire? It's not that he wanted anything bad to happen to his dad. In fact, if he could, he'd sneak him one of the syringes to protect him from the disease. But at the same time, he didn't want his dad thinking they were gonna skip off together in some kind of bullshit happy ending.

"I'm getting ahead of myself, though. We can talk about that later." His dad turned to his bike again. "So once you turn on the ignition, you hold in the clutch with your hand like this, and you kick down into first gear."

As his dad went on with his little motorcycle lesson, Shy's thoughts drifted to his family back home. He pictured their faces. His mom's. His sister's. Miguel's. What would he do if he found out something had happened to them?

"Just tell me the truth," Shy finally said, cutting off his dad. "What do you know?"

The man paused, staring at Shy.

"I deserve the truth."

His dad took a deep breath and blew it out slow. "Look, I spoke to Teresa only a few hours before the earthquakes," he said. "Miguel didn't make it. He died of the disease."

Shy just stood there, staring at his dad. His body going cold. He'd almost expected this part, but it still hit him like a brick. "I thought they had him on meds, though."

His dad nodded. "I'm telling you what I heard."

Shy turned away, imagining Mr. Miller's face. Imagining how the man's expression would change if he stuck him with a knife. "What about Mom and Teresa?"

"Look, Shy," his dad said. "If you just stay here a little longer—"

"Come on, Pop," Shy said, begging this time. "Just . . . please. Tell me what you know."

"I don't know anything. Not for sure."

Shy shifted his gaze to the ground, wanting to believe that was it, but he knew his dad was holding something back. "What do you *think*, though?"

"I'll say this, okay?" His dad lifted Shy's chin so their eyes met.

Shy's ears were already ringing in anticipation. Because he could sense it. The news he was about to hear would change everything.

"A day after the earthquakes," his dad went on, "I got through to a guy I used to work with in Chula Vista on my phone. This was right before the last of the cell towers went down." He took a breath and let it out slowly. "Otay Mesa's gone, *mijo*. All the surrounding towns, too. Anyone who survived the earthquakes was wiped out by the fires." He paused. "They're all gone, *mijo*. Down there was hit harder than any other place in the state."

Shy's stomach climbed into his throat, and he kneeled down and stuck his palms against the dirt.

He pictured his mom. Dead.

His sister. Dead.

There was no longer anything for him back home. Or anywhere else. Because maybe he was dead, too.

His dad tried to pull Shy up by his shoulders. "Listen to me, Shy. We'll get through this together. Because I realized something. You're all I ever had in this world. I mean that shit honestly."

Shy stayed on his hands and knees, staring at the dirt, for several minutes. The faint sound of his dad's empty words raining down on his head. When he'd imagined this moment earlier in the morning, he saw himself shouting at the sky. And sobbing.

But he didn't do either of those things now. He just sat there, numb, his eyes out of focus.

A loud crashing sound made him finally look up.

It came from somewhere on the property.

"What the fuck?" he heard his dad mumble.

Shy then heard the loud revving of an engine. Same one as before, only closer now. Then he saw a black SUV drive right through a row of thick hedges, into the Wild West lot.

Shy scrambled to his feet.

Two men dressed in black jumped out of the vehicle on the far side of the horse run and pulled out handguns.

Before Shy could react, the men were marching forward and firing, their bullets cutting tracks in the dirt beside his feet.

29
Empty Trailer

Shy's dad shoved him onto the dirt behind the fake horse stables as shots rang out around them. Shy scrambled to his feet in a panic, watching his dad hop on his bike and kick-start the engine and motion for Shy to get on. Shy peeked around the side of the stables. The two men were advancing across the horse run. They stopped firing their weapons long enough for one to shout directions at the other. Then they split up, the leader moving toward the perimeter of the lot.

"Come on!" his dad shouted, smacking the seat behind him. "Lemme get us outta here!"

Shy's breath came in great, rapid gulps. Behind the shed was a slight hill that led to a small, barn-style house. He peered around the side of the stables again. The other man was heading directly toward them, gun raised. Shy didn't know what to do or who these people were or what they wanted. But he knew he couldn't leave with his dad.

"I said get on!" his dad shouted again. "Now!"

Shy took off up the hill instead, a few shots ripping through the trees to the right of him. He dove behind a large camera crane and lay there, sucking in breaths and looking up at the sky and listening. He heard the sound of the idling truck, and he heard his dad's bike zipping out from behind the stables, and he heard a faint commotion down near the main lawn.

The one thing he *didn't* hear was gunfire.

Shy gathered himself and lifted his head to take another look. He spotted his dad gunning it right at one of the armed men. The man fired two shots, missing both times, then turned to run just as Shy's dad barreled into him, sending the gun and the man flying.

His dad swerved so sharply he had to put a foot down to keep his balance. The gunman scrambled across the dirt for his weapon.

Shy's dad took off, but just then the other gunman emerged and shot him in the shoulder.

"Dad!" Shy shouted.

He watched his dad instinctively reach for his shoulder, causing the bike to crash right into the driver's-side door of the idling truck. He quickly righted himself and lurched forward again, busting right through the flimsy wooden fence that surrounded the lot.

A wave of relief passed through Shy as he watched his old man gun it down the path that led to the main lawn.

The man Shy's dad had hit slowly picked himself up off the ground and stood there, fumbling with his weapon. The other man was still marching toward the part of the fence Shy's dad had just toppled, firing random shots. He turned toward an older man who stood frozen in the middle of the paved path and shot him in the forehead. The old man buckled instantly, the back of his head cracking against the pavement.

Shy scurried out from behind the camera crane and took off running the other way.

He raced through a few nearby lots, no idea where to go or how to escape, until he found himself on the Cruise Ship set again, where he ducked behind a café cart. He kneeled there trying to catch his breath, trying to think. He needed to get back down to the trailers to find Carmen and Marcus and Shoeshine, but he was afraid to take the main path. The men were shooting at anything that moved. And they'd eventually make their way down to the lawn, where they'd find the greatest concentration of people.

Darius had warned them about people throwing bottles and shooting out lights, but this seemed different. These guys were trying to *kill* everyone.

Shy imagined Carmen down there somewhere, caught in the cross fire. His heart pounded inside his chest. He had to protect her.

Then he pictured his mom.

And the things his dad told him about back home.

All of it wiped out.

Which meant . . .

Shy heard a few more pops of gunfire. They sounded farther away now. He sucked in a deep breath and forced himself out from behind the cart, out of the Cruise Ship lot.

He hurried down the main path, in plain sight. He kept waiting for someone to pop out of the bushes and blast him in the back. But there was nobody.

When he got down to the main lawn he slipped behind a skinny tree and took in the chaotic scene. One of the gunmen was hunkered down behind the back wall of the cafeteria, firing shots into a screaming crowd of people running every which way. There were a few bodies motionless on the ground. The other gunman lay facedown in the grass about twenty yards from the cafeteria. He wasn't moving either. Three security guards were on the opposite side of the lawn, firing at the remaining gunman.

Shy cut through the row of caution-taped office buildings, emerging near the back row of trailers. He found his own and flung open the door and stuck his head inside, shouting his friends' names, but the trailer was empty. Even their things were gone.

He let the door slam closed and looked around, anxiously. Where *were* they? And where was his dad?

People all around him were opening and closing their own trailer doors and calling out names, some openly sobbing, others slinking by, their eyes darting all around. One man raced past Shy carrying a screaming toddler over his shoulder. Shy was about to take off in that direction, too, when he heard someone shout his name over the commotion.

He spun around and saw Marcus hurrying toward him.

"Take this!" Marcus shouted, tossing Shy his backpack. "Follow me!"

They cut through the edge of the main lawn, where the guards were taking cover behind the massive trash bin. His dad was there, too, reloading a handgun. He glanced at Shy before turning back to the remaining gunman and firing.

Marcus grabbed Shy by the arm. "This way!" The two of them raced toward the front gate.

A large crowd had gathered around Darius and several other guards who were trying to calm them down. "Trust me, people!" Darius shouted. "It's still safer than outside!"

"Shy!"

He spun toward Carmen's voice. She and Shoeshine stood

about twenty yards to the left of the crowd, half hidden behind a cluster of baby palms. Shoeshine had the duffel bag.

As Shy and Marcus hurried toward them, Shy saw a rolled-up sheet hanging down from a thick tree branch on the other side of the brick wall. "Shoe says we can use it to scale the wall!" Carmen shouted.

Shy nodded watching Marcus grab ahold of the sheet first and start climbing. It only took him a few seconds to make it to the top, where he pulled himself over the side and dropped out of sight.

Carmen went next.

Then Shy.

After Shoeshine finally made it over, still gripping the duffel and favoring his stitched-up leg, they hurried down the middle of the road, past the front gates.

At the first intersection, Shy spotted a second black SUV—same model as the one that had crashed into the lots. A trailer hitched to the back carried two brand-new metallic-gray motorcycles. The eyes of the man inside the SUV grew wide as he watched the four of them hurry by.

They ducked down a narrow residential street, and Shy kept glancing back, expecting to find the SUV on their heels, the driver leaning out his window aiming a gun at them.

But it never happened.

The street behind them remained empty.

Eventually Shy quit looking.

30
Union Station

There weren't any trains running.

That much was clear right away.

During their hour-long walk to Union Station, Shy had prayed there might be *something*. But Marcus was right, it was a pipe dream. The roof of the tall, iconic building was half caved in, and a train that had apparently crashed into the station lay wrecked on its side across several tracks.

Shy studied the sloppy red circles painted all over the walls and doors and windows. The mess of flies buzzing around the exterior. There were more bodies inside. Probably a grip of them.

He watched Carmen and Marcus approach the high arcing front doors, thinking about the last time he'd been at the station. The day his old man dropped him off at the curb with a one-way ticket back to San Diego. The station had been packed with people coming and going, wheeling their luggage around, hugging loved ones.

Now it was a ghost town.

Carmen waved for Shy to join her and Marcus, but he was done with dead bodies. Anyway, he needed a minute to himself. He was still shook from getting shot at like that. Out of nowhere. And he kept replaying what his dad had told him about back home. Which made him question *everything*.

What did he expect would happen when they made it to Arizona? *If* they made it to Arizona. Yeah, they'd pass along the vaccine to scientists. And maybe it would save some lives. But would those people be any more deserving than his mom and his sis and nephew? Or what about all those innocent babies in the nursery?

Then there was the issue of Carmen.

He'd have to tell her what he knew. That everyone back home was gone. Including their families. But how do you break that kind of news to the girl you're trying to protect?

Shoeshine sat against a palm tree behind Shy, writing in his journal. The guy looked so peaceful. His pen moving methodically across the page. The tree's large fronds swaying in the wind above him.

Shy wondered how Shoeshine had become so emotionally detached about everything. Was it a trait that came with age? Was it his time in the military? Or were some people just born that way?

"Jesus!" Carmen shouted.

Shy turned and watched her rush out of the train station and lean over the cracked concrete and throw up. Marcus was right behind her. He slammed the door closed and marched away covering his mouth.

"Are there a lot?" Shy called to them.

"They're stacked on top of each other," Marcus said. "Must be thousands, man. It's even worse than the hospital."

Carmen was on her hands and knees, staring at the concrete in front of her face.

Shy turned back to Shoeshine, who was still just sitting there, writing in his journal. He probably hadn't even bothered to look up.

Now that his family was gone, Shy needed to become more like this.

Callous to the world.

It was the only way he'd be able to keep going.

31
Billion-Dollar Companies

Shoeshine led them east along the train tracks that emerged behind Union Station. The sun beat down on Shy's face and his thick mess of tangled hair. The air was so dry his lungs were on fire. If he started coughing, he'd never be able to stop. The plan was to walk the tracks until they were past the congested part of the city. Then they'd jump over to the 10 Freeway, which also ran east, and look for a car with keys and gas or some older model that Shy might be able to hot-wire.

But for now they just walked.

Shy's shirt was soaked with sweat, especially the patch trapped between his backpack and skin. He held the pack away from his body for long stretches to air his shirt out, but eventually he gave up and let the sweat streak down his ass and the back of his legs. Shoeshine limped in front of him, using a gnarled stick he'd found as a makeshift cane, the duffel slung over his shoulder. Marcus carried his radio, which played DJ Dan just loud enough so they could listen. Carmen tightrope-walked on one of the metal rails.

Shy watched how she'd wave her arms around every so often to keep her balance, like he imagined a little girl might. Seeing her this way made his secret about their families turn his empty stomach.

In an hour they were in the heart of downtown LA, and Shy was blown away by the devastation he could see. Skyscrapers fallen on their sides, creating massive craters in the earth. Streets with gaping holes. Traffic lights shattered on the sidewalks, and large stretches of scorched concrete and asphalt. Little shantytowns had sprung up in some of the empty lots, tents packed tightly together, heads bobbing in shadows behind them. A few smaller tent clusters rested right on top of a fallen church.

About a mile outside Chinatown they passed a group of little kids running in and out of a large overturned Dumpster that had been torched by fire. Shy saw motionless bodies lined up along one extended stretch of sidewalk, and he saw two kids in a nearby alley, standing over a large, bloated man, poking him with sticks, and he saw the Staples Center, where the Lakers played, covered in spidered glass, the glare coming off the massive building forcing the four of them to shield their eyes. All the red spray-painted circles told Shy that the home arena of his old man's favorite NBA team was now a giant coffin.

Shoeshine led them onto the 10 Freeway, where several cars were flipped on their hoods, many of the driver's-side-doors flung wide open where people had escaped. They checked inside all the vehicles that were still upright, but it was rare that they found keys, and when they did, the gas tanks were always empty.

At the point where the 10 intersected with several other freeways, Shoeshine broke the silence. "You all should know we're being followed."

Shy turned around to look, but all he saw was a sea of abandoned cars and the back view of the ruined city.

"I don't see anything," Carmen said.

Marcus turned down his radio and looked all around. "By who? The Suzuki Gang? Wouldn't we hear their bikes?"

The city beyond downtown was quiet. Even when Shy closed his eyes and concentrated, the only thing he heard was the wind.

Shoeshine peered straight ahead as he walked with his stick. "We knew that company would eventually start looking for us." He glanced at Shy. "Going on the radio like you all did just narrowed the search."

"LasoTech?" Marcus said. "Nah, man. They probably think we died on the island with everyone else."

"Not when a ship with their men never returned," Shoeshine said. "Think about it from their side. There's a letter out there that explains everything they've done. And there are syringes full of a vaccine that backs up the letter. Maybe all this is at the bottom of the ocean somewhere, but billion-dollar companies don't operate on maybes."

Shy kept glancing behind them. He'd told Carmen the same thing, that the company would be looking for them, but hearing Shoeshine say it made it more real. He fingered the good-luck ring inside his pocket hoping they were just being paranoid.

But then another thought occurred to him. "Are you saying those guys that busted into the lots this morning were LasoTech?"

"That's right," Shoeshine said.

Carmen shook her head. "You didn't hear what Darius told us, Shoe. They'd been having problems with people on the outside all along."

Shy pictured the two gunmen hopping out of the SUV. They'd shot at everyone, but they went after him and his old man first. What if he'd been their actual target?

"You told them exactly where we were," Shoeshine said.

Marcus shook his head. "On the radio? Nah, man. We purposely didn't use our names."

Shoeshine stopped walking. "Who cares what your names are? Think about it, boy. Group of kids goes on the air talking about leaving the Sony lots. By choice. Because of an important trip they have to take."

Shy glanced at the freeway behind them again. He still didn't see anything, but he knew Shoeshine was right. Which made him feel like an idiot. They'd gone on the radio to try and connect with their families, but their families were gone. So all they'd done was tell LasoTech where to find them.

"Shit," Shy said. "So what now?"

Shoeshine stared at the freeway ahead of them. "We need to make a stop in San Bernardino."

"San Bernardino?" Carmen said.

"Thought we were in a hurry to get to Arizona," Marcus said.

Shoeshine pointed his stick east. "It's on the way, about sixty miles from here. We don't find a car that runs, we're looking at two-day walk at least. So it's best we get moving."

"What's in San Bernardino?" Shy asked.

Shoeshine turned to him. "I know a guy there who stores weapons. We need to be able to protect ourselves."

Shy looked up at the clear sky as the four of them continued walking. No helicopters. And he still didn't hear any trucks or motorcycles. He didn't understand why Shoeshine was so convinced they were being followed.

32
East into the Desert

By the time the blazing hot sun was directly overhead, they were a good distance outside the city limits. The freeway lost a lane on either side and there were fewer cars to check and the towns they passed were smaller and more spread out but they were just as devastated by the earthquakes and fires. Shy wiped his sweaty brow with the back of his wrist and studied their surroundings. He was aware of even the slightest sound in the distance.

They had been taking turns ducking their heads into each car they passed, but so far none had both keys and gas. Eventually Shy told Carmen: "Let's face it, we're hoofing it all the way to Arizona."

She looked annoyed but didn't say anything.

He wondered if now was a good time to talk about back home. The longer he waited, the harder it would be to explain why he hadn't told her right away. He cleared his throat. But when he opened his mouth, he couldn't find the words. So he looked ahead again and continued walking in silence.

The farther east they got, the more spread-out things became. A strip mall on the right side of the freeway here, a Cineplex there. Big signs promised fast-food joints and coffee shops and hotel chains, but nearly every place they passed was caved in and abandoned. They didn't stop anywhere to investigate. Instead they ate on the move—granola bars and crackers—and took baby sips of bottled water. Shy stared at the road in front of them, trying to swallow his emotions like Shoeshine, but his mind kept circling back to everything he'd lost.

They'd been walking for hours when a helicopter appeared like a tiny dot in the sky.

"Whoa," Shoeshine said, putting a hand up for them to stop.

"What is it?" Carmen asked.

Shy pointed to the sky, watching Shoeshine scan the freeway around them.

"There," the man said, motioning them toward a wrecked white Suburban about twenty yards away.

Shy looked up again as the four of them hurried toward the Suburban. The helicopter was heading directly toward them. Shy held his breath and climbed underneath the car with the others to hide.

They waited in silence for several minutes, listening to the sound of the chopper grow louder and louder, until it was directly overhead, stirring up everything on the road. Shy's heart climbed into his throat, and he looked at Carmen and Marcus.

But then the chopper seemed to continue on its way.

Shy craned his neck so he could watch it move west along

the 10 Freeway and then veer north, toward a small town they'd passed earlier. The chopper dipped closer to the ground and just hovered in place for a while. Suddenly the side door slid open and a man wearing a Red Cross jacket appeared with a large wooden crate, which he began lowering by rope.

Shy let out his breath, relieved.

Carmen started to climb out from underneath the Suburban, but Shoeshine stopped her. "Just hang tight for now."

There was a bit of a commotion underneath the helicopter as the man in the Red Cross jacket let the crate fall to the earth, then reeled up the rope. He tied it to another crate and began lowering that one, too.

"It's just a food drop," Carmen said to Shoeshine. "Not everyone's out to get us like you think."

Shoeshine nodded, pulling the duffel closer to his chest.

After dropping the second crate, the helicopter continued farther west. When Carmen made a move to slide out from underneath the Suburban, it wasn't Shoeshine who stopped her this time. It was Shy. The helicopter was clearly making relief drops. But Shy figured it was still best to wait until it was completely out of sight.

33
Marcus's Decision

As soon as the sky grew dark, they began looking for a safe place to spend the night. Without the sun the desert air was chilly, and they had to break out their jackets. Shoeshine led them to a deep, tree-covered gutter on the opposite side of the freeway, and Shy climbed down into the dry gut of the thing with the others and ate another granola bar and sipped his water. From a sitting position, the gutter walls reached just over their heads. Between the walls and the scrawny trees overhead, it seemed unlikely that anyone would spot them in the dark.

"Best get your rest now," Shoeshine said. "We need to be back on the road again by daybreak." Shy watched the man take his journal out of the duffel bag and unlock it with the key around his neck.

"What we *need* to do is find a damn car that runs," Carmen said. "My feet are killing me."

"'Cause you're the only one, right?" Marcus said.

"I was saying it about *all* of us, asshole." Carmen shook her head and looked to Shy. "This *vato* talks too much."

Marcus waved her off.

Shy watched Carmen crumple up her wrapper and slip it inside the front pocket of her backpack. He had decided that tonight he'd tell her everything he knew about back home. He'd take her down the way a bit, where she could react to the news in private. And he'd hug her. Or listen if she wanted to talk. Whatever she needed. But he had to get the bad news over with. Tonight.

Carmen took one last sip of water and screwed the cap back on and glanced at Shy. "Wake me up when we're there, Sancho."

"Wait," Shy said, sitting up straight. "You're going to sleep?"

"Humans tend to do that shit at night," she answered.

"And since you all are Mexicans," Marcus butted in, "you're used to sleeping in gutters, right? Didn't your forefathers have to do that shit when they snuck into this country?" He put a fist to his mouth, grinning.

"Yo, Carm," Shy said, "you hear something? Sounds like Marcus's voice, but I can't see his black ass in all this dark."

"Soon as you locate that nappy-headed fool," she said, "slap him for me. I'm too tired to get up."

The three of them cracked up a little.

After everything they'd been through, it felt good to cap on each other the way they used to back on the ship.

Shy watched Carmen position her backpack directly behind her, lay her head on it and gaze up at the sky. It was only a couple minutes before her eyelids slid down her eyes and her breaths grew long and heavy.

So much for breaking the bad news tonight.

Marcus turned on his radio, and he and Shy listened to the DJ talk about the latest death toll estimates. According to a government leak, the disease was now believed to be responsible for more than twice as many deaths as the earthquakes and fires combined.

"Yo, Shy," Marcus said after they'd been listening for a while. "Could I talk to you a minute?"

"Yeah, what's up?"

Marcus glanced at Carmen, then Shoeshine, who was busy writing. "I mean in private."

Shy got up and followed Marcus down the gutter, stepping over the occasional empty beer can or fast-food wrapper, until they were twenty or so yards away. They sat across from each other, against the angled gutter walls, but Marcus didn't talk right away, he just looked up at the night. There were tons of stars out and a half-moon that hung so low and heavy in the sky, Shy felt like he could almost reach out and grab it. Just enough light came off the moon for him to see Marcus.

"What's up?" Shy asked again.

Marcus shrugged and looked down at his hands. "I just been thinking about shit, I guess."

A long silence followed.

Shy knew from their time together on the sailboat, it always took Marcus a while to say what was on his mind. At least when it was something serious. Shy would have to bring up whatever he'd been thinking about first, to get the guy talking. But everything on his mind tonight was stuff he could only share with Carmen.

So he just sat there.

And waited.

Eventually Marcus turned to small talk. He told Shy for the hundredth time he should go for Carmen—even if she *did* have an attitude. When Shy brought up Carmen's fiancé, Marcus waved him off and said after everything Shy and Carmen had been through together, there was no way she'd be able to go back to her old life. "Nothing bonds two people more than going through hardships together. Trust me. I even got a soft spot for that crazy old bastard over there." He motioned down the gutter, toward Shoeshine.

Shy knew there was some truth to that. At this point, he probably felt closer to Carmen, Marcus and Shoeshine than any of his boys back home. But he doubted it was strong enough to make someone ditch the person they planned to marry.

"Seriously, though," Shy said, eager to change the subject, "what'd you drag me over here to talk about? I know it wasn't to lecture my ass on relationships."

Marcus sat there, shaking his head for a while. But then a surprising thing happened: he started opening up.

He told Shy how everyone at his college and on the cruise ship thought of him as this tough, gangster type because he was from Compton. And because of how he dressed. "That shit cracks me up sometimes," he said. "'Cause if you actually talk to the brothers I grew up with . . . they'd laugh in your face. Back home folks see me as a straight-up nerd, man."

"Serious?" Shy knew Marcus was good at school, but he couldn't see him as a nerd.

"Swear to God." Marcus chuckled a little. "I mean, I had the grades, right? But it's more than just that. I always had my face buried in a book. Especially comics. And I barely ever went to parties. Fools used to call me 'the Milk Drinker' when I did. I'd walk in the door and some girl would shout that shit out. 'Hey, everyone! The Milk Drinker's here!'"

"No way," Shy said. "I saw you drink on the ship."

"I'm talking about back in high school, though." Marcus shook his head. "Anyways, I'm not trying to tell my life story or anything. But it does sort of fit with what I wanted to tell you."

Shy watched Marcus rub his eyes, like he was suddenly exhausted.

"I got some bad news, I guess." Marcus turned to face Shy. "I'm going home, man. First thing tomorrow morning."

"Home?" Shy repeated. This caught him totally off guard. "Wait, why'd you come all this way, then?"

"Like I said, I been thinking about shit." Marcus shoved his hands in his jacket pockets and leaned back against the gutter wall. "I ain't no hero, bro."

"What, you think *I* am?"

"I saw the look on your face in the hospital, Shy. When you said you were going to Arizona. You *meant* that shit. I went along with it 'cause . . . I don't know. I guess I thought I was supposed to." Marcus pulled his hands out of his pockets and rubbed his eyes again. "And that's not a good enough reason to do something, I decided."

Shy searched his head for something deep he could tell Marcus, something that would make the guy see their Arizona trip in a totally different way. None of them were heroes. It was like Shoeshine said, they'd just found themselves on this journey. And they had to complete it. Or maybe Shy could bring up what his dad had told him back at the Sony lots. That his mom was gone. His sister and nephew. Maybe the only reason he was going to Arizona was because he had nowhere else to go.

But it didn't seem right for Shy to use his family that way, as a tactic to try and change someone's mind. So he just sat there, shaking his head and fingering the diamond ring in his pocket.

"Anyways, I wanted to tell you first." Marcus kicked Shy's foot to make sure he was paying attention. "I know I give you a hard time and shit, but, for real . . . you been a good friend to me, Shy."

"Same with you," Shy said. He had a strange feeling in his stomach. This might be the last one-on-one conversation he and

Marcus ever had. They'd already lost so many people from their group on the cruise ship. But this was different.

"Anyways," Marcus said.

Shy wanted to say something else, just to keep them talking a little longer, but everything that came into his head seemed sentimental. Marcus would probably laugh at him. So he just sat there instead, staring at the dirty gutter floor.

"I feel like a punk, you know? I'm not gonna lie." Marcus shook his head. "But at the same time, I don't even care."

"You're not a punk," Shy told him.

Marcus coughed into his fist and peered down the gutter at Shoeshine and Carmen. "Anyways, next time I see you, kid, I expect you and Carm to be all arm in arm and shit." He turned back to Shy. "That girl's annoying as hell sometimes, but, hey . . . at least things would never get boring, right?"

They both smiled.

Secretly, though, Shy was trying to picture the rest of the trip without Marcus. For some reason he couldn't really do it. They'd been through so much together.

Day 48

34
Circle of Poison

When Shy awoke the next morning he was surprised to find himself alone. He rubbed his eyes with balled fists and looked up and down the gutter, but there was nobody. Their stuff was gone, too. He hooked his arms into his backpack straps and climbed to his feet, and that's when he saw it.

In the middle of the eastbound lanes, maybe twenty yards from where he stood, a large circle of motionless bodies surrounded a commercial van. "What the hell?" Shy mumbled.

He climbed out of the gutter and started toward the freeway, his heart already pounding. The sun was just coming up over the far-off hills to the east, spilling light over the strange scene. Shy focused on the bodies again, all of them on their backs, arms by their sides. There were at least two dozen. Perfectly arranged. The van between them was facing the shoulder.

Shy was relieved to see that Marcus hadn't left yet. He was wedged between the van and an overturned Volvo, peering into the van's cracked windshield. Carmen and Shoeshine stood on the outside of the circle of bodies, staring at a small box.

"What happened?" Shy called out, as he crossed over the freeway median to join them.

Carmen was first to look up. "They did it to themselves. Can you believe that shit?"

There were boxes scattered all around the bodies. Shy reached down and picked one up.

"It's rat poison," Carmen told him.

"Rat poison?" Shy scanned the label, spotting the skull and crossbones in the upper right-hand corner. He turned back to the van just as Marcus slid open the side door and stuck his head inside. The big logo on the side was for a pest control company. The group must have raided the thing.

But why?

And how come the bodies were so neatly arranged?

Shy looked around the freeway again. There was a large, orange-painted storage facility beyond the shoulder. Past that, a strip mall. And one of those big McDonald's that has an outside play area for kids.

"Couldn't have happened more than a few days ago," Shoeshine said.

Shy watched the man kneel over one of the bodies. A middle-aged woman in a gray tracksuit.

Carmen nudged the body closest to her with the toe of her shoe. "How could you even *do* that to yourself?"

"Were they sick?" Shy asked.

Shoeshine peeled open the woman's eyelids with his fingers. "Doesn't look like it." He used his stick to help himself stand.

"Yo, check this out!" Marcus shouted from the driver's seat

of the van. He was holding a set of keys out the rolled-down window.

"Shut up!" Carmen shouted, tossing aside the box she'd been holding.

"There's even a little gas." Marcus hopped out of the van and bounded toward them. He stopped just inside the circle of bodies and tossed Carmen the keys. "Hang on to these while I check the back."

Carmen turned to Shy and Shoeshine. "Let's drag some of these bodies out of the way so we can take the van."

Shoeshine cupped a hand to his ear and aimed it at the sky. He had an odd expression on his face.

"Yo, you're seeing this, right, bro?" Marcus was pointing at Shy. "One last contribution. Don't say I never did nothing for you all." Just as he started back toward the van, a loud blast echoed in the distance.

Marcus stumbled, grabbing the lower right side of his back. He turned toward Shy, his eyes impossibly wide, and crumpled to the ground.

Carmen screamed.

Shy held his breath and crouched instinctively, looking all around.

Two armed men in gas masks had appeared in front of the McDonald's. They were advancing toward the freeway. Two more shots were fired, the bullets ricocheting off the concrete near Marcus. The men ducked behind a trash bin.

Shoeshine dove on top of Marcus. "Get in the van!" he shouted over his shoulder.

Shy grabbed Carmen and pulled her past the bodies, toward the pest vehicle. Three more shots rang out, sparking the concrete near their feet. Then Shy heard another familiar sound.

He looked back, saw a government helicopter lifting into the sky from behind the storage facility.

35
Still Hands

Shy and Carmen sprinted behind the overturned Volvo.

He took the keys from her and opened the passenger-side door of the van, then dove over the bucket seat, to the driver's side, and fumbled to get the right key into the ignition.

More gunfire.

One of the bullets tore through the back wall of the van. Another shattered the small back window. Carmen crouched in the seat beside him, her hands covering her ears.

Shy's heart was in his throat as he pulled himself all the way into the driver's seat. He kept his head as low as possible as he turned the key and pumped the gas. The engine turned over and stalled.

"Come on!" Carmen shouted, pounding the dash.

Shy glanced outside. The gunmen were fifty yards away now and closing fast. They'd figured out that Shy and his group were unarmed, that they were sitting ducks.

Shy pumped the gas and turned the key again. This time the van started up. He revved the engine and cranked the gearshift into reverse.

"Hurry!" Carmen shouted as Shy slammed his foot down on the gas, peeling out backward across the freeway. When the van made it between the gunmen and Shoeshine and Marcus, Shy hit the brakes and threw it into park and shouted at Carmen: "Let's get 'em in the van!"

Carmen leaped out of the passenger-side door.

Shy climbed out after her and slid open the side door and he and Carmen lifted Marcus into the van while Shoeshine brushed away loose tubes and hoses and boxes so they could lay him on his back.

Shy looked up.

The helicopter was almost directly above them now, its blades whipping the air all around. The side door was wide-open now, too, and a man with a gun leaned out and started firing.

Shy dove inside the van just as a bullet shattered the windshield. Shoeshine leaned over Shy, pulling the door closed and shouting at Carmen: "Drive!"

Carmen scrambled into the driver's seat, flipped the gearshift into drive and stepped on the gas. The van lurched forward, thumping over a few of the bodies. She steered them into the fast lane and gunned it, slowing only to slalom around a stalled car or a buckle in the concrete.

The sound of gunshots continued.

Shy crouched near the back of the van, pulling in deep breaths and covering his head with his hands. He kept expecting bullets to pierce the sides of the van, or the roof, but they didn't. After a few seconds he raised his head slightly and looked out the shattered back window.

"Get down!" Shoeshine shouted.

The gunmen on foot were no longer firing at the van. Their attention was on an SUV that had shown up out of nowhere. It looked exactly like the SUV that had crashed into the Sony lots. The man driving aimed a gun out his window, but he didn't fire at the pest control van—he shot at the gunmen on foot.

One was hit in the shoulder.

Shy watched him fall to the pavement.

The SUV screeched to a stop and the driver leaned out his window and fired at the other gunman, who dove behind the overturned Volvo. After that, the van was too far away for Shy to see. He looked to the sky again. The helicopter had pulled off their van, too. It was circling back toward the shoot-out.

"I said get down!" Shoeshine repeated.

"They let us go," Shy told him.

"Do what I said!"

Shy ducked away from the window, his heart pounding in his throat as he tried to makes sense of things. Why was the guy in the SUV shooting at the two men on foot? Weren't they together? And what about the helicopter?

He turned to look at Marcus. The left side of his friend's shirt was soaked in blood, and he was blinking hard, like he was trying to wake himself up.

"Is it bad?" Shy asked. As soon as the words left his mouth he knew it was a stupid question.

Shoeshine didn't answer. He was too busy pressing one of his spare shirts against Marcus's wound.

"Who were they?" Carmen shouted from the front of the van.

"LasoTech!" Shy shouted. "Right?"

Marcus began to moan.

Carmen glanced over her shoulder at Shy, then looked back at the road. "What about that guy in the SUV, though?"

Shy shook his head and looked out the rear window again. The helicopter appeared to be landing several miles to the west of them. "Maybe he was with the Suzuki Gang. I don't even know."

"The men on foot were LasoTech," Shoeshine said. "So was the helicopter. They're the ones with the resources."

"What about the SUV then?" Shy said.

Marcus's moaning grew louder.

Shoeshine held Marcus in his arms and began rocking him. "Everything's gonna be okay," he said into Marcus's ear. He repeated this over and over. "Everything's gonna be okay. You hear me? Everything's gonna be okay."

Shy watched them for a few seconds, cringing at the amount of blood. Nothing made sense. Not the circle of bodies or the shooting or the SUV or Shoeshine's strange embrace of Marcus. Shy wiped his hands down his face and turned his attention to the shelves built into the walls of the van. All the chemicals and strange contraptions. He wanted to believe Shoeshine. That everything would be okay. Even for Marcus. But he couldn't shake the sight of all that blood. Or how wide Marcus's eyes got after he was shot. Or the moaning that now filled the van.

How could this happen?

Marcus was supposed to be on his way home by now.

Shy sifted through dusters and sprayers and fogging equipment, wondering if any of it would be useful. Strange-looking vacuums with dozens of attachments. He turned on a UV flashlight and aimed the powerful beam of light into the drawers near the bottom of the shelves as he opened them one by one. He studied the jars and bottles for a few minutes before realizing what he was looking for. This was where the people they'd found circled around the van had found their poison.

He pushed aside a dual-headed plastic container of insecticide concentrate, and found the rat poison. There were only a few boxes left. A part of Shy understood why the people did it, even if they *weren't* sick. At this point, everything was so bleak in California. And it was only getting worse. They wanted to take control of how and when their lives came to an end.

But at the same time it pissed Shy off. How could they willingly take their own lives when so many of those who'd died would give anything for another breath? He pictured all the people he'd seen die since the ship was pummeled by that first tsunami wave. Passengers in his muster station and Supervisor Franco and Toni and Rodney and the oilman and countless others, including everyone who'd lined up on the beach back on Jones Island, thinking they'd been rescued.

And that didn't even count his mom.

He grabbed a box of the poison and let it fall to the floor of the van, and then he stepped on it. He didn't even know why.

"Shit!" Carmen shouted.

Shy scrambled to the front of the van. "What now?"

"The gas light came on."

Shy sat in the passenger seat and stared at the gauge.

The fuel light was blinking bright red. He looked out the side window. Still nobody following. "Shoe!" he called toward the back of the van. "The gas light just came on. We should just go as far as it'll take us, right?"

When Shoeshine didn't answer, Shy turned all the way around. He saw Shoeshine caressing Marcus's hair and kissing his forehead as he continued rocking him. It weirded Shy out a little, but at least Marcus had stopped moaning. Maybe Shoeshine knew what he was doing.

Shy turned back around and glanced at the gauge again, then looked through the spidered windshield at the road ahead. "We can probably make it another fifteen, twenty miles," he told Carmen.

She let out a deep exhale. "I can't stop *shaking*."

Shy looked down at his hands. He was surprised to find them perfectly still. His heart had calmed, too. It didn't make sense considering all they'd just been through.

"I swear to God," Carmen said, "if Marcus doesn't make it . . ."

Shy looked into the back of the van. Marcus seemed more alert now. Shoeshine even had him talking a little. That had to be a good sign. But then Shy focused on the blood. He turned around and sat there, watching the road, sometimes glancing down at his steady hands.

36
The Plan

The farther east they got, the clearer the freeway became. Carmen was able to keep them at a steady forty-five mph. Shy went back and forth between checking the gas gauge and watching the stunted towns on either side of the freeway. They passed Pomona and Montclair and Ontario. They passed a few more tent communities. They passed a large group pushing shopping carts full of their belongings near the shoulder of the freeway—all of them stopping to stare at the shot-up pest control van careening down the freeway.

They'd just passed a sign announcing WELCOME TO RANCHO CUCAMONGA! when Shy spotted something in his side mirror. He stuck his head out the window and watched the small dot slowly evolve into a helicopter.

It was far away, and he had no way of knowing if it was the one from before.

Still.

His heart sank.

"You see what's behind us?" he asked Carmen.

She kept her eyes on the road. "*Chinga!* What is it?"

He adjusted his side mirror so she could see.

Carmen slammed the wheel. "What now? We're running on fumes already."

"Take the 15 East up ahead," Shoeshine called to her.

"Where's *that* gonna take us?" Shy asked, spinning around. He was surprised to see Shoeshine sitting against the side of the van with his journal in his lap. Marcus was sitting up, too, pressing the shirt against his side and staring blankly at a bullet hole in the roof of the van.

Shy spun back to his mirror. He watched as the helicopter got closer and closer, until it was directly behind them.

Just then the van's engine started to sputter and cough. "What am I supposed to do?" Carmen shouted, pumping the gas pedal.

Shoeshine was suddenly hovering over her shoulder, pointing through the windshield. "Get us to that underpass!"

A man leaned out the open door of the helicopter and fired a shot. Shy ducked as the bullet burrowed into the hood of the van.

"Fuck!" Carmen cranked the wheel toward the median and then quickly straightened out.

"What's happening?" Marcus shouted.

The helicopter flew slightly ahead of the van and turned, giving the man hanging out the door a clear shot. "Get down!" Shy yelled. The side mirror exploded into pieces.

Carmen swerved again.

As the bridge ahead of them grew closer, an idea came to Shy. "Turn off the engine!" he shouted.

"What?" Carmen shouted back. "We're too far!"

Another shot pierced the hood of the van.

"Just do it!" Shy shouted. "Coast in neutral the rest of the way! I have a plan!" He was surprised Shoeshine didn't ask any questions. The man just climbed back to Marcus and took hold of the duffel.

Carmen shut off the engine and let the van coast.

The gunman fired off two more rounds, one shattering the driver's-side window, the other puncturing a back tire. The helicopter then rose slightly to avoid the bridge.

As soon as the van was underneath the bridge, Shy shouted, "Stop here!"

Carmen hit the brakes, and the van screeched to a stop.

The engine stalled.

Shy scrambled into the back and cranked open the sliding side door and motioned everyone out. Carmen climbed into the back and jumped out first. Shy and Shoeshine carried Marcus out onto the shoulder of the freeway, where they laid him on his back. Shoeshine limped back to the van for the duffel while Carmen grabbed their backpacks.

Shy couldn't see the helicopter, which meant it was hovering directly above the bridge, waiting to pick them off when they came out. Dirt and debris swirled all around, getting in his eyes, coating his teeth.

If his plan didn't work, they were done.

He jumped back into the van and slid the door closed. He grabbed Shoeshine's makeshift cane and crawled up to the driver's seat and started the van again, his breaths coming in great, rapid gulps. He shifted it into neutral, then snapped the stick over his knee and jammed one half between the gas pedal and the steering column.

It stayed.

The engine screamed.

Please let this work, he kept repeating in his head.

Please let this work.

Please let this work.

As he slid halfway out the driver's-side door, though, the stick popped out. He quickly jammed it back in place again, making sure the gas pedal was pressed all the way to the floor. Then he cranked the van into drive and dove out onto the hard concrete.

Shy watched from his stomach as the van lurched forward, careening out from underneath the bridge.

The helicopter quickly emerged, following closely behind the van, the man hanging out the open door firing shot after shot through the back windshield, through the side, through the roof. The van continued on several hundred feet until the man shot out the front right tire. At that point the pest control van veered sharply toward the shoulder, where it clipped the back half of a pickup truck and flipped over. It landed on its side with a tremendous crash and slid into the median where it burst into flames.

Shy was on his feet now, sucking in breaths, watching the fire. He looked back at Carmen. She was watching it, too. Shoeshine had his back turned, hovering over Marcus.

Shy spun back around when he heard a flurry of gunshots. The helicopter was hovering directly over the flaming van, the gunman still hanging out the door and unloading his weapon. He kept firing until he ran out of ammo, and then the helicopter rose slightly and lingered there awhile, waiting to see if anyone would emerge from the fire.

"Go on," Shy mumbled. "Get the hell outta here."

Carmen was beside him now. Both of them standing in the shadow of the bridge, watching the chopper.

To Shy's great relief, it dipped its nose, spun to the east and started flying off. He moved out from under the bridge slightly to watch it go.

"Holy shit," Carmen said, grabbing Shy by the wrist.

Shy turned to her, nodding. His plan had actually worked.

Carmen stared at the fading dot in the sky with him for several seconds, her chest rising and falling. When the chopper had all but disappeared she turned to Shoeshine and Marcus and shouted: "They're gone!"

Shoeshine didn't turn around, though.

Shy saw he had Marcus in his arms again, rocking him back and forth rhythmically. But now he was kissing his ear every once in a while, too.

Carmen looked disturbed. "What's he doing?" she asked Shy.

"Hey, Shoe!" Shy called out. When the man still didn't turn around, Shy motioned for Carmen to follow him.

37
The Pure of Heart

"How bad is it?" Carmen asked.

Shoeshine gave her an odd smile. "He's going to be just fine. Aren't you, boy?"

Shy watched a wide-eyed Marcus look up at him and Carmen in shock. His face covered in sweat. "I'm okay," he managed to say.

"You have my word," Shoeshine told Marcus. "Everything's going to be fine because the three of us love you. And there's nothing in this world as powerful as love. You know that, boy?"

Marcus nodded and swallowed hard. He made a move to lift his bloody shirt, to look at his bullet wound, but Shoeshine brushed his hand away and continued pressing one of his spare shirts against Marcus's wound.

Blood was caked all down Marcus's right side. It wasn't just the two shirts anymore, it was his jeans, too. And Shoeshine's jeans. Shy cringed and turned to look up and down the freeway. There wasn't much around. A few caved-in fast-food places. A torched motel. Marcus needed medical attention immediately. Or else he'd bleed out. But where were they supposed to take him out here?

"Young fella," Shoeshine said to Shy. "You did good. That was the right move with the van."

Shy nodded.

"You see?" Shoeshine let go of the duffel bag long enough to pat Shy on his shoe. "You're becoming who you already are."

For half a second Shy felt a swell of pride, but he quickly shook himself free of it. None of that mattered now. Not with his friend in such a bad way.

"We gotta do something," Carmen said.

"You think we can carry him?" Shy asked Shoeshine. "Or should I try and find someone to bring here?"

"Let's take a minute to catch our breath," Shoeshine said, and he resumed rocking Marcus in his arms.

"We don't *have* a minute!" Shy snapped. "He needs help *now*!"

A tear streaked down Carmen's face as she kneeled next to Marcus and took his hand. "We'll get you help," she told him. "I promise."

"I'm okay," Marcus answered. His eyes shifted to Shy. "I'm okay," he said again, like he actually believed the lies Shoeshine was feeding him.

But Shy knew better. Even if he took off running right this second, how long would it take him to find someone who could help? And if they carried Marcus, how far would they be able to get him? Especially once it started getting hot again?

Shy turned back to Shoeshine. "How close are we to San Bernardino?"

"We're *in* San Bernardino," Shoeshine answered.

This gave Shy a glimmer of hope. "So you know somewhere we can take him?"

"Of course I know somewhere we can take him." Shoeshine closed his eyes as he continued calmly rocking Marcus. He used his big leathery hands to massage Marcus's temples and around his ears.

Carmen stood up and looked at Shy. "What are we waiting for? We have to *go*."

"Shoe," Shy said. "Come on, man."

Instead of answering, the man began humming in Marcus's ear. It only took a few seconds for Shy to recognize the song. It was the same one Shoeshine had hummed to the two girls they'd buried near the motor home. Shy's heart started beating faster.

"Shoe, come on," Carmen tried again.

Shoeshine leaned forward and kissed Marcus on the ear again, then positioned his hands on the sides of Marcus's face and hummed louder.

"Shoe," Shy pleaded.

"I'm okay," Marcus said, his wide eyes darting every which way.

Shoeshine hummed and rocked Marcus back and forth, back and forth, and then he made a sudden jerking movement, tweaking Marcus's head so violently in his hands that Shy could actually hear his friend's neck snap, and he watched Marcus's body immediately go slack, his head falling against Shoeshine's chest and his eyes rolling back.

"Jesus fucking Christ!" Carmen screamed, turning away.

Shy lunged away from Shoeshine and Marcus, sick to his stomach. He covered his face with his hands and walked out from under the bridge, his whole body trembling. He kneeled down and spit on the concrete.

"Jesus Christ, Shoe!" Carmen screamed again. "What the fuck are you doing!"

Shy pulled at his own hair. He was so sickened by what he'd just seen and heard he couldn't think straight. Then he hopped back up and marched over to Shoeshine, shouting: "You killed him, Shoe! You fucking killed Marcus!"

Shoeshine cracked open his eyes lazily and looked up at Shy. But he didn't say anything. And he was still rocking Marcus's lifeless body.

Shy was choking on anger now. He clenched his fists, wanting to crack Shoeshine in the side of the face. Or kick him in his stitched-up leg. Or snap *his* neck.

But he didn't do any of that.

He just stood there in disbelief. Carmen beside him sobbing.

Shoeshine finally stopped rocking. He slipped out from under Marcus's lifeless body and struggled to his feet to face Shy. "Those who are pure of heart will not suffer unnecessarily."

Rage pulsed through Shy's body.

He was so pissed at Shoeshine he could feel his veins raising under his skin. But it wasn't just Shoeshine. He was pissed at the gunman who shot Marcus, too. And he was pissed at the earthquakes and the tsunamis and his decision to board a Paradise cruise ship in the first place. But all that combined couldn't match the rage he felt for LasoTech. And Addie's dad. There was no way he'd be able to go on living with this much rage bubbling inside.

"You don't get to decide!" Carmen screamed at Shoeshine. She wiped her wet face and glanced at Shy between sobs. Then she turned back to Shoeshine. "You don't get to decide for someone else!"

Shoeshine slung the duffel bag over his shoulder, then reached down and lifted Marcus's body into his arms and began carrying him out from under the bridge like a small child. He was limping badly. Near the shoulder he stumbled a bit and had to kneel down. "Help me get the boy out onto the field so I can bury him," he said, looking back at Shy.

"You don't get to decide," Carmen said again. But this time her words came out softer.

Shy realized the blood on Shoeshine's jeans wasn't from Marcus. He could tell because it was still spreading. And it was in the same spot where the man had been shot. He must have torn open his stitches somehow.

Shoeshine stood again, still staring at Shy. "We do what has to be done, young fella. And we do it without ego or sentimentality. All life is one life."

Shy glanced at Carmen, who was sobbing uncontrollably.

He was so confused. Just last night he and Marcus had a long conversation in the gutter. And Marcus broke the news that he was going home.

Now Marcus was dead.

Shy flashed on Shoeshine tweaking his friend's neck again. The awful sound it made. How his body went limp and his eyes rolled back.

Shy wasn't naive. He'd seen all the blood leaking out of his friend's gunshot wound. And he knew there was no one around to help. But did that give Shoeshine the right to end Marcus's life so violently?

Shoeshine shook his head and struggled to his feet again, cradling Marcus's body. He began limping out onto the field by himself, leaving Shy and Carmen to mourn under the bridge.

38

Incompetent Burial

They didn't have anything to dig a grave with, so they placed Marcus's body in the gutter at the shoulder of the freeway and covered him with sand and leaves and what little chalky dirt they could dig up with their bare hands. The three of them worked beside each other in silence for over an hour. Carmen was no longer crying. But she wouldn't look at Shy. Shoeshine was favoring his injured leg so much Shy wondered how he'd be able to continue now that they would be on foot.

A single bird circled lazily overhead, like it was watching them.

Twice they had to duck inside the gutter to hide from a passing vehicle. The first time it was the black SUV that had appeared back near the circle of bodies. Shy could tell by the spidered windshield and the bullet holes in the door. The SUV rolled by slowly, its driver scanning both sides of the freeway, no doubt looking for Shy, Carmen and Marcus. But then Shy saw something else. The SUV was pulling a trailer that held two brand-new metallic gray motorcycles. It was the same SUV he'd seen outside the Sony lots when they were leaving. The driver had tracked them all the way out into the desert.

The second vehicle was even more menacing. A jacked-up black Hummer. There were two people inside wearing military-style gas masks even though the windows were rolled up. Shy shook his head as he watched the vehicle disappear down the freeway. How many people had LasoTech sent after them? All because of the duffel bag resting inside the gutter near Shoeshine's feet.

When they'd covered Marcus the best they could, Shoeshine kneeled beside the makeshift grave and said a few quiet words Shy couldn't make out.

Carmen shot Shy a dirty look and stormed off.

Shy stayed, though, studying the man. His gray hair was wild and partially burned. But his braided chin beard was still perfectly intact, like that part of him was indestructible or somehow other-worldly. Who was this man who could snap Marcus's neck with his bare hands? Shy realized he didn't know any more about Shoeshine today than he did back when Shoeshine rescued him and Addie in the middle of the ocean.

Then a strange thought occurred to Shy. Maybe Marcus was the lucky one. Everything worthwhile had seemingly been destroyed by the earthquakes and fires. The disease that feasted on anyone in its path. And now LasoTech hit men were hunting them down like dogs. All this for what? So Shy could walk through the scorching-hot desert, starving and dehydrated, for the next several days?

He played with the ring in his pocket as he watched Shoeshine hover over his friend. Was this a life he even wanted anymore? Everyone he'd ever cared about was gone.

Everyone except Carmen.

When Shoeshine finally moved away from the makeshift grave, Shy took his place. He stood there for several minutes, remembering his friend back on the ship. Doing all that hip-hop dancing on the outdoor stage. A crowd of people staring. "We won't forget you," Shy mumbled. Then he turned and followed Shoeshine and Carmen through an open field of dried-out shrubs just north of the freeway. All of them walking a good distance from one another. Carmen's eyes still puffy from crying. Shoeshine limping badly, but still leading.

As they approached a small tent community on the far side of the field, Shy glanced back one more time at the stretch of freeway where they'd just buried Marcus.

A sickening feeling spread through his veins. There were several birds circling above Marcus now. Vultures, he realized. Waiting until it was safe to descend.

39
Arrowhead in the Mountainside

A few men from the tent community gathered to watch Shy, Carmen and Shoeshine approach. Cutting through their area suddenly didn't seem like such a good idea. But to Shy's surprise the men didn't do or say anything. They let them march right into their long line of tents.

"It's a damn miracle," Shy said under his breath. "I figured everyone wanted to shoot at us."

Carmen glanced at Shy but didn't say anything.

Shy saw a few small kids playing with toy trucks, and he saw a group of women gathered around a large pot that hung over an open flame, and he saw a kid around his age leaning against a tree, watching them. It didn't take long to pass through the entire community, and then it was more open field. Shy and Carmen followed a limping Shoeshine in silence, toward a cluster of brown hills to the north.

Hours spiraled by.

The temperature rose with the blurry sun, and soon the dry heat pressed down on Shy, making it hard to breathe. He was exhausted—from the walking and the stress of everything that had happened. His shins ached. His left knee creaked. He took off his shirt and wrapped it around his head, the way he had every day on the sailboat. Back then, he would've given anything to set foot on dry land like this. Now all he wanted to do was throw himself in the cold ocean.

Carmen tied her hair in a knot at the back of her head. Shy tried to talk to her a few times, but she only gave one-word answers.

Shoeshine led them over rolling hills, through tiny run-down neighborhoods built on potholed roads, up a steep paved street that cut through a more modern-looking housing development, which had been badly damaged in the earthquakes. They passed very few people, and nobody hassled them about zones. They just stopped whatever it was they were doing and watched.

By the time the sun was directly overhead, Shy had fallen a few steps behind and he concentrated on the rhythm of his own footsteps. He forgot about Carmen and Shoeshine, and he forgot about the relentless desert heat and the sticky sweat running down his back, and he forgot about the wind whistling past his ears and the buzz of insects and the yips of distant coyotes. He simply walked, occasionally fingering the ring in his pocket. At first he thought about Marcus. Then he thought about what his dad said about back home. But soon he wasn't thinking about anything at all. His mind went blank. And he realized a blank mind was sometimes a powerful thing. Maybe this was why those Buddhist people always sat around meditating. It was like you existed beyond yourself. Or not at all. He couldn't decide which.

Before Shy knew it, the sun began to fall and the temperature dropped. He had to put his shirt back on.

Shoeshine finally stopped at the edge of an overgrown Little League field and pointed his walking stick across a large valley. "You all see that arrowhead in the mountain?"

The sun was setting, but there was still enough light for Shy to make out a faded white shape in the otherwise brown mountainside.

"Some Native Americans believed a giant flaming arrow struck the mountain in ancient times," Shoeshine went on. "Others believed the arrow pointed to a healing hot spring in the valley." He paused for a few seconds. "But the truth is, the world is never quite as magical as we want to believe. The arrow is nothing more than a natural formation of quartz."

Shy stared at the mountainside.

The white part really was shaped like an arrowhead.

"And how do *you* know all this?" Carmen's tone told Shy she wasn't going to forgive Shoeshine anytime soon.

"Because it's where we're going," Shoeshine answered.

During their never-ending walk, Shy started wondering if Shoeshine had done the right thing. Marcus had lost a whole lot of blood. There was no way he was going to survive without a hospital. It would've been even worse to let him suffer. Hard as it was to see, what else could they have done?

Shoeshine switched the duffel to his other shoulder and started walking down a narrow paved street, toward the distant arrowhead.

"It won't leave my head," Carmen said, turning to Shy. And then she did something that caught Shy completely off guard. She moved forward and hugged him tightly.

He reached his hands around her back awkwardly. Trying to soothe her. But he didn't know how to soothe anyone. "Shoe would never hurt Marcus if he didn't have to," he said. "Remember how he draped his own body over Marcus's, back where we found the van?"

Carmen didn't say anything.

Shy cleared his throat. "Me and you both know, Carm . . . He was losing mad blood. You saw it."

Carmen sniffled. "But how could he just . . . ?"

Shy held her in silence, staring at the arrowhead in the distance. Carmen was already devastated about Marcus. How would he ever be able to tell her about back home? It wasn't possible.

Carmen pulled away to wipe her face. She looked up at Shy and took a deep breath, then set off after Shoeshine.

Shy did, too.

It was dark by the time they came upon a giant statue of a Native American pointing down a narrow dirt path. The moon gave just enough light for Shy to make out the face of the statue as he walked by.

A few minutes later, they encountered a tall chain-link gate with a large sign tacked onto it.

"What's it say?" Carmen asked.

Shy went right up to the sign and read the words out loud. "'Caution. This property is condemned. Do not enter.'"

"You made us walk miles and miles to get *here*?" Carmen barked at Shoeshine.

Instead of answering, the man put his thumb and middle finger between his lips and whistled loudly. A few coyotes yipped in the nearby mountainside.

Shy peered through the gate. He could see the outline of a large, old building. And an old water fountain. Then he spotted two men in cowboy hats emerging from behind the fountain, both holding shotguns.

"Uh, Shoe?" Shy said, backing up a few steps. "You sure we didn't make a wrong turn somewhere?"

"Nightwatch?" one of the cowboys called out. "Nightwatch, is that really you?"

"It's me all right, Dale," Shoeshine called back.

To Shy's surprise, the two men set down their guns and hurried toward the gate. The taller, overweight one pulled a key out of his pocket and unlocked the dead bolt, and the other man began unraveling the thick chain, opening the gate.

Shy and Carmen looked at each other.

"Wait, you *know* these guys?" Carmen asked Shoeshine.

Both men wrapped Shoeshine in a tight bear hug, but he managed to turn his head toward Shy and Carmen. "I used to work here," he said.

Day 49

40

A Distorted Voice
from the Past

Shy awoke early the next morning to the sound of someone pounding on the door. It took him a few seconds to get his bearings.

The two men with shotguns had led him, Carmen and Shoeshine through the gate and across the grounds to a small building positioned directly behind the massive crumbling structure they'd seen from the path. The men took them inside and got them each a big glass of water and then led Shy and Carmen to an open bedroom. All Shy remembered after that was making a beeline for the single bed across the room from the one Carmen chose.

He'd been so exhausted from walking in the hot desert sun all day, he must have passed out before his head even hit the pillow.

More pounding on the door.

Shy opened his eyes and saw the comb-over man's letter lying on his chest. Apparently he *hadn't* fallen asleep right away. He folded the beat-up pages and stuck them back into their beat-up envelope, and that's when he discovered something else.

Carmen was under the covers next to him.

The other bed had clearly been slept in, so she must have crossed to his side of the room at some point during the night. They were both fully dressed, but still. They were lying in a single bed together. Her thick, wavy hair spread out around her beautiful, peaceful-looking face. Which was only inches from *his* face. He could lean over and kiss her on the forehead if he wanted, like two married people waking up for work.

After everything that had happened with Marcus the day before, it was the most ridiculous possible time to be getting butterflies over a female. But that's exactly what was happening. They were flapping their wings all through Shy's stupid stomach, even when he ordered himself to calm the hell down.

The knocking woke up Carmen now, too. She stretched her arms and slowly opened her eyes, and when she realized she was in bed with Shy she quickly slipped out from under the covers and crossed to the other side of the room, where she pretended to be preoccupied with one of her pillowcases. "Who *is* that?" she said without looking up.

Shy shrugged and sat up, wondering what it meant that Carmen had climbed in bed with him. He remembered what Marcus had told him in the gutter. That he and Carmen should be together. But the whole idea of that got messed up because he started thinking about Marcus again. Who he'd never see again. He still couldn't believe it.

Shy pushed these thoughts out of his head and shouted: "Just come in already!"

The door slowly creaked open and a harried-looking older woman with a frizzy gray ponytail stuck her head inside. "Is one of you named Shy?"

Shy looked at Carmen.

Last night he'd been under the impression that the two cowboys were the only ones who lived here.

"That's you, right?" the woman said, pointing at Shy. "I mean, I assumed 'Shy' was a guy's name—though technically it's not really a name at all, is it? It's an adjective. But whatever."

"I'm Shy," he told her.

The woman was wearing Chicago Bears pajamas and her eye makeup was a little messed up. "I'm Esther," she said, stepping the rest of the way inside the room. She was short and round, like a circle. "I read people's palms. I know, I know, you're probably thinking I'm some sort of witch, or one of those people who looks into crystal balls, but it's not like that. My aunt taught me how to read palms when I was six, and I've been doing it ever since. Mario says I have a gift. Anyway, you need to come with me, Shy." She turned to Carmen, adding: "You should come, too. I hate when women get left out. I guess you could say I'm technically a feminist, though I don't go around burning my bras like some people."

Shy shot Carmen another look. She shrugged and tossed aside her pillow and followed the woman out of the room.

Shy had no idea where they were or what to expect, but maybe there was an important reason this woman had been sent for him. He slipped the comb-over man's letter back inside his backpack and followed Carmen and this strange woman, Esther, and when he passed through the doorway he felt a sudden and overwhelming sadness that Marcus was no longer with them.

* * *

Turned out the people who lived here were "mentally challenged" adults. At least, that was the way Esther phrased it as she led them through the building.

The day before the earthquakes, there had been thirteen residents, three counselors and the guy who ran the place, Mario. But as soon as they found out how bad the damage around the rest of the state was, the counselors all left in a rush to try and get back to their families. Most of the residents took off, too, leaving only five people: Esther, the two cowboys, an older resident named Larry, who never spoke, and Mario. The place was called Bright House, according to Esther, and they operated out of this ten-room building constructed on the property of an old, abandoned resort, which the city had been trying to evict them from.

Esther stopped in front of a closed door at the end of the hall. "This is the technology room I was telling you about. Dale's good at computers. He thinks he's gonna work for NASA someday, and who am I to squash a person's dreams? Mario has two generators, and he lets Dale use one for taping a radio show he likes."

She pushed open the door.

The two cowboys sat in front of a portable table that held some elaborate-looking, old-school radio equipment with rabbit-ear antennae. The taller, heavier guy looked up and said: "Your name's Shy, right?"

Shy nodded.

"I *thought* that's what Nightwatch said last night. Did you know two weeks ago, someone went on the radio looking for you?"

Shy frowned. His first thought was his mom and sis. But that was impossible. Then he thought of his dad.

"Dude, come in," the heavier cowboy said. "You gotta hear this."

"I'll leave you to it then." Esther started to leave but then stuck

212

her head back in the room and said: "Oh, do either of you guys want a palm reading later?"

She seemed so earnest Shy felt bad for her. He doubted they got too many visitors way out here in the middle of nowhere, even *before* the earthquakes.

Carmen glanced at Shy, then gave Esther a smile. "I'd love a palm reading," she said.

"Really?" Esther grew even more excited. "Great. I'll find you later. And I'll tell you everything I see." She waved at Shy and Carmen and left the room, pulling the door closed behind her.

Shy and Carmen sat at the table and the heavier of the two guys said: "I'm Dale. And my friend here is Tommy."

"Pleased to meet you," Tommy said, pinching the front rim of his cowboy hat. He was younger and scruffier than Dale, and he had yet to make eye contact.

They all shook hands.

Shy had never been around mentally challenged adults before, and he didn't know how to act. They had seemed mostly normal to him last night. And now, too. If anything they just seemed nicer than most people you meet. In a childlike way.

"Where's Shoeshine?" Carmen asked.

"Who?" Dale said.

"Nightwatch," Shy said, remembering the name the cowboys had been calling him last night.

"Oh. Still sleeping," Tommy said, pointing up at the ceiling. "His room's above us."

This surprised Shy. Shoeshine had never slept in later than him, even back on the sailboat. He always rose before dawn. *Always*. Shy looked at the ceiling, too, suddenly nervous.

Dale pointed at his radio, drawing Shy back into the conversation. "The minute I heard Nightwatch say your name, I knew it sounded familiar. So last night, after you guys went to sleep, me and Tommy came in here and listened to some old recordings of DJ Dan's radio show—do you guys know about DJ Dan?"

Shy glanced at Carmen and nodded.

He was reminded of Marcus again. The way he always had a radio.

"Anyway, on this one show a couple weeks ago, some guy from the Suzuki Gang came on and said he was looking for a kid named Shy, and I thought: How many Shys could there be in the world? It's a weird name, no offense."

"None taken," Shy said, remembering his old man saying he'd gone on the radio looking for Shy. At the time, he hadn't believed it.

Tommy pointed at the radio. "Just let 'em hear it already."

"I *know*, Tommy," Dale said. "I needed to catch him up first, okay? Jeez." He turned back to Shy, shaking his head. "Anyway, you wanna hear it?"

"Uh, yeah," Shy said, suddenly overcome by nerves. Because what if it *wasn't* his dad? What if it was some kind of warning from LasoTech? Or Jim Miller himself?

But the second the recording began, those fears faded away.

It was definitely his old man.

MAN: Doesn't matter if you're sick or healthy, man or woman, grown person or child . . . you need to stay where you are. No more traveling from zone to zone. For any reason. Or there will be consequences. Understand? [*Coughing.*] And I'm also looking for a kid—

DJ DAN: What consequences?

MAN: Hang on. [*Rustling.*] The kid's name is Shy Espinoza. Seventeen, with short brown hair and brown skin.

Sort of tall and thin. Anyone can give me information on this boy's whereabouts, there'll be a reward. Just get in touch with DJ Dan here, and I'll keep checking back.

DJ DAN: What are the consequences for moving from zone to zone? And who will issue these consequences?

MAN: Us, man. We're out patrolling. . . .

Dale stopped the recording and looked at Shy, excited. "That's you, right?"

Shy nodded.

A different kind of butterfly feeling now flooded his stomach. His dad really *had* gone on the radio looking for him. He'd even offered a reward. Shy didn't know how to feel about this. Maybe he was wrong to reject his dad back at the Sony lots.

Carmen touched Shy's arm and gave him a comforting look.

Shy turned back to Dale. "Would it be possible to listen to the rest of those recordings?"

"Sure," the cowboy said. "But that's the only one that mentions you."

"I know. I'm just curious."

Dale gave Tommy an awkward thumbs-up and turned his attention back to his machine and began punching buttons. "Why don't we start with the first one I ever recorded."

Shy was still trying to wrap his head around things. While he was creeping through the Pacific Ocean on a sailboat, half starved and baking in the sun, his dad had been searching for him. And then at the Sony lots, his dad had tried to teach him how to ride a motorcycle. It proved the guy was genuinely trying.

But at the same time, should it really take a natural disaster to make someone want to be your dad?

Dale cued up the first recording and hit Play, and Shy listened to the DJ introduce himself and explain why he was starting a radio show in the middle of a catastrophe. He'd lost everything, he said. His entire family. If he didn't find something to do, or some way to give back, he'd be lost, too. Before the earthquakes he'd been a sound engineer at a radio station. He'd never actually been in front of a microphone. But he had all the satellite equipment. So here he was, starting a radio show. His focus would be on spreading information to survivors like himself.

In the first few recordings, DJ Dan explained everything he knew about the earthquakes and the fires and where to get medical attention. Then he began interviewing people about where they were when it happened, and how they survived and who they were separated from. Then he started talking about the disease, too, and how quickly it was spreading. He gave information about how to get help from the government, where to find food drops, how to get medicine. He explained the zone system that was beginning to emerge and gave reports about the border rumored to be going up in Arizona.

Shy's heart sank when the DJ began talking about San Diego. The area near the border was one of the most devastated regions in the state. People were calling it Ground Zero. The few who had survived the earthquakes and fires there were the first to contract Romero Disease.

Shy glanced at Carmen, whose stare was fixed on the radio. She wasn't even blinking. He knew he should have already told her what he'd learned from his dad, but maybe this got him off the hook.

Shy was still thinking about back home when a distorted female voice then came on the DJ's show. It made him sit up in his chair and listen more closely. He didn't recognize the voice, but the cadence of the girl's speech, and what she was saying, gave him a strange feeling. And she was using the name Cassandra.

The voice explained a few details about the makeshift border in Avondale, Arizona—where Shy, Carmen and Shoeshine were heading—then shifted into an unexpected story about getting stuck in the tide with some guy at the beach. When she said the word "Shinola," Shy's whole body went numb.

Shinola was the shoe polish brand he'd told Addie about when they were stranded on the broken lifeboat.

It was *her*.

No one outside of Otay Mesa knew that story.

She was reaching out to him in code, distorting her voice to prevent someone from recognizing it. Like her dad. Or anyone else affiliated with LasoTech.

"What's wrong?" Dale asked Shy. "Do you know who this is?"

Shy ignored Dale.

He kept listening.

There was a company that wanted to wipe out the Shinola brand, Addie said in her distorted voice, which meant there was a company that wanted to wipe out *Shy*. And everyone with him. The company, Addie went on, knew the sailboat had made it back to California. And it knew about the vaccine. And the letter.

In other words, LasoTech knew everything.

Addie ended the interview in a rush:

It's important for the Shinola company to understand two things. I have the missing page. And not every government helicopter is there to drop off food. . . .

When DJ Dan's voice came back on, Shy spun toward Carmen. "That was Addie."

She nodded. "I had a feeling."

"You did?"

"I could tell by your face."

Shy looked at Dale and then turned back to Carmen. "She was warning us."

"No," Carmen said, "she was warning *you*."

Shy motioned toward the radio. "Dale, can you play that whole interview again?"

41
Shoeshine's Surprising Apology

Shy listened to every single one of Dale's recordings before walking upstairs with Carmen, to the room where they were told they'd find Shoeshine. Shy pushed through the door without knocking. "They know everything, Shoe," he said as he walked in. "And they're not gonna stop until . . ."

Shy paused when he saw that Shoeshine was stripped down to his *chones*, dressing his own ugly thigh wound over a white towel covered in splotches of blood.

Shoeshine set aside the rifle he'd had on his lap and quickly covered his thigh and pulled his shirt over his head. But Shy had seen everything. Shoeshine's stitches were ripped to shreds. And there was a nasty layer of pus near the borders of the wound, like it might be getting infected. And Shoeshine had a long, thick scar running down his chest.

Carmen gasped and covered her mouth with her hand. "What happened to your stitches?"

"Just a little tear," Shoeshine said, hiking his pants back up and doing his belt. "But I got off lucky compared to some."

Shy glanced at Carmen, who shifted her eyes to the floor. The three of them were quiet for a few seconds. Shy cringed. Shoeshine's wound made him flash back to the blood caked to Marcus's side. And he still couldn't believe what he'd just heard on the radio. Addie. Warning him. Was it possible her dad had taken her off the island by force? That she had no idea about LasoTech's plan to gun down all the people on the island?

Maybe Shy was wrong about her.

"I'm sorry you all had to see that back by the freeway," Shoeshine said, breaking the silence. "He was a good kid."

Shy watched Carmen nod and lean back against the wall.

It was the first time either of them had heard Shoeshine apologize. For anything. But instead of making Shy feel better, it stressed him out. He'd seen the man's wound. What if Shoeshine planned to stay here? What if he and Carmen were on their own from this point forward?

"Anyways," Shy said, pushing these thoughts out of his head. "We just heard something on the radio you need to know about."

Shoeshine stood up, fully dressed now, and listened as Shy recapped everything he'd learned from Addie's interview. Laso-Tech knew their sailboat had made it back to California, and they knew what was inside the duffel.

Shoeshine stared at Shy for a few long seconds. "And here I thought you were coming to me with new information, young fella."

"But we know *for sure* now."

Shoeshine folded up the bloody towel and set it down at the foot of the bed.

Carmen pointed at the rifle. "You already got the weapons we came for?"

Shoeshine lifted a long gun bag off the floor, set it on the bed and unzipped it. "There's one for each of us. And plenty of ammo. We can no longer afford to be on the road unarmed."

Shy was relieved. Shoeshine was coming with them.

"So are we leaving now?" Carmen said. "The sooner we get this duffel to Arizona, the sooner we can be done with all this hero bullshit."

Shoeshine shook his head. "From now on, we only travel at night."

"So we'll be harder to see," Shy said.

Shoeshine sat back down on the bed. "And so we can avoid the heat. We'll cover more ground that way. Especially the deeper we get into the desert." The man loaded ammunition into the rifle beside him, snapped the barrel back into place, put on the safety and slipped it into the gun bag.

Shy looked at the clock on the wall. "So what are we supposed to do until dark? It's barely two o'clock."

"Rest," the man said. "And eat. Try and get your strength back."

42
Modern-Day Buddha

Seconds after Shoeshine kicked Shy and Carmen out of his room, they ran into an older, balding Mexican man who introduced himself as Mario. "Well, isn't this convenient?" he said, clapping his hands together with a grin. "I was just looking for you two."

Shy knew Mario was the guy who ran the place, so he held out his hand and introduced himself. Carmen did, too, saying: "Thanks for letting us stay here last night."

"From what I understand, you guys aren't leaving until tonight. So I thought I'd show you around." Mario glanced at Shoeshine's closed door. "I realize the world is crumbling all around us, but there's no reason I can't still be a good host."

Shy followed Mario and Carmen down the long hall and out the front door. As they passed the gate they'd come through the night before, he thought he heard the vague sound of a motorcycle engine. He stopped and listened closely, peering through the gate, but all he saw was dust floating across the dirt road in the distance.

"You okay?" Carmen said, stopping too.

"You hear that?" he asked her.

"What?"

"It was probably just a coyote," Mario said. "Or a deer. There's wildlife all around this property, looking for handouts."

As they resumed walking, Shy's brain started spinning. Maybe he was just being paranoid, but he could've sworn he heard a motorcycle. What if LasoTech had tracked them all the way out here? What if they had helicopters waiting down by the freeway? Addie's words kept spinning though his head: "They know."

"They know."

"They know."

Mario led them to the other side of the massive, half-collapsed hotel, pointing things out along the way: a row of overgrown tennis courts, a giant, dilapidated gazebo, a drained Olympic-sized swimming pool full of dirt and weeds. He listed all the movie stars from the forties and fifties who used to vacation there when the resort was the place to be. They were all names Shy had never heard of, but he tried to picture the place cleaned up and packed full of guests.

How weird to think that people were born in different eras, with different adversities. A world war for one generation. Earthquakes and a deadly disease for the next. He wondered if there had ever been a time when shit was just peaceful. When a kid his age could just hang out with his friends and not worry about getting bum-rushed by some greedy pharmaceutical company.

They went down creaky wooden stairs into a dense, overgrown section of forest where Mario pointed out natural springs that smelled like rotten eggs. He explained that the sulfur springs were the big draw back when the resort was at the height of its popularity. There were over a dozen pools of various sizes and temperatures, and according to Mario, indigenous people had made use of the sulfur water's healing powers long before the mountainside was claimed by settlers.

"Do people still use them?" Carmen asked.

"My residents and staff do," Mario said. "Or at least they did before everyone ran off."

Carmen wanted to know more about the movie stars who used to visit the resort as Mario led them back up to the hotel. Shy followed a few steps behind, staring at a distant helicopter and thinking some more about Addie's warning on the radio. The chopper was so far away he couldn't even hear it, but that didn't mean it wasn't LasoTech. They were probably scouring every inch of land between LA and Arizona. If so, Shy didn't see how he, Carmen and Shoeshine were going to make it to the Avondale border. A few rifles wouldn't slow down a rich company that had access to helicopters and trucks and automatic weapons. Maybe this whole duffel bag trip was one big suicide mission.

Shy stopped in front of the hotel where Mario and Carmen were standing, and the three of them stared at all the damage in silence. The building was ten stories of peeling white paint and broken columns. The entire left-hand side had caved in during the earthquakes. The roof sloped toward the overgrown lawn on *both* sides, and all the front windows were boarded up.

Mario shook his head. "For twenty years I've been trying to raise enough money to buy this place outright. The plan was to renovate the hotel and create the largest special needs residence in the country. But I could never quite get to my number. And then, of course, the earthquakes hit. . . ."

Shy looked up at the helicopter again. It was still a long ways away, but he could vaguely hear it now, which meant it was closer.

He wished it would hurry up and be night already so they could get back on the road. There was nothing left to do here but wait, and the waiting was probably the worst part of all.

"I have to tell you," Mario said, turning to Shy and Carmen, "your friend is truly one of a kind."

It took Shy a few seconds to realize Mario was talking about Shoeshine.

"So he really worked here?" Carmen asked.

Mario nodded. "For just about five years. He was our night watch."

"That's what you called him, too, right?" Shy said.

Mario nodded. "He insisted."

Shy had to crack a smile, his first since he and Marcus had their talk in the gutter. It was good to know some things never changed. "So what else can you tell us about him?" Shy asked. "He never talks about himself."

Mario chuckled. "I don't know much. He mostly kept to himself." The man paused to look up at the circling helicopter. It seemed to be getting farther away again. "I remember he was always reading books and writing in journals."

"He *still* does a journal," Carmen said.

Shy's interest was piqued. "Do you have any idea what he writes about?"

Mario shook his head. "I asked him once. But all he'd tell me was some mumbo jumbo about recording the world. I do remember this, though. Soon as he finished a journal, he'd burn it in the fire pit out front and start a new one."

"He'd *burn* it?" Carmen said with a frown. "Why?"

Mario shrugged. "Your guess is as good as mine."

Shy imagined himself sneaking a peek inside Shoeshine's journal. It was locked, but he knew if you peeled down a corner of the leather cover you could at least make out a few lines.

"We did have a beer in town once," Mario said. "The night he put in his resignation. I wanted to thank him for all he'd done for me and the residents, and he humored me. When I asked where he was from, he didn't give a straight answer. But he did tell me he came from a family of wealthy landowners."

"Rich people?" Shy was shocked. Shoeshine definitely didn't strike him as someone who came from money.

"That's what he said." Mario cleared his throat. "He also told me that the day he turned thirteen he packed a bag, hugged his parents and walked off their property."

"Why?" Shy and Carmen said at the same time.

"Let's see if I can remember his exact words," Mario said. "'A safe, happy life behind gates is no life at all.' I guess he hasn't seen his family since that day."

"That's harsh," Shy said. He couldn't imagine walking away from his family at *any* age, much less thirteen.

"I remember when he told me that," Mario said, "I called him a modern-day Buddha. Nightwatch—or Shoeshine, as you call him—laughed with me a little. Then he set his empty glass down on the bar and shook my hand. Next thing I knew he was walking out of the bar carrying his bag over his shoulder. I hadn't seen him for almost seven years when you all showed up late last night."

Shy tried to imagine Shoeshine seven years younger. Did he have the crazy gray hair back then? What about the magical braided chin beard? Shy glanced up at the sky again. The helicopter was nowhere to be found.

Mario cleared his throat. "I also brought you out here to ask a favor."

Shy nodded along with Carmen.

"Nightwatch wouldn't tell me exactly where you all are going," Mario said. "And I'm guessing you won't tell me either."

"We can't," Shy said. "Sorry."

"It's probably better if you don't know," Carmen added.

Mario nodded. "Well, I'm guessing it's not all that close. Is that fair to ask?"

Shy glanced at Carmen. "It's not close," he admitted.

Mario looked past them, back toward the building. "He's in no condition to walk, I don't think. Maybe I can at least help out in that department." The man nodded at Shy and Carmen. "Keep an eye on that old guy for me, will you? Last night when I spoke to him, something didn't seem right to me."

"His leg's hurt pretty bad," Carmen said.

"He got stitched up a few days ago," Shy added, "but they got messed up."

Mario stared up at the clear blue sky for a while, like he was thinking. "I was afraid it might be something like that." He shook hands with Shy, and then Carmen. "You'll do that for me, won't you? You'll keep an eye on him?"

43
What the Lines Say

"Did Mario take you to see his car?" Esther asked as she led Shy and Carmen toward her room.

Shy looked at her, confused. "His car?"

"I'll take that as a no." Esther opened her door and flipped on the lights. "He has this fancy old car he shows everyone and their mother. But I guess he's too preoccupied now." She pointed for Carmen to sit in one of two metal folding chairs in the center of the room.

Carmen looked at Shy and shrugged, then sat in the chair closest to her.

Esther stood behind the other one. "I'm so tired of doing readings for the same people over and over and over." Shy couldn't believe how fast she was talking. He understood she was excited, but it was more than that. She was acting like this was the greatest thing that had ever happened to her. "Finally I get to do someone new!"

Shy stood just inside the doorway, looking around the small room. The shades were drawn and the walls were painted purple and black. The sheets on the single bed were black, too, and next to the bed was a dresser covered with candles, big and small. He watched Esther walk over to her dresser and start lighting the candles, like she was getting ready for some kind of séance.

"Lights, please?" she said to Shy.

He flipped off the overhead light.

"You can sit here." She directed Shy toward a black beanbag he hadn't noticed in the corner of the room. "And please try not to disturb us."

"Yeah, Sancho." Carmen smiled. "Keep your ass quiet over there."

"I'm surprised you're even here," Esther added. "I figured you'd be in the tech room with Dale and Tommy."

"Me?" Shy said. "Why?"

"Supposedly that DJ guy is making some announcement. I don't know. Something like that."

Shy moved over to the beanbag and dropped into it with a hiss. After listening to hours and hours of recordings this morning, he needed a break from the radio. If it was up to him, he and Carmen would be in one of those sulfur pools right about now. Or they'd be asleep. But Carmen insisted he escort her to the big palm-reading session. She acted like she was excited about the reading, but Shy knew the truth. She wanted Esther to be happy.

Carmen was good like that.

Esther took Carmen's left hand and turned it over in her lap. She ran her fingers across Carmen's wrist and the inside of her thumb and forefinger and took a series of long, dramatic breaths. Then she began tracing the lines inside Carmen's palm, making odd humming and tongue-clicking sounds.

Shy tried not to laugh out loud as he watched the woman furrow her brow in concentration. He'd never believed in stuff like palm readings or astrological signs. Reality wasn't in someone's hand. It wasn't in the stars. Reality was helicopters chasing your ass down the freeway. Reality was a big truck crashing into the Sony lots and two LasoTech dudes aiming guns at you. Reality was what happened to Marcus. And Shy's family. And all those babies he'd seen in the hospital nursery.

"Oh yes," Esther said, tilting her head to the side slightly. "I see it clearly now. You, my dear, have suffered a devastating loss. A loved one, I believe. This is what the gods have given to you this past year. Before the earthquakes even. Someone in your family."

Carmen glanced at Shy, raising her eyebrows. "My dad?" she asked, turning back to Esther.

"That's it!" the woman exclaimed. "Oh my. So much pain. So much confusion."

Shy rolled his eyes. The art of palm reading was keeping shit so vague it could be taken a million different ways. He hoped Carmen understood that.

"But this line here," the woman continued, pressing her thumb into the middle of Carmen's palm. "You will not suffer the same fate yourself. No, I see a long, long life."

"That's what I like to hear," Carmen said.

"The gods will make sure of it. You will grow old and see the world change quite drastically." Shy watched Esther blink dramatically as she began tracing a different line. "But what about this one here?" she said. "Your love line."

"What about it?" Carmen said, her expression suddenly serious.

Shy was surprised to see Carmen actually getting into it. He leaned forward a little in the beanbag, waiting to hear what non-sense would come out of Esther's mouth next.

"Very interesting," the woman said, nodding.

"What?" Carmen said.

"There's someone waiting for you."

"There is?" Carmen glanced at Shy again. "Who's waiting for me? Where is he?"

"I see him clearly," Esther went on. "He's pacing back and forth on some kind of field. A park maybe. Near a body of water. He's waiting for your safe return."

"What park?" Carmen wanted to know. "Like a *park* park? With swings and shit?"

Esther dropped Carmen's left hand and picked up her right. "The left hand is what the gods have given you," she explained, "but your right hand tells what you're going to do about it."

"You hear that, Carm?" Shy said. "Ol' girl's running a two-for-one up in here."

When Carmen didn't laugh, Shy waved them both off and leaned back in the beanbag. He couldn't believe she was taking it so seriously. She'd heard the recording about San Diego this morning. There wasn't anyone waiting for *anybody*. Yet here Carmen was, holding out her palms and hoping her damn fiancé was pacing back and forth in some park, dreaming of her return.

"He's not where you imagine, though," Esther said. "He's somewhere else. Somewhere far away from home."

Esther started saying something about tree roots, but Shy was no longer listening. Not really. He was thinking instead. About Marcus and the last talk they had. About Shoeshine's thigh. About his entire family being taken away, and how lonely he felt now. And then he thought about the trip they would resume as soon as the sun went down. Getting to Arizona was all he had left, he realized.

What if they actually made it, though? What would he do then?

His mind drew a blank.

And then Shy found himself remembering Addie. The two of them sitting across from each other in their broken lifeboat. All the talks they had. And how they huddled together those last few nights to keep warm.

Shy climbed out of the stupid beanbag. "Yo, this shit's getting a little corny for my taste," he announced. "I'm outta here. Peace." He walked right past Carmen and Esther on his way to the door.

He was surprised that neither of them even looked up as he left the room.

44
The Rainbow Connection

Shy was halfway through reading the comb-over man's letter—for maybe the eight thousandth time—when Carmen barged into their room. She stood over him, hands on hips. "Uh, what do you think you're doing?"

He didn't look up. "Reading a letter?"

"I mean *why, pendejo!*" She sat on the edge of his bed and snatched the pages out of his hands. "You're just gonna mess it up. And then what good does it do us? Without this, *nobody* will believe us." She stuck the pages back in the envelope and slipped the envelope inside Shy's backpack.

Shy sniffed the air. He was pretty sure Carmen's breath smelled like vodka. "I need to keep reminding myself what those assholes did," he told her.

Carmen just sat there, staring at him.

Shy linked his fingers behind his head and looked away. He wished it was dark already. If it was dark they could go *do* something, instead of just sitting around reading each other's palms.

They were both quiet for a few minutes, until Carmen got up from the bed and grabbed Shy's arm. "Come with me."

"What now?" Shy sat up, acting annoyed.

"I thought you wanted to go check out the hot springs." She pulled Shy to his feet and pointed at the towel slung over her shoulder.

This caught Shy off guard. "Wait, for real?"

"Shoe said we should get some rest, right? What's more restful than soaking in some damn hot springs?"

Shy's heart sort of kicked into gear as he followed her out the door.

Carmen reached down and stuck her hand in the most secluded of the mineral pools. "This one's not even that warm," she said. "But it definitely still smells."

Shy stood a few feet back, looking up into the sky. No helicopters in sight. In another hour or so the sun would set, and they'd start getting ready to go. But first . . . He was curious to see if Carmen would really get in the water. He sat on a large, flat rock at the side of the sulfur pool and watched her. The overgrown trees were packed so tightly around them it felt like their own little private world.

Carmen kneeled near the lip of the pool and ran her right hand back and forth in the water. "I wonder if these minerals are as good for your skin as everyone says." She scooped some of the water out and rubbed it into her cheeks and forehead and neck.

"Nasty," Shy said.

"What?" Carmen wiped her face on her shirt sleeves. "I'm

about to have perfect skin now, like my shit was airbrushed. You'll wish you did it, too, when you get mad pimples."

"At least I won't smell like a damn Easter egg."

Carmen scooped some more water and splashed it at Shy.

He dove backward, managing to avoid most of the water, but a little splattered on the bottom of his jeans and shoes. "Come on, Carm! Damn!"

"I guess now we both smell like eggs." Carmen stood up and stared into the water, then turned back to Shy with a mischievous grin. "Might as well go all the way in, right?"

"Go 'head," he told her. "I'll be the lifeguard."

"You're the one who wanted to come out here in the first place. Now you're gonna punk out?"

Shy glanced over his shoulder. They were alone. He didn't know why, but he had this weird feeling they were about to get busted.

By who though?

And for what?

There were no rules anymore.

He kept having to remind himself.

"You're going in like that?" he said, pointing at Carmen's clothes.

She shook her head and stepped out of her kicks, one at a time. "Nah, like *this, vato.*" She pulled her T-shirt over her head and started undoing her jeans.

Suddenly Carmen's beautiful brown body was in front of Shy. Her heavy chest weighing down her bra. Her bare arms and shoulders. The quote inked above her belly button—so close now he could almost read the words. She'd lost a little weight since the day their ship went down, but she still looked incredible.

Shy swallowed hard watching her tug down her jeans and step out of them.

Carmen turned and slowly lowered herself into the pool. "Oh, man, it feels good in here," she said, wading to the other side. "Come on."

Butterfly wings were beating frantically inside Shy's chest as he kicked off his own shoes and dropped his shirt and jeans. Hundreds of wings going at once. Thousands. He climbed in after Carmen in only his boxers, wondering if she was staring at his excitement. What if she laughed at him? Or what if she hopped out abruptly because he was reading the situation all wrong?

Shy met eyes with Carmen again.

Beautiful and brown and staring into him.

This morning she'd climbed into his bed. Now they were damn near skinny-dipping. What did it *mean*?

"Feels good, right?" Carmen said.

"Feels perfect," he told her. Because it did. The temperature and the wild trees that hid them and the endless desert sky.

He breathed in the egg smell and glanced down at what he could see of Carmen's wet body. Even after everything they'd been through, she was still the sexiest girl he'd ever been around—or sexiest *woman*. He never understood that. When did "girl" officially become "woman"? Because he didn't want to mess that up when it came to Carmen. Someone should be explaining things like that to kids in high school.

There are no rules, he told himself.

Or anything else.

Shy went all the way underwater, and when he came back up he brushed his hair out of his eyes and leaned his back against the rocky ledge and looked at Carmen, sitting across the water from him, both her arms resting on the pool's edge.

He didn't know what to do.

Or how to act.

He needed a haircut.

"What if this was the rest of our lives?" Carmen said. "Relaxing in natural springs every day."

"Up in the mountains," he said.

"Behind some old hotel where famous people used to go."

"Shit, I'd be down for that." Shy tried to imagine it. Him and Carmen fixing up the hotel all by themselves. Slapping on a new coat of paint. Hanging with the Bright House folks every once in a while. Reading books like Shoeshine. "We'd probably even get used to the smell," he said.

"I'm *already* used to it." Carmen floated her hands on the water's surface for a while, then looked up at him again. "Hey, Shy?"

"Yeah?"

She smoothed her wet hair behind her ears. "Did it weird you out this morning, hearing her voice on the radio?"

"Who, Addie?"

Carmen nodded.

He paused, trying to think. "I guess so. Yeah." But he didn't know if that was the right answer, so he added: "Why?"

Carmen shook her head. "It's just . . . it sounded like you and her had this, like, secret language."

Shy frowned. "You mean the Shinola thing?"

"How come I never heard of that?"

Shy rubbed his eyes with wet fists and wiped the sulfur water away from his nose. "I guess while we were out there I told her some stuff. Like how I got my name. There wasn't much else to do."

"How come I don't know that story, though?" Carmen asked. "Did you get closer to her than me while you guys were stranded?"

"Not even," Shy assured her. But inside he felt kind of weird. Carmen was the one who stopped them from getting any closer. She was the one who made the rules. "I could tell you now," he said.

"Okay." Carmen splashed away a dead bug floating on the surface of the water. "'Cause I wanna know stuff like that, too," she told him.

The way she was acting surprised Shy. It wasn't like *he* had a fiancée waiting for him in a park somewhere. He'd tell her anything she wanted to hear.

Shy rubbed a little water on his face—in case it really did prevent pimples—and then he told her the CliffsNotes version. "I guess when I was little, my old man used to have this saying whenever I knocked something over. At least, according to my mom and sis. He'd be like, 'Damn, this kid doesn't know shit from Shinola.' Which is a saying from back in the day. After a while he started calling me Shinola as a nickname. And then he shortened it to just 'Shy.' I guess it sort of stuck. Obviously."

Carmen furrowed her brow. "How could he say that about his own son?"

"Don't ask me."

She shook her head in disgust. "Yo, if I ever see that *pinche puto* again, Shy, I'm kicking him in the *huevos,* for real. So he can't have no more kids."

"Go for it," Shy said. He cracked up inside a little, thinking about how different the two girls' reactions were to his Shinola story. Addie had gotten all depressed-looking and said it was the saddest thing she'd ever heard. Carmen wanted to fight.

Shy watched her go all the way under again and come up with her head tilted back so she could smooth the water out of her hair. He'd always loved Carmen's wild hair. It was thick and wavy and sort of reckless, but it was soft, too. She had the kind of hair everyone in the mall turned to check out—especially other girls.

"I think it's my turn to ask a question," Shy said. He pointed at the part of her that was underwater. "What's it say on your stomach?"

"My tattoo?"

Shy nodded. He'd been wanting to ask her this since back on the ship.

Carmen looked at him for a few long seconds. "It's not that big a deal. Just some saying I always liked."

Shy waved her off. "Must like it a whole lot to ink it onto your stomach."

Carmen grinned. "I guess you got a point."

"So?"

She sighed and rolled her eyes but stood up and took a few steps toward Shy so he could see for himself.

"'Someday we'll find it,'" he read aloud, "'the rainbow connection. The lovers, the dreamers and me.'" He looked up at her. "Who wrote that?"

"Kermit," she said.

"Who?"

"What, are you deaf now, *ese*? Kermit the fucking Frog, okay?"

"Wait," Shy said, trying to process. "Like, from the Muppets?"

"Hell yeah, from the Muppets. Don't talk shit about it, either." She sank back into the water. "To this day that damn song makes me cry every time. I'm not afraid to admit that shit, either."

Shy couldn't help it, he started cracking up. He'd expected some deep quote or passage from a poem. Like Edgar Allan Poe or Shakespeare or something else from back in the day. The last thing he would've guessed was Kermit the Frog. When he looked up he had little tears in his eyes from laughing so hard. He thought Carmen might be pissed, but she wasn't. She was laughing right along with him. Which made him crack up even harder.

Both of them laughed and laughed for days.

After all they'd been through, it felt amazing to let go. Laughter-tears flooded Shy's eyes, blurring everything, and he slapped at the surface of the lukewarm sulfur water. Carmen tried to explain through her laughter how the lyrics reminded her of childhood, back when everything was simple, and how they made her believe she'd one day find true happiness, but the fact that Carmen was trying to justify her Kermit tattoo just made Shy lose it even more.

When they finally settled down, Carmen took a deep breath and reached for the towel to wipe her eyes. She leaned back against the pool wall across from Shy and said: "I'm glad my dreams make you laugh."

"Me too," Shy said. "I needed that shit."

Carmen shook her head and stared at the water in front of her. "Do you ever get the feeling you were born in the wrong time and place?"

Shy made his face go serious. "Like how?"

"I don't know," she said, wiping her eyes again. "It's just . . . what if everything was different? What if we existed decades before this disease was ever invented? Or centuries before? Or what if we were born in a completely different country? Like Russia or France or Argentina?"

Shy nodded. "I guess I sort of *do* think about that," he said. "Especially since our ship went down. And everything that happened with Marcus. And"—he made sure Carmen was looking at him—"what the DJ said about San Diego."

Carmen's eyes dropped to the water again.

It seemed strange to Shy that she still hadn't brought up what they'd heard about back home. It was like she was trying to pretend it never happened, which didn't seem healthy.

"But I was thinking about this a couple days ago," Shy said.

"Maybe there's *always* been a drug company trying to get rich off people like us. Throughout history."

Carmen nodded. "I wonder if it'll ever change."

Shy thought about it for a couple seconds. "I wish I could be there to see it. The people who finally decide to stand up to that shit."

They were quiet for several seconds, then Carmen waded slowly across the pool toward Shy, saying: "Hey, maybe you could tell me about our space versions one more time." She reached for his hand underwater, made it so their fingers linked together.

Shy's heart started thumping its ass off.

He'd only seen this look in Carmen's eyes one other time. Back on the cruise ship. When they were sitting outside her cabin door together, talking. Brazilian beats playing quietly on her laptop computer. An empty bottle of wine between them.

It was the only time they'd ever hooked up.

45
Space Versions

Shy tried to maintain his cool, but inside he was panicking. This was everything he'd ever wanted. But at the same time, what would happen after? It was like when he used to stand on the highest deck of the cruise ship, at night, and look down. Sometimes he wanted to jump. He wanted to fly free into all that dark, whispering water. But he never did, because what if that was it? What if it was the end?

He swallowed hard and cleared his throat. "You sure you're ready for all that?"

"After everything we been through," Carmen said, "I think I need to hear it again." She stared straight into his eyes without blinking, like she was reaching for something inside his chest, something true, something beyond the physical world.

Back on the ship Shy had claimed there was a "space version" of him and Carmen that lived on a distant planet somewhere. And this version was together. They were in love. And he came up with some hokey hand-holding test that led to them hooking up.

This time, though, they were *already* holding hands.

And it felt even better than he remembered.

"I'm saying, though," he told her, "it's some powerful information."

"I think I can handle it," she said.

But before he even got a word out, Carmen pulled him closer, so that their faces were only inches away. He looked into her dark brown eyes and breathed in her breath. "By the way, were you drinking with Esther?"

Carmen's lips broke into a little grin. "You should've stuck around for the end of the palm reading." She reached out and poked Shy's stomach and said: "You know what?"

"What?"

"I like your body."

"Me too," he heard himself say. She'd never said anything like that before. "I mean, I like *yours*," he said.

"You can touch me if you want." She never broke eye contact.

Shy's heart was in his throat now. He could feel himself brushing up against her, and he didn't know if he should feel embarrassed. "But what about—?"

Carmen put a finger to his lips to shut him up.

"Okay," he mumbled through her finger.

And then he reached through the water, slowly, and touched her bare knee, gently. When she didn't pull away, he shifted to the under part of her thigh.

Her skin was so soft.

So warm.

He tried to imagine if *he* was her fiancé and he could touch

Carmen's thigh like this whenever he wanted. After breakfast. Or in the middle of the night. He slid his hand down to her shapely calf and held it tight and stared deep into her eyes, trying to reach inside *her* chest now.

"I had a feeling," she whispered in his ear.

"What?" he said.

"I just . . . I like how your hands feel." She put her palm on his chest and looked down into the sulfur water, at his excitement. And this time he didn't move, didn't pull back. Because if she really wanted his truth, this was it. This was how he felt.

And there were no rules.

There was only him and Carmen.

In an abandoned sulfur pool movie stars used to soak themselves in.

They leaned in at the same time, and when their lips touched, Shy was lost. His fingers tracing the Muppet quote on her stomach, like he'd always wanted to. The pool dissolving into microscopic particles that swirled around them, like a whirlpool, then morphed into thousands of tiny hands that lifted Shy and Carmen up above the dilapidated resort, above the mountaintops, above the birds measuring the sky with their wings, and all the living creatures of the earth spoke to him.

You're lost, they said.

You're broken and alone.

But you're still here with us, and it's a gift.

All life is one life.

46
The Ring

It was over in an embarrassingly short amount of time.

Shy watched Carmen climb out of the pool and dry off with the towel she'd brought with her. Then he watched her step back into her jeans and pull her shirt over her head, the material quickly falling over her Muppet tattoo.

He felt like apologizing, he didn't even know why.

Instead, he stepped out of the pool and took the towel she was holding out for him. As he began drying off, he cleared his throat and said: "Hey, Carm. You okay with everything?"

She smiled. "Of course I'm okay, Shy."

"I just mean . . . So you're not gonna write out new rules or anything?"

She laughed a little—which struck Shy as a good sign. "Oh, I'm sure there'll eventually be new rules. I'll let you know when I figure them out." She looked past Shy, toward the trail. "But, hey, the sun's about to set. We should probably go find Shoe."

"Definitely," he said.

She took a couple steps forward and kissed him on the lips. It was a short kiss, but it lifted a huge weight off Shy's shoulders. "Hurry up and get dressed," she told him.

As he was zipping up his jeans a thought occurred to him: the ring.

He pulled it out of his pocket and held it out to her, excitedly. It took her a few seconds to notice what he was holding, but when she did, she froze. And her face shifted into a slight frown.

Shy cleared his throat. "Look, it doesn't mean anything, okay? I promise. I know you already got someone. But since the day I got this thing . . . I always thought you should have it."

Carmen backed away a little, shaking her head. "But it *does* mean something, Shy. You *know* it does."

"I'm not even saying for you to wear it," Shy told her. "Put it in a drawer somewhere. When all this is over. Dude, take it to a pawnshop. Whatever you want."

Carmen looked up at the sky and yanked at her wet hair. "God, Shy, I love that you think so highly of me." Her eyes fell on his again. "But I don't deserve it."

"Says who?" Shy said.

"Anyone who could've seen what we just did. What *I* just did." She shook her head. "Listen, I could never accept that ring, okay? Not until I find out for sure about Brett."

Shy lowered the ring, ashamed.

He'd never felt so small in his life. Like he might disappear into thin air. "But no one else would even know," he argued.

"*I'll* know."

Shy slipped the ring back in his pocket, trying to act like it was no big deal, like they could just move on and go find Shoeshine and continue on their stupid trip. But secretly he was crushed. One of the best moments of his life, being with Carmen, now felt like one of the worst moments of his life. She wouldn't even take his ring as just friends.

He turned away from her and started drying his floppy hair, ignoring the egg smell embedded into the towel.

"Come on, Shy," Carmen pleaded. "I know how I sound to you right now, but symbols like that still mean something—" She stopped abruptly and spun around to the dense stretch of trees behind them.

Shy heard it, too.

The sound of footsteps and snapping branches.

"Shy!" a distant voice called out. "Shy, you there?"

Shy could sense Carmen staring at him, but he couldn't look at her. Not yet.

"Shy!" The voice sounded closer now. And he was able to make out who it was. Dale.

"Yeah!" Shy called back.

In a few seconds Dale pushed through the overgrown tree limbs, followed by Tommy. Both of them out of breath. Dale looked at Shy, then Carmen. He seemed like he was hopped up on meds or something.

"What is it?" Shy asked.

"It was just on the radio," Dale said between breaths. "DJ Dan. We were listening and—"

"He made an announcement," Tommy said.

Dale nodded, excitedly. "It's all over."

"What's all over?" Shy asked.

"*Everything*," Dale said. "What's happening to California."

This time Shy *did* look at Carmen. She had her hands on her hips, her face frozen in a frown. "What are you talking about?" she said.

"This one drug company," Dale explained, pausing to suck in another breath, "according to the DJ, they found a cure for Romero Disease. A pill. The epidemic is over."

"Shut up," Carmen said.

Tommy nodded. "Swear to God."

Dale gave Tommy an awkward high five and turned back to Shy. "Tomorrow they're gonna start passing the pills out to everyone in California."

Shy's whole body went numb.

He and Carmen stared at each other.

"It's amazing news, right?" Dale said. He laughed and shook his head. "These people . . . they're heroes. They saved all of our lives."

"You don't happen to remember the name of this company, do you?" Shy asked, though he was pretty sure he knew the answer.

"Of course I do," Dale barked. "I wrote it down as soon as I heard it. They're called LasoTech."

47

Reports from the Wreckage

DJ DAN: . . . estimating that the total number of deaths due to Romero Disease is now more than triple the number attributed to the earthquakes. Which is why last night's announcement is so critical. New details continue trickling in, and we'll update this story throughout the coming days, but here's what we know as of right now:

A pharmaceutical company called LasoTech has developed a new medication to treat the disease. If taken once daily, for twenty-one consecutive days, this medication not only treats the symptoms—as first reported—it *cures* the disease.

LasoTech founder Jim Miller said in a press release this morning that his team began working on the new drug well before the earthquakes. LasoTech was also the first company to fund research on the disease back when it was only affecting a few poor neighborhoods near the Mexican border. When its offshore lab flooded, however, they lost over fifty percent of their work. Looters destroyed the rest. So they had to start from scratch. Even the president of the United States has acknowledged LasoTech's perseverance. He has asked Congress to work directly with Mr. Miller to distribute the medication across the West Coast in the coming weeks. Mr. Miller also revealed in his press release that he has personally sponsored several crusader groups for the past several weeks. These groups have provided food and water and medical supplies and sometimes even transportation through the desert.

LasoTech and several other pharmaceutical companies are now hard at work trying to come up with a vaccine that will protect the uninfected. We're told that only then will the president take down the border protecting the rest of the country. So for now, at least, the travel ban continues.

Meanwhile, many have resorted to extreme isolation in order to avoid contact with the infected. The walls protecting the most well-known safe haven, the Sony lots, may have fallen yesterday, but others still remain. Residents of Coronado, a small island off the coast of San Diego, have managed to destroy a portion of the bridge connecting the island to the city, cutting themselves off from the rest of the population. The Strand, the only other way to get onto the island, is now completely underwater.

A large community of yachts has come together a few miles off the coast of Santa Barbara. People move from boat to boat and live off seaweed and whatever fish they catch. They have no access to government drops, and drinking water is scarce, but they refuse to come back to the mainland for fear of the disease.

One of the largest isolated populations is a tent community deep in the California desert. Over five thousand people are now gathered together in the scorching heat. They have access to weekly drops, but they've also managed to tap wells and erect greenhouses where they harvest crops like radishes and spinach.

The most surprising of the isolated communities has to be state penitentiaries like San Quentin and Pelican Bay. We've heard that Avenal State Prison now boasts a population of over ten thousand. Prisoners who once longed to escape their cell walls now guard the perimeter of the prison, making sure no one sneaks in. . . .

Day 50

48
Today Versus Tomorrow

They were five miles west of Indio when the old-school gas gauge officially inched into the red. Shy stared at it for a few seconds, discouraged, before peering through the back window of the vintage ride Mario had insisted they take. It was a cherried-out 1953 Buick Skylark convertible, Mario's pride and joy, according to Dale and Tommy. The man had tossed Shoeshine the keys during the big goodbye scene, telling him: "I don't know where you all are going, but if you're involved, I trust it's somewhere important. Might as well get there in style."

Now here they were, creeping east on the 10 Freeway in the dark. Headlights off to keep a low profile. Shy and Carmen were supposed to be looking for a gas station off the freeway—no matter what condition it was in—but Shy's mind was still stuck on the news.

LasoTech had saved the day.

LasoTech was now working directly with the government, and Jim Miller, Addie's asshole dad, was being celebrated as some kind of hero.

The shit made Shy want to vomit.

Or break something.

The shadowy landscape had become more mountainous outside of San Bernardino. Shrubs were scattered along the shoulder. Power lines dipped and rose and dipped again. They had all the car windows down and the air smelled like dust and clay and fire and Carmen's wild hair, which blew into Shy's face from the front seat, constantly reminding him of the sulfur pool.

And how was Shy supposed to process those two competing emotions? Rage against an evil company and nervous excitement about a girl. *Woman!* It was like trying to push together the plus sides on two bar magnets.

Shy moved Dale's spare radio from his lap onto his right knee and tried to focus in spite of the classical music the DJ had been playing for the last few hours.

"Is that one up there?" Carmen said, pointing through the windshield.

Shy could vaguely make out a sign about a half-mile in the distance. But he didn't see an actual gas station.

Shoeshine peered into the rearview mirror before taking the next off-ramp.

There was a gas station all right, but it had been reduced to a charred pile of rubble. Shy counted six big holes in the ground where the pumps must have been. He wondered if the underground tanks had exploded in the fire.

Shoeshine parked the Skylark across the street and cut the engine, and the three of them stared at the debris.

"Be back in a minute," Shoeshine said, climbing awkwardly out of the driver's seat.

"Wait, where you going?" Shy said, suddenly nervous to be alone with Carmen.

The man stuck his head back in his window. "Sometimes an old man like myself has to relieve himself, young fella. It's a prostate thing. You'll get there one day."

"Oh." Shy watched Shoeshine limp away, relying heavily on his walking stick. There was no way the man would make it anywhere without the Skylark. They had to find gas.

Shy took a deep breath and focused on the back of Carmen's head. "Hey, Carm. I wanted to apologize about what happened back at—"

"Look," Carmen said, spinning around to face him, "I've been thinking about this since we left. If anyone should be apologizing it's me, okay? I just . . . I couldn't fight it anymore. And I know that doesn't say much about me, right? But when you took out that ring—"

"That's what I'm talking about, though," Shy said. "I don't even know why I did that." He fingered the ring in his pocket, feeling encouraged. If Carmen said she couldn't fight it, then it meant she was drawn to him, too. It wasn't all in his head. "But here's what I wanted to tell you," he continued. "I know you got someone, all right? And I know as soon as we get to Arizona—"

"*If* we get to Arizona."

"Exactly. *If* we get to Arizona. I know you're gonna start looking for the dude. And I respect that. For real. But look at shit, Carm." He pointed at the gas station, which was barely visible in the dark. "Everything's different now. People are dropping like flies. They're hiding out in prisons. I'm not worried about tomorrow right now. I'm worried about today."

Carmen nodded a little and kept looking at him. "That's actually a pretty smart way to say what I've been feeling, Sancho." She turned around farther so she could look him directly in the eyes. "I'm not claiming it's right, but who decides that shit now anyway? Right and wrong. Everything's changed."

Before Shy could respond, he heard a loud retching sound in the dark somewhere. He couldn't see anything outside his window, though. "Damn."

"Sounded like Shoe," Carmen said. "You think we should go look for him?"

Shy nodded and reached into the duffel for the flashlight Dale had given him. But as soon as he opened his door, there was Shoeshine, walking through the dark toward them. Shy followed the man with his eyes as he went around the front of the Skylark and climbed back into the driver's seat.

"You okay?" Carmen asked.

Shoeshine turned to her. "Who, me?"

"Sounded like you just got sick out there," Shy said from the backseat.

Shoeshine craned his neck to look at Shy. "Believe you got the wrong black man, young fella."

Shy and Carmen shared a frown as Shoeshine turned the key in the ignition. The man was definitely trying hide how bad off he was. Shy remembered the pus he'd seen on Shoeshine's wound.

The engine turned over several times before finally catching and roaring back to life. Shoeshine studied his mirrors for an unusually long time before pulling back onto the road.

49
The Rifle Bag

They were running on fumes by the time Shy pointed out the next gas station. Shoeshine pulled off the freeway and coasted up the off-ramp, then steered them over a narrow bridge, onto the north side of the freeway.

"There," Carmen said, pointing through the dark at a small empty parking lot beside the boarded-up gas station.

Shoeshine pulled into one of the stalls and shut off the engine. "She's not gonna move from this spot unless we get her some gas."

Shy counted four pumps this time, all covered in caution tape. A dented pickup truck was parked next to the station, like there might be someone staying there. "So how's this supposed to work anyway?" he asked. "You can't pump gas without power, right?"

"We need to find something we can use as a siphon," Shoeshine answered, distracted. He was staring back at the bridge they'd just crossed. Shy followed Shoeshine's gaze. But it was just an ordinary overpass. As far as he could tell, there was nothing else there.

After a few seconds, Shoeshine turned to Shy and Carmen. "If there's gas left, there's gonna be someone claiming it. So keep your eyes open." He grabbed the duffel and pushed open the driver's-side door.

Shy pulled the rifle bag onto his lap.

"Wait," Carmen said. "So we're just gonna, like, knock? It's the middle of the night."

Movement in the shadows made Shy freeze. Two hooded figures were standing in front of the door to the station, aiming handguns at the Skylark. "Guess we don't have to worry about the knocking part," he said.

One of the figures held up a megaphone. *"Get out of the car with your hands up,"* he announced in a high-pitched, muffled voice. *"And do it slow."*

Shoeshine stepped out first, still holding the duffel, and raised his hands.

Shy and Carmen shared a look. "I think they're just kids," he told her.

"Still," Carmen said. "I have a bad feeling about this."

But they had no choice. They were out of gas. Shy stashed the rifle bag by his feet and stepped out of the car, raising his hands. Carmen did the same.

The two figures approached cautiously.

When they were just a few steps away, Shy saw under their hoods. He was right. Two kids in hospital masks. Twelve or thirteen, tops. No shoes. It made him feel a little better, though there were still two guns in his face.

The shorter kid took the megaphone from the bigger one. *"You're not allowed to be on the road this late. We could shoot you right here and nobody would even care."*

The taller kid snatched back the megaphone and whacked the other kid on the side of the head. "They're right in front of us, stupid. You can talk regular now."

The shorter kid rubbed his head through his hood and glared at his friend.

"We just need some gas," Carmen said.

"You and everyone else," the taller kid said. "But we claimed this station right after the earthquakes. Paulie's dad used to work here."

"Exactly," the shorter one said.

"So if you want gas," the taller one went on, "you gotta trade something."

"What are you looking for?" Shoeshine said.

"Weapons," Paulie said.

Shoeshine looked at Shy, then looked into the back of the car. He was signaling for Shy to grab the rifle bag. Shy shot back his best "are you crazy?" look. There was no way they were going to get past LasoTech security without a way to defend themselves. Shoeshine had said so himself. It was the whole reason they'd stopped in San Bernardino.

"Go on, young fella," Shoeshine said. "Get 'em the rifles."

Shy couldn't believe it. He shot Carmen a confused look, then reluctantly reached back into the Skylark for the rifle bag.

The taller boy nodded, and motioned for Shy, Carmen and Shoeshine to follow him toward the boarded-up station.

50
Twinkies and Spoiled Milk

There were three more kids inside the sour-smelling station, all of them putting on hospital masks and rubbing their eyes like they'd just woken up. No adults that Shy could see. The place was trashed, too. The food shelves were mostly picked clean and the refrigerator was full of empty cartons and wrappers and there were wrappers all over the cracked cement floor. In the dim candle-light, Shy spied five worn pieces of cardboard against the far wall. Their beds, he assumed. Folded Shammys for pillows.

The DJ Dan show played quietly on a small clock radio near the cleaned-out cash register. Still just classical music which meant the DJ was asleep.

The taller kid opened up the gun bag to inspect the rifles. He took them out one by one and held them up to a row of burning candles, looking into each muzzle and then peering through the sight. "I'll give you a five-gallon can for all three of 'em," he said.

"Well, we need to hold on to at least one for protection," Shoeshine answered. He shifted the duffel bag from one shoulder to the other. Having the duffel seemed careless to Shy. They should have left it in the Skylark.

"What you need," another kid said, "is some gas in your tank. Otherwise you're stuck here with us."

"And you can't be stuck with us," the taller one said. "You know we could just take these for nothin' and send you on your way, right? But I like to be fair. For karma reasons."

"Where you all trying to get, anyways?" the smallest kid, Paulie, said. He hopped up onto the table next to the cash register and pulled down his mask, revealing his dirt-covered face.

The taller kid snapped his fingers, and Paulie quickly put his mask back on.

"Come on, Paulie," another kid scolded him. "Even if they got a cure now we still don't wanna catch nothin'."

"Okay, okay," Paulie said through his mask.

"We're on our way to Arizona," Carmen told them.

The kids gave each other strange looks. The tall kid even laughed a little, saying: "You know they built a fence out there, right?"

"Don't you listen to the radio?" another kid asked.

"We know about the stupid border," Carmen snapped.

Shy noticed that the tall kid who'd ushered them inside the station had lowered his gun. He wondered if they could steal the gas somehow and keep the rifles. It was five against three, but they were just kids.

One of them moved a sheet of plywood away from the front window and pointed outside. "What kind of car is that out there? It looks historical."

"It sure is," Shoeshine said. "You're looking at a 1953 Buick Skylark convertible. Mint condition. You ever seen a classic car like that?"

The kid shook his head.

"Little different than that pickup you got parked out front," Shy said. He could tell Shoeshine was up to something, and he decided to try and play along.

"My daddy left me that truck," Paulie said.

"Where's your dad now?" Carmen asked him. "He stay here, too?"

"My daddy's dead," the boy answered. "Just like everyone else is dead."

"Paulie!" the tall kid snapped, shooting him a dirty look.

Paulie shrugged and glanced at the floor.

Shy knew from this little back-and-forth that there weren't any adults around. It was just these five kids. Alone. Living on Twinkies and spoiled milk. They'd probably made a pact to keep it to themselves.

"We're sorry for your loss," Shy said in a sympathetic voice. He glanced at Shoeshine, who gave a subtle nod.

"Nobody else is gonna die, though," another kid said, "now that they got that medicine that cures you. We heard it on the radio."

"We heard that, too," Shoeshine said. "Soon it'll all be over, and you boys'll be back in school."

"The school's burned down," one of the kids said.

"Then they'll build you all a brand-new one," Shy said. "It'll probably be mad nice, too."

It went quiet in the station for a few seconds. Carmen frowned at Shy, trying to figure out what he was doing. But Shy didn't know, either. He was just following Shoeshine's lead, assuming he had a plan.

264

"You know what?" Shoeshine said, tapping his walking stick against the cement floor. "I just thought of a new offer I'd like to propose." He cringed a little, like his leg was hurting, then he motioned toward the front window. "How would you all like to *own* that classic car out there?"

"What are you talking about?" the tallest kid said.

Now Shy understood.

It was a way for them to keep the rifles.

"Where we're headed," Shoeshine said, "we're really gonna need all three of those rifles. I'd be willing to trade the Skylark for your pickup, though. Long as you fill it full of gas."

Paulie hopped down from the counter excitedly. "It's already got a full tank, mister. And you got a deal." He turned to the tall kid. "Right, Quinn?"

Quinn went to the window and looked out at the Skylark. He wasn't as quick to jump on Shoeshine's offer, even though all the other kids were urging him to take the deal.

It surprised Shy that Shoeshine was willing to give up Mario's car so quickly. But at the end of the day, it didn't matter how they got to Arizona, as long as they got there.

"Lemme explain something to you guys," Quinn said, turning back to his buddies. "Having a fancy car doesn't do anything for us right now. It's what you can *do* with it. And we stick all kinds of stuff in the bed of that truck."

"Yeah, but we got the Jeep for that," one of the kids argued.

"You heard him," Paulie said. "Now that they got a cure, it'll all be over soon. Anyways, it was *my* dad's truck. I should have some say."

Quinn stood there a few seconds, staring back and forth between the Skylark and his boys. Shy could tell the kid liked being in charge, having everyone waiting on his answer.

"You kept it in real nice condition," Quinn finally said to

Shoeshine. "Maybe it'll be worth something when things got back to normal."

"Be worth a lot," Shoeshine told him.

After another short pause, Quinn said: "You know what? Screw it. We got a deal."

The other kids broke out in a cheer. It showed how young they really were. Shy had to hold back a smile.

"Shoot, I'll even throw in a five-gallon can of gas," Quinn said. "That way you'll for sure be able to get all the way to Arizona." He turned to one of his boys. "Go put a can in the bed of the truck."

Shoeshine tossed Quinn the keys to the Skylark, and Quinn tossed him the keys to the truck. Shy was impressed with Shoeshine's negotiating skills. Especially considering how he seemed to be in pain throughout the whole exchange. Now they'd be able to get back on the road and stop staring at the gas gauge. They still had a few more hours before the sun came up.

One of the kids hustled into the back of the station for a can of gas. The other kids began pleading with Quinn to let them take the Skylark for a test-drive. "We gotta make sure it runs before we let 'em go, right?" one argued.

Quinn reluctantly handed over the keys, saying: "You better not scratch it up, though."

"You'll want to put a little gas in first," Shoeshine said. "We brought her in here bone-dry."

Quinn pointed at Paulie. "You can put in the gas, but you're not driving."

Paulie nodded and hurried out the front door with the two other kids. Quinn watched them go, a slight grin on his face. Even after everything they'd been through, Shy thought, they were still just kids. He wondered if Shoeshine felt that about him and Carmen.

"We barely just got that thing," Carmen said, sidling up to Shy.

"Least we still got the rifles," he told her.

"True." She didn't look too happy. "Why's this trip even matter anymore, though? They already got a cure."

"Yeah, but they don't have a letter that proves everything LasoTech did." Shy could feel the anger begin to stir again. "If we just let shit ride, everyone will keep thinking those dickheads are heroes."

Shy watched through the window as the kids disappeared around the side of the building, then reappeared with a second gas can, which they carried down to the Skylark. They poured some gas into the tank, then climbed inside the old car and started up the engine. They sat there for a few minutes, turning on the headlights, rolling the windows up and down, honking the horn, opening and closing all the doors, then Shy heard the grinding sound of the driver stripping the gears as he backed out of the parking space.

Quinn laughed at the sound. "Stupid kids."

Shoeshine joined Shy, Carmen and Quinn at the window, and they all watched the Skylark jerk out of the gas station and merge onto the dark, empty road.

As the car rolled through the first stop sign, Shy suddenly spotted a large blur rapidly approaching from the opposite direction.

A black Hummer.

"Look out!" Carmen shouted through the window.

But it was too late.

51
Sick and Alive

The Hummer smashed right into the front grille of the Skylark, crunching the hood and shattering the windshield and sending the old car spinning across the dark and narrow road.

An earsplitting scream filled the station. Shy turned and saw Quinn breaking free of Shoeshine's grip, pushing through the front door of the station and racing toward the crash.

"Oh my God!" Carmen kept repeating. She grabbed Shy by the arm, her face frozen in shock.

Shy stared at the flames devouring the front half of the Skylark, illuminating the heads of the kids inside.

"Get down!" Shoeshine shouted at him and Carmen.

Shy spun around as Shoeshine whipped one of the rifles out of the gun bag and aimed it at the window, kicking the duffel toward Shy. Shy quickly scooped it up and slung it over his shoulder and ducked under the windowsill next to Carmen, both of them breathing hard and staring at each other wide-eyed.

It was the same black Hummer they'd seen when they were burying Marcus near the freeway. Shy was sure of it. But how could LasoTech possibly have tracked them here in the dark?

Shy peeked over the windowsill again. Carmen grabbed at his shirt to try and pull him back down, but he had to see. Three men dressed in black had jumped out of the Hummer. One turned and shot Quinn in the chest. Then the stomach. The boy's body falling limp to the pavement. The other two raced up to the inflamed Skylark and raised their handguns and fired round after round through the side windows and the windshield, lighting up the desert night.

"Jesus," Shy whispered.

The men didn't stop shooting until all movement inside the car had stopped, then one of them circled the thing, opening each door and searching the bodies inside. The man shook his head and pointed at the station.

All Shy's blood rushed to his head and his breaths were coming way too fast. The men had just massacred four kids without hesitating a second. Massacred them in the hopes that they were Shy, Carmen and Shoeshine. And now they were marching toward the station, weapons drawn.

Shoeshine took a few steps forward, aiming his rifle at the window. Shy pulled the duffel off, thinking he should hide it. He stashed it under the counter and hurried behind Shoeshine and grabbed a rifle and cocked it like Shoeshine had shown him back at the Bright House and turned toward the front window. Carmen staring at him.

The three men in black cut through the gas pumps, toward the station, and glass suddenly exploded all around Shy. Shoeshine shoved Carmen away from the window and fired back, dropping one of the LasoTech guys with a single shot.

Bullets whizzed through the window and Shy took cover behind one of the empty shelves, listening to shots pepper the wall behind him, sparking off the cement floor, shattering the glass cooler. Without thinking about anything at all, Shy found himself on the move, in a crouch, back toward the window. He settled the barrel of his rifle on the windowsill beside Shoeshine, who was reloading and took aim and fired two shots in quick succession.

To his surprise, one of the two remaining men dropped to the pavement, not ten feet in front of the station door, grasping at his chest. Shy took aim again and finished the guy off with a shot to the midsection. Then he took aim at the other guy, realizing he'd just killed a man.

His heart was in his throat.

He felt sick and alive.

It was so easy. A slight curl of his right pointer finger and a man's life was gone forever.

He fired again but missed.

The man spun back around and took off at a sprint toward the Hummer, somehow avoiding another shot from Shy and one from Shoeshine. He swung open the door of the Hummer and scurried inside and soon the engine came roaring back to life.

"I'm going after him!" Shoeshine shouted, limping toward the door and pushing through.

Shy was still aiming his rifle out the window, even though he no longer had a target. Carmen had to grab him by the arm and yank him out of his trance. Shy grabbed the duffel from behind the counter and they both sprinted out of the station, racing around the building after Shoeshine, who had already started up the truck and was cranking it into reverse.

Shy dove headfirst into the passenger side door with Carmen, their bodies momentarily tangled as the truck lurched forward.

Two more shots rang out.

But they didn't come from inside the truck.

Shy righted himself and peered cautiously through the windshield, expecting to see the man inside the Hummer shooting at them, but what he saw instead was the massive vehicle swerving.

One of the back tires had blown out.

Pure luck, Shy told himself.

But then a third shot rang out, and one of the Hummer's *front* tires exploded. This time the vehicle veered so sharply to the right it crashed through the guardrail and went hurtling over the side of the overpass.

For half a second the world went deafeningly silent.

Shy squeezing the duffel bag straps in his right hand.

Then he heard the earthshaking crash of the Hummer hitting the freeway below, followed closely by a booming explosion. Smoke rose up over the side of the bridge and drifted toward their truck.

Shy sucked in breaths, staring at the gap in the guardrail and trying to wrap his head around what had just happened. All three of them were still holding rifles, even Carmen, like they were some kind of mismatched posse in the Wild West.

Then Shy spotted it through the smoke. A motorcycle speeding down the freeway on-ramp, heading east. The driver must have shot out the tires of the Hummer as he passed.

None of them spoke as Shoeshine pulled the truck up to the lip of the bridge, and they jumped out and hurried to the guardrail to take a look.

The Hummer was upside down on the freeway and lit up by high-arcing flames. There was no sign that anyone had climbed out alive. In the distance, Shy could no longer make out the shape of the mysterious motorcycle speeding away.

Day 51

52
California Ghost Town

Something moved in the bushes.

Shy turned quickly enough to see what it was this time—a small Mexican boy spying on them. He stood up and called to the boy: "Hey! Nobody's gonna hurt you!" But the kid was already hurrying away in a chorus of rustling leaves and snapping branches.

For a second or two Shy was convinced it was his nephew, Miguel. But then he remembered. Miguel was dead. Same as the rest of his family.

Shy sat back down on the log next to Carmen. "It's just some kid."

"Yeah, 'cause kids never lead to anything fucked-up, right?" There was more than a little sarcasm in Carmen's voice.

"Good point." Shy glanced over at the bushes again.

Nothing.

"Anyways, like I was telling you," Carmen continued, "if it was just some random *vato* heading east on his motorcycle, why'd he shoot at the Hummer then? Wouldn't he wanna slip by without calling attention to himself?"

Shy picked up a small rock and tossed it into the lazy river in front of them. He studied the tiny splash it made.

"Nah, he was going after them," Carmen said. "Had to be. You saw the way he shot out those tires. I agree with what Shoe said."

"Maybe you guys are right," Shy said, still staring at the water. Shoeshine believed the man who'd shot out the Hummer's tires was a crusader from the other side. They'd heard on the radio about regular folks who had come to California to try and protect the unprotected. The fact that the guy had ridden off so quickly proved to Shoeshine that he wasn't used to encounters like that. He was still getting his feet wet.

"The point is," Carmen said, "we don't know. So it's probably not even worth speculating about. All we can do is hurry up and get the damn duffel to Avondale."

Shy glanced over at Shoeshine, who'd settled in about twenty yards down the riverbank from them, where he was writing in his journal again. After the Hummer incident, Shy, Carmen and Shoeshine had scrambled back into the truck and driven east for miles and miles, talking very little about what had happened. When the first few rays of daylight spilled out onto the two lanes of freeway in front of them, Shoeshine pulled off in a town called Blythe, which he said was on the border of California and Arizona, less than a hundred and fifty miles from the Avondale border. He maneuvered the beat-up truck through back roads to the secluded stretch of river they were at now, fifteen miles north of town.

Carmen picked up a small stick and rolled it between her fingers. "When we drove past the Skylark," she said to Shy, "did you by any chance . . . ?"

"Look inside?" he said.

She nodded.

"I did."

It was dark, but Shy had seen enough. Four small shot-up bodies lying all over the seats. Blood dripping off what little glass was left in the windshield. He remembered thinking how this wasn't some video game where you could just hit Pause and go grub out on your mom's empanadas. This was real. This was *permanent*. These kids who were mouthing off only minutes ago were now dead.

But Shy had seen something else before Shoeshine drove them away from the gas station, something he didn't mention to Carmen.

The tweaked body of the man he'd shot and killed.

Back when their sailboat had first landed in California, Shy wouldn't have been capable of shooting *anything*, much less a person. Didn't matter what the situation was. But something inside him had changed. When he'd pulled the trigger at the station, and saw the man drop, he realized something terrifying.

Killing was easy.

People thought there was this huge chasm between life and death, but really there was nothing. Not when you had a gun. You could end someone in the blink of an eye. With the twitch of a finger. Before you even knew what happened. And the world didn't stop like everyone probably thought it did. It just kept right on spinning. It didn't give a shit about your karma or your act of violence. That part was all in your head.

Shy was yanked out of his thoughts when he heard more rustling in the bushes. He turned and saw that it was the young

Mexican boy again. This time he was with a slightly younger girl who looked just like him. His sister, probably.

Shy and Carmen stood up.

The girl rattled off something in Spanish, but it was too fast for Shy. In order for him to understand Spanish, he needed it to be spoken slowly.

"She wants to know where we came from and if we're sick," Carmen told him.

"I know what she said," Shy lied.

Carmen turned back to the kids, but before she could answer, Shoeshine called out: "*Perdónanos, amigos. Sólo estamos pasando de camino a Arizona. Le aseguramos que ninguno de nosotros está enfermo.*"

Shy stared at Shoeshine.

So did Carmen.

How was it possible that some old black Buddha dude spoke better Spanish than Shy? It made him feel ashamed. Like some kind of fake Mexican. No wonder his old man nicknamed him Shinola back in the day.

The boy stepped forward. "If you are not sick," he said in a stiff version of English, "my grandma has an offer to feed you back at our camp."

"That's very generous," Shoeshine said.

When Shy caught the boy staring directly at him, a weird butterfly feeling flooded his stomach. It was creepy how much the kid reminded him of his nephew.

The brother and sister led Shy, Carmen and Shoeshine down the river, about a hundred yards from where they'd parked the truck. They moved into a dense patch of tall bushes, away from the water, and when they emerged, Shy stopped in his tracks and stared at the surreal sight. A couple dozen tents were set up in and around half-decayed old housing foundations and rusted-out vintage cars that sat on busted axles. Tagged cement walls, positioned randomly throughout the mostly flat desert landscape, seemed to sag and crumble with age. To the right of Shy was what looked to be an old, dilapidated baseball field, the dugouts no more than a few scattered cement blocks covered in weeds.

"What *is* this place?" Carmen asked.

"No idea," Shy said. The people he saw milling around, he realized, were all Mexican. Like *Mexican* Mexican. Like maybe some of them didn't have their papers.

Shoeshine wiped his sweat-drenched face with the arm of his short-sleeved shirt. "Welcome to Midland, California," he said. "Sixty, seventy years ago, this place looked a lot different from what you see now."

The boy that had led them there turned around. "Please come!" he called out, waving them toward a small pocket of tents near the overgrown baseball field.

As they started walking again, Carmen said to Shoeshine: "You sure you're okay to walk?"

"Of course I'm okay to walk." Shoeshine stepped slowly and deliberately now, putting a ton of weight on his walking stick. If they didn't have a gassed-up truck, Shy knew there was no way the man would be able to take even one night of walking.

"Maybe there's someone here who could look at your stitches," Carmen said.

"Not interested." Shoeshine stopped and pulled the duffel off his shoulder. He handed it to Shy, saying: "But I will ask that you carry this from now on, young fella."

"No problem." Shy took the bag and slung it over his shoulder, happy to help however he could.

"This used to be a company town owned by U.S. Gypsum," Shoeshine continued. "Folks from all over came to mine the gypsum in these parts. The company sold the stuff to Hollywood, where it was used as fake snow. There's a little history lesson for you. There were over a thousand people living here at its peak, but when Hollywood found a cheaper alternative, this place dried up almost overnight, became the ghost town you see today."

"How do you know so much about this place?" Shy asked.

Shoeshine grinned. "I mined the gypsum here briefly in my youth." He wiped his brow again and let out a chuckle. "I was just a kid back then. Not even eighteen."

They walked a long stretch in silence.

Shy did the math in his head. Sixty years back, and the guy was probably in his teens. Wouldn't that put Shoeshine in his midseventies now? He'd known the guy was old, but not *that* old. Which made all the stuff he'd done since the ship went down even more insane.

Shy remembered what Mario told him and Carmen back at the Bright House. That Shoeshine had been born rich and then left home without even saying goodbye to his family. One day, Shy vowed, after all this was over, he and Shoeshine were going to sit down and have an actual conversation. And he wouldn't settle for Shoeshine's usual cryptic answers. He'd get the whole story out of the guy.

There were cactus shrubs all over the place. Rolling tumbleweeds. Faceless plastic shopping bags that were lifted into the air by the wind, then dropped back down to the gravelly sand. The air was so hot and dry Shy couldn't stop wiping sweat from his brow.

Shoeshine pointed his stick to the left of where they stood. "About a half-mile that way are the Blythe Intaglios. Every day after work I used to go hang out by the biggest of them and walk the perimeter."

"The Blythe what?" Carmen asked.

"Intaglios," Shoeshine said. "A group of giant figures scraped into the earth by ancient people. The largest is one hundred and seventy-one feet long and was created thousands of years ago. I used to stare through the fence at it for hours, trying to imagine the lives of the people who'd created it."

Carmen shot Shy a look.

He shrugged subtly, watching the man stare off in the direction of his ancient artifact. It was the most he'd ever heard Shoeshine say about himself at any one time. And he'd never seen him look so nostalgic. It made Shy wonder if the man felt closer to him and Carmen now. Like they were actual friends.

The two kids eventually led them to a large, weathered tent with a gaping hole near the front flap. There were several tiny old Mexican ladies sitting on overturned crates, talking while they sewed and folded laundry. A small fire crackled inside a circle of uneven rocks.

One of the old ladies pushed off her crate when she saw the boy and girl coming. She gave a big smile and hugged them both, glancing at Shy and his crew. She said something to the boy and girl, and the boy spun around and called out: "My grandma says to sit. She will make food so you're not hungry from your travels."

The woman shuffled toward the fire and lifted a pan off the ground. She placed it directly onto the open flame and used a pair of tongs to lift some type of shapeless dough out of a plastic container another lady held out to her. The dough hit the pan with a sizzle, and the rich corn smell immediately wafted into the air, making Shy's stomach buzz in anticipation.

Carmen tapped Shy's elbow. "Dude, where the hell *are* we? And how come *they're* not worried about us having the disease?"

"I don't even know," Shy told her. "But I'm gonna eat first and ask questions later."

"Good plan."

Shy watched Shoeshine lower himself slowly onto the crate the old woman who was cooking had just vacated. The man then turned to the Mexican ladies and spoke to them in perfect Spanish. In a few seconds they were all laughing together like old friends.

53

A Quiet Swim in the River

After killing a plate of beans, some kind of mystery meat, and thick corn tortillas—and thanking the grandma profusely—Shy and Carmen followed the boy and girl back to the river, leaving Shoeshine behind with the old Mexican ladies. The boy pointed to the water. "Every day we swim here. You can swim, too, with us?"

Shy glanced at Carmen.

She shrugged. "We're not leaving till the sun goes down anyway, right?"

Shy turned and saw the boy and girl already stripping down to their *chones*, their skinny little brown bodies slick with sweat. "Let me ask you a question," he said to the boy. "Why are you guys being so nice to us?"

A confused look settled over the boy's face.

"*Nadie viene aquí*," the girl said.

The boy nodded. "It gets boring with just old people." He grabbed his sister by the wrist and the two of them took off toward the water, laughing. They dove in, one after the other, and splashed their way out to where they could no longer touch.

"Screw it," Shy said, stashing the duffel bag behind a boulder and turning to Carmen. "My ass is going in. It's hot." He pulled off his shirt, tossed it onto the duffel.

Carmen pulled off her shirt, too, leaving only her bra and panties. "Just try and keep your hands to yourself this time, all right, Sancho?"

"I was about to tell you the same thing." Shy cracked up a little when he saw her Kermit tattoo again. But he realized something. He liked Carmen even *more* for being so into the damn Muppets. If they ever made it across the wall in Avondale, he decided he'd watch more episodes so he could see what it was all about.

They waded in slowly, and the cold water brought Shy's exhausted body back to life. It was such amazing relief from the hot sun, which was now directly overhead.

The boy splashed Shy in the face, laughing wildly.

Shy wiped his eyes and spit into the water. Before he could splash back, the boy lunged forward and got Shy into a weak, playful headlock, shouting: "I am WWE champion of the world!"

"*¡Ya!*" the girl shouted at her brother. "*¡Deja a mi novio!*"

Shy easily tossed the boy aside. "What'd she say?" he asked.

The boy shook his head. "My sister sometimes is like a crazy person."

Carmen waded closer to them. "You need to talk some sense into that girl, dude. You're her big brother."

The boy turned and splashed Carmen, too.

Shy and Carmen splashed the boy back, and Shy wiped the water out of his eyes again, cracking up, because the whole thing reminded him of going to the pool at the Y back when he was little. He watched Carmen and the boy go at it for a few seconds, then he went all the way under, letting the crisp, clean river water run into his mouth before spitting it out.

After a few minutes of playing with the kids, Shy drifted off by himself. So did Carmen. They looked at each other every once in a while and smiled, but mostly they just treaded water in their own little worlds.

Shy remembered beating his hands through the water just like this in the middle of the Pacific Ocean, watching his Paradise Cruise liner slowly sink in the distance. And he remembered swimming toward the broken lifeboat where he and Addie were stranded for several days.

Addie.

He hadn't thought of her since he heard the recording of her distorted voice on the radio. So much had happened since then. Him and Carmen in the sulfur pool. And the Skylark. And the kids from the gas station.

After a while Shy decided it was best to stop remembering and just float. He concentrated on the water lapping all around him. And he listened to the boy and girl laugh and splash in the distance, shouting things at each other in Spanish. Beyond them he heard the cries of far-off birds. Hawks, he was pretty sure. He knew because when he was little his old man used to stop him whenever he spotted a hawk circling the sky. Didn't matter where. In the liquor-store parking lot. Or leaving school. And they'd just stand there watching it together. In silence.

Shy realized something as he breathed in the desert air and continued floating. He was happy. At least, in this very moment. His stomach was full. The river water was cool. There were no helicopters above them. No clouds. Just the bright blue sky. And he was with Carmen. They weren't flirting this time. They weren't

285

even talking. But just having her close by made everything better. He didn't even care that their time together was only temporary.

After a couple hours or so of just floating around, Shy saw that the boy and girl were slowly wading back toward shore. "You guys done already?" Shy called to them. "I could stay in here all day."

"I can show you something," the boy called back.

The girl didn't seem too excited about this. Shy could tell by the look on her face. "What is it?" he asked the boy.

"Just please. Come."

54
The Other Side of the Hill

Shy followed the boy back toward the ghost town, only this time they veered toward the hilly stretch a few hundred yards behind all the tents. It was just the two of them now. When the girl refused to go with her brother, Carmen walked with her back to camp.

The sun was already beginning its slow descent, but it was still scorching hot. An awful smell had materialized, and it seemed to grow stronger the farther they hiked. Like rotting manure. Shy covered his mouth as he followed the boy up the small, rocky hill.

He decided he liked this kid. Maybe it was his resemblance to Miguel. Or the fact that his family had been so nice. Shy felt like he needed to do something for him. And the one thing he could do was protect him from Romero Disease. Anyway, what was the point of having a lifesaving vaccine if you never actually saved a life? Shy began using his diamond ring to rip open the second extra compartment Shoeshine had sewn into the gut of the duffel.

The boy stopped at the edge of a steep drop-off and stared at the valley below.

Shy fumbled with the duffel, opening up the tear he'd just made while at the same time trying to cover his nose and mouth with his arm to block the overwhelming stench. It wasn't working. He looked up from the duffel to see why they'd stopped and found himself staring down at a field of rotting corpses. The valley was a giant graveyard.

Some of the bodies looked like they'd been dumped weeks ago, and a pack of vultures picked the meat off their bones and tore through their clothing. But what made Shy even sicker was the fact that at least two of the bodies were still moving.

They were *alive*.

"What the hell *is* this place?" Shy asked.

"If you are diseased," the boy said, "you have to come here to die so no one else is sick."

Shy stared at one of the moving bodies—he could tell it was a man by his clothes—who was furiously scratching at both legs. "They come here on their own?" Shy asked.

The boy nodded. "If their eyes become red."

"Jesus." Shy crouched down and studied the rest of the bodies. There were at least twenty of them scattered among the tumbleweed. He thought of Addie and her dad. And everyone else associated with LasoTech. The supposed "heroes" who'd created a supposed "cure" for Romero Disease. It disgusted Shy. In reality they'd murdered each and every person who'd had to die in this kind of agony.

Like Shy's grandma and his nephew.

And Rodney.

And Carmen's dad.

Shy turned to the boy, who was still staring down into the valley. He had to use one of the precious vaccines, not just for the boy but for Miguel, too. For his whole family. When he finally loosened the extra pouch inside the duffel, he slipped out one of the syringes and held it behind his back. He just needed to figure out a way to vaccinate the boy without him knowing.

A few seconds later it came to him.

WWE.

"My sister never will come here with me," the boy said. "But I have to. Every day."

"I get it," Shy told him. "Out of respect, right?"

The boy grew fidgety. He shoved his hands in his pockets, then pulled them out and crossed his arms and looked up at Shy. "I come," he said, "because my mom is down there, too."

"Your mom?"

The boy nodded, his eyes glassy.

"Shit, man. I'm sorry." Shy turned back to the valley. He couldn't imagine the heartbreak the boy must feel every time he looked down into the valley. All those bodies. And the vultures. And the smell. His mom.

Shy took the kid by the arm and told him: "Come on, man. Let's get out of here. They're probably waiting on us."

As they started back down the hill, Shy occasionally glanced at the boy. He seemed like such a good kid. Tough, too. No kid should have to be this tough. Shy cleared his throat after a few minutes. "You know, me and you are actually a lot alike."

The boy looked up at him, his eyes no longer glassy.

"For real," Shy said. "We both got sisters. And grandmas who can cook. And we both lost people to this bullshit disease."

The boy nodded and looked straight ahead.

"And you know what else?" Shy said.

"What?"

Shy nudged the boy's arm. "We're both WWE fans."

He gave Shy a little smile.

"But lemme ask you this, little bro. You ever heard of a move called the Triple Shinola Throw-Down Deluxe?"

"There is no move like this," the boy argued. "I know all moves they say on TV. This is fake."

"Fake my ass. It's only the best wrestling move ever invented." Shy stopped in the middle of the overgrown baseball field. "Here, I'll show you."

The boy stopped, too. A big smile on his face.

Shy set down the duffel bag and got into a wrestling position, the syringe now unwrapped and sticking out of his back pocket. "First, you pop 'em one in the throat with the heel of your hand." Shy faked hitting the kid in the Adam's apple. "Then, when he's pissed off, you use his weight against him. Charge me."

The boy moved forward, and Shy grabbed him by the shoulders, while at the same time crouching so that he was able to flip the boy over his shoulders, onto his back. Just as the boy hit the ground, Shy reached for the syringe and stuck him in the leg.

"¡Ay!" the kid exclaimed.

"Jesus, man!" Shy shouted, tossing away the empty syringe and scrambling to his feet.

The boy got up, too. He reached for his leg, looking at the ground, and Shy made a big production of grabbing for his right arm. "Yo, you got mad spiders around here or some shit?" he asked, frowning. "I think I just got bit by a spider."

The kid attempted to look around at the back of his own leg, but he couldn't quite manage it.

"Damn, man," Shy went on. "Guess I shouldn't be horsing around out here in tarantula territory."

"You saw a spider?" the boy asked innocently.

Shy nodded. "I can't stand those bastards, man." He was still rubbing his arm. "Anyway, now you know what the Triple Shinola Throw-Down Deluxe is."

The kid's smile came back. He gave Shy a little shove, saying: "I don't believe you."

As they continued walking, a bright spot opened in Shy's chest. Nothing he could do would help bring back the boy's mom, but at least now he was safe from Romero Disease.

In the distance Shy spotted Carmen walking toward them from the tent community. As she got closer, he could tell she was upset. "What's the matter?" he called out.

Carmen held out a set of keys on her finger. "Shoeshine says it's time to leave," she told him.

"The sun hasn't even set yet."

"And he also says . . ." She covered her mouth, like she was trying not to cry.

"What?" Shy asked, worried. "Is he okay?"

Carmen dropped her hand and took a deep breath to compose herself. "He's not coming with us, Shy. He says we're on our own now."

55
Blythe Intaglios

"Come on, man," Shy pleaded, as he inched the truck alongside Shoeshine, who was limping down a long dirt path. "Just get in. We *need* you."

Shoeshine wiped his brow on his shirt and waved Shy off. "It's *your* time now, young fella."

"You're wasting your breath," Carmen told Shy. She was in the passenger seat, turning the flashlight they'd found in the glove compartment on and off. "I tried everything I could think of before you came back."

Shy was sweating his ass off. Even though the sun was starting to set, the heat was stifling. And it wasn't like the truck had working AC. "I'm just gonna keep following you then," Shy told Shoeshine. "Guess now we'll *never* get this vaccine across the border."

The man coughed and kept limping along.

Shy and Carmen had left camp in a rush. They didn't even get to say a proper goodbye to the boy or his sister or the old ladies. When Shy showed up with the boy, Carmen told him Shoeshine had already set off down the road. And he wouldn't tell her where he was going. Shy took off immediately to fetch the truck.

Now here they were. Barely traveling two miles an hour. Wasting precious gas.

Something had to give.

"For real, Shoe," Shy tried again. "Don't you wanna see what this border's all about? Don't you wanna see the looks on those LasoTech guys' faces when their asses get cuffed by the FBI?"

The man just kept creeping along with his walking stick, mopping his brow every few seconds with his shirtsleeve. Coughing. He looked bad now. *Really* bad. His limp was more exaggerated, and his clothes were soaked through with sweat. For the first time since Shy had known him, his braided chin beard had even come undone.

They went on like this for another fifteen, twenty minutes, until Shoeshine suddenly stopped in front of a rusty chain-link fence that looked out of place in the middle of the desert. Shy put the truck in park and grabbed the duffel and got out with Carmen, the two of them walking right up to the man. "See, you can't get rid of us that easily," Shy said.

Shoeshine pulled the bottom of his shirt up to mop his drenched forehead. He coughed into his hand. "There's no pretty way to say it," he told them. "But this is where it ends for me."

"What are you even *talking* about?" Carmen barked. She turned to Shy, disgusted. "You know what? I'm not trying to listen to this shit no more. He needs a doctor, Shy. I said we'd take him to one, but he *still* doesn't wanna come. It's just stupid." She threw her hands in the air and stormed off.

"Carm!" Shy called to her. "Hang on!"

She didn't turn around, though. Just kept marching away from them, out into the desert.

Shy looked at Shoeshine. "Fine, you don't give a shit about yourself. But what about *us*, man? We'll never make it without you, Shoe. You're the one who's been leading us this whole time."

"Am I?" Shoeshine asked.

Shy frowned. "Hell yeah, you are."

"Or have we all been following *you*, young fella? Think back to your time on the ship. The man in the black suit. Addie and her father. Carmen. Myself. What if I told you we're all reacting to your actions?"

"There's no way," Shy said.

"And now out here in the desert," Shoeshine told him. "You can't even see it, can you? You have no idea who else you're leading."

Shy shook his head, beyond frustrated. Shoeshine was doing his stupid riddle thing again. And Shy didn't have *time* for riddles right now.

Shoeshine gripped the chain-link fence in front of him. Shy stared at the back of the man's singed gray hair for a while. And then it dawned on him where they were. The ancient figures scraped into the earth. The ones Shoeshine said he was obsessed with back when he was young and mining gypsum for Hollywood.

Shy cleared his throat, said: "This is one of those intaglios, isn't it?"

"This here's the largest," Shoeshine said, pointing through the fence. "It's hard to see from the ground like this, but like I said earlier, it's a hundred and seventeen feet long."

Shy stared through the fence, but he couldn't really make it out. "Why's this thing so important to you anyway?"

"It marks a different time," Shoeshine said, without turning away from it. "Back when humans moved freely across the land, like animals. Before capitalism set its invisible trap."

"Some people still live free," Shy said. "*You* do."

Shoeshine chuckled and looked back at Shy. "It's not the same, I'm afraid." He coughed and mopped his brow again, then pointed at the duffel hanging over Shy's shoulder. "Do me a favor. Make sure my notebook ends up in the Hassayampa River. It's on the way to Avondale. You'll see the signs."

"What do you mean?" Shy asked, confused.

"I need you to chuck it in the river for me."

Shy studied the black key hanging around Shoeshine's neck, the one that unlocked the man's journal. "Why do you spend so much time writing in there if you're just gonna throw your words in a river?"

"For me the power is in the writing itself," Shoeshine said. "Not the record of it. Once the word is on the page its energy is lost. Once a journal is full, it's no different than dead skin to be shed."

"Okay, fine," Shy said, sensing this might be his last conversation with the man. There was still so much he wanted to know. "But why that particular river, then? Why not throw it in the one here?"

"According to legend," Shoeshine told him, "when a man drinks from the Hassayampa River, he will never again be able to tell the truth. I'm afraid that's where my thoughts belong. Much as we try, young fella, no one man can ever own the truth. Not even a small sliver of it. Truth is not a fixed thing. It evolves and morphs and inverts. What is true today may not be true tomorrow." Shoeshine coughed and glanced at the fence again. He was eager to be on his way. "But you'll do that for me, won't you?"

Shy shrugged. "I'll do it." Deep down, though, he knew he'd never be able to throw out any part of Shoeshine.

Shoeshine tossed aside his walking stick. "I have one other favor to ask, and then you should be on your way. Can you give an old man a boost?"

"Over the fence?" Shy said, surprised. "You're going *inside*?"

"It's time."

Shy stared at the man, searching his head for ways to stall him. "Can I ask you something first?"

The man nodded.

Shy glanced through the rusted fence, trying to come up with some kind of worthy question. "I know you were in the military," he started. "And Mario told us you left home when you were young. And you never went back. And you obviously worked a bunch of different jobs. But that's all I really know. Which is *nothing*. You've always been this huge mystery to me. Ever since I met you."

Shoeshine looked disappointed. "Don't do that, young fella."

"Do what?"

"Try and label everyone you meet." The man coughed again. "It's lazy."

"I'm not trying to label—"

Shoeshine covered Shy's mouth with one of his big leathery hands. "I'm exactly what you see, young fella. Nothing more. Nothing less."

Shy jerked away from the man's grip and stared.

He realized he'd never get a straight answer out of Shoeshine. Not even at the very end.

"So am I gonna have to climb this myself?" Shoeshine asked.

Shy had stalled enough.

He linked his fingers and held them low enough for Shoeshine to use as a step. When the man's shoe was securely in his hands, he hoisted him up over the chain-link fence, watched him land in the dirt on the other side with a thud.

Shoeshine struggled to his feet and brushed himself off. He didn't say goodbye or even turn around. He just set off slowly toward the ancient figure, limping worse now that he was without his stick.

Shy could see the figure more clearly now. He made out one of the giant hands. And then the head. And he realized Shoeshine was limping to where the heart of the figure might be. And that's where he sat down, facing away from Shy, craning his neck so he could look up into the colorful sunset sky. He remained in that position for several minutes before slowly lowering himself onto his back, where he became still.

Shy stood there for a long time, staring at Shoeshine.

He didn't know how to feel, because he never knew the man. Not really. He only knew that some powerful presence, or energy, had left him. And he knew he'd never encounter anything like it again for as long as he lived.

Eventually Shy turned and started back toward the truck, where he found Carmen already sitting in the passenger seat. He climbed in the driver's side and closed the door and started the engine. Out of the corner of his eye, he saw Carmen reaching across the cab toward him, and inside he cringed. He thought she was going to wipe away one of the tears that had managed to sneak down his cheek.

But she didn't.

She pinched something near his chest and lifted it for him to see.

Shy froze.

The thin rope Shoeshine had always worn around his neck was now around Shy's neck. And at the end of it was the black key that unlocked the man's journal.

56
The Living

Shy drove in silence as Carmen slept in the seat beside him. He watched the sun slowly disappear in the rearview mirror, listening to hour after hour of DJ Dan on the radio. The man reported about the slew of new crusader groups flooding into California now that a cure for the disease had been found. One group offered food and water to the hungry just west of the border. Another offered religious services. A bus caravan had been established in the desert, taking passengers east every few hours, toward the border. A group of Catholic nuns had begun searching for orphans in downtown Los Angeles.

Just before ten at night, the DJ stopped the classical music he'd been playing and said, in an excited voice, that he had his most significant announcement since the earthquakes hit California.

Shy turned up the volume.

LasoTech, which had already produced a pill that was said to cure Romero Disease, had once again beaten out all other pharmaceutical companies. They'd now developed the first-ever *vaccine* against the disease. The president had just made the announcement in Washington. The press secretary was expecting a statement from LasoTech founder Jim Miller as soon as he returned from a crusader mission in the desert. If this vaccine proved effective, the DJ explained, the disaster would essentially be over and the country could finally begin picking up the pieces.

"Sweet," Shy mumbled sarcastically. "Now they're vaccinating everyone, too. Who the fuck needs *us*?"

Shy turned off the radio.

He glanced at Carmen, but she was still asleep.

It hit him how truly exhausted he was, too. He rolled down his window and let the cool air beat against his face as he thought about their trip to Avondale. It was all but meaningless now. LasoTech had won. Shy and Carmen could still turn over the letter that connected LasoTech with the start of Romero Disease. But who were authorities more likely to believe, two Mexican kids trying to sneak across the Avondale border, or a company that had just saved the country?

And would anyone even care now?

When he got tired of the wind, Shy rolled up his window and listened to Carmen's quiet snoring. He crept them along the freeway in the dark, picturing Shoeshine laying himself onto the ancient figure scraped into the earth. And the kids lying dead inside the Skylark. And the corpses rotting in the valley. And Marcus and his mom and sis and nephew.

So many people lost.

And for what?

* * *

It was just after midnight when Shy finally came across a sign for the Hassayampa River—the one Shoeshine had told him to look for. He took the off-ramp and maneuvered the truck down to the mouth of the river and cut the engine. He grabbed the flashlight out of the center console and turned to Carmen. She was still asleep, though, so he opened the door quietly and walked to the edge of the river, where he peered down into the water. A blurry full moon danced across the surface.

The river itself was disappointing—if you could even call it a river. It was more like a creek. Or a glorified puddle. Shy figured if he got a running start he could probably leap right over the whole damn thing.

He took Shoeshine's journal out of the duffel and aimed his light on the beat-up leather cover, the metal lock. He stood there for several minutes, debating whether or not he should just toss it in the water. It was what Shoeshine wanted. And it was the right thing to do. But deep down Shy had always known he wouldn't be able to do it. Now that he had Shoeshine's key, he had access to the man's secrets. And how was Shy supposed to pass that up?

He glanced back at the truck, making sure Carmen was still asleep, then he sat down on a flat rock near the river's edge and brought the journal up to the black key Shoeshine had somehow transferred onto his neck.

To Shy's surprise, the lock was a fake.

The journal didn't need a key. All you had to do was open the thing like you'd open any other journal. Weird. Shy distinctly remembered Shoeshine reaching the journal up to his key every time he pulled it out of the duffel. Was he just messing with them? And if the heavy black key didn't open the journal, what *did* it open?

Shy shook his head.

Shoeshine seemed even stranger now that he was gone.

Shy flipped to the first page and shined his light on the simple two-word title. It seemed kind of odd for someone to title a journal. But then again, Shy had never kept a journal. What did *he* know about these things?

On the next page he found a loose map that showed their path to Arizona. He pulled it out and looked at it more closely. The double line drawn from Venice Beach, heading east, ended just outside of Blythe, exactly where Shoeshine had ended.

Shy then paged forward and read the first bit of actual text. His entire body went cold when he saw his own name in Shoeshine's neat handwriting.

It was a description of Shy standing on the Honeymoon Deck back on the cruise ship. He was handing out bottles of water to passengers taking a break from some party going on inside. Shoeshine described a man who walked outside wearing a suit that was too small. And he described Shy walking up to that man, holding out a water bottle. And the two of them talking about vacation homes.

The comb-over man.

Shy slammed the journal closed.

It was too weird.

Just thinking about it messed up his stomach, like he was about to get sick. How could Shoeshine know what Shy and the comb-over man said that night?

Shy stood and opened the journal back up and reread the two-word title. He pulled out the loose map, folded it up and shoved it in his pocket. And then he did something that surprised even *him*. He chucked Shoeshine's journal right into the water.

He aimed his light so he could watch the thing sink out of sight, but what he saw instead was some kind of crazy witchcraft spectacle. The whole river lit up bright red and began furiously bubbling where the journal had sunk. And he heard human screams all around him, coming from every part of the desert. Or maybe it was the cry of animals. And the sand around his feet began to swirl furiously, pulling him down into the earth.

When he crouched and put his hands on the ground, it stopped.

The whole thing only lasted a few seconds, but it freaked him out so much he was left sucking in breaths and holding himself.

He rubbed his eyes and looked all around. It was like nothing had ever happened. The water was calm. The sand was still. The endless desert was eerily quiet.

Shy grabbed the duffel bag, hurried back over to the truck and climbed back inside the cab, glancing at Carmen, who was still asleep. He pushed the key inside the ignition and turned it, but the truck didn't start.

He tried again.

Nothing.

"You gotta be shittin' me," he said, looking back toward the river. He half expected to see some kind of Loch Ness Monster climbing out of the water, charging the pickup. But there was nothing there.

Had he imagined everything?

Shy hopped out and grabbed the extra gas canister from the bed of the truck and poured it into the gas tank, then re-capped it and climbed back into the cab and tried the key again.

Still nothing.

Carmen woke up and rubbed her eyes. "What's going on?"

"Fuckin' thing won't start," Shy said, pumping the gas pedal. He tried again, but the engine was no longer even turning over.

Shy climbed out of the truck again and slammed the door and kicked the front left tire and pounded the heel of his hand against the hood.

Carmen came around the front of the truck. "I don't know if I can walk all that way, Shy. My legs are done."

Shy let his head fall against the driver's-side window. His legs were done, too. And if it turned out LasoTech's vaccine really worked, what was the point anyway?

He pictured the words in Shoeshine's journal again. It made him feel light-headed. Why would he write about *Shy*? It didn't make any sense.

It was Carmen's turn to slam a hand against the hood of their broken-down truck. "What are we gonna do?" she said.

Shy shook his head. It was the most defeated he'd felt since their sailboat hit land.

"We never should've come out here!" Carmen shouted. "Fuck Arizona. And fuck this fucking duffel bag." Carmen lunged forward and kicked the bag right out of Shy's hands.

He hurried over and picked it up. He didn't even know why.

It went quiet between them for a few seconds. Then Carmen let out a heartbreaking sigh and repeated her question: "What are we supposed to do, Shy?"

He turned and met her gaze, but he couldn't even muster up enough energy to respond.

Day 52

57
First Come, First Served

Shy led Carmen up a long, relentless hill, the early-morning sun just starting to peek its head out in the distance. His legs were numb and heavy. His feet were blistered. He was hungry and thirsty, and he couldn't stop thinking about those couple of lines he'd read in Shoeshine's journal. Lines about *him*. It didn't make any sense.

Carmen was in bad shape, too. She'd slowed down dramatically. And she hadn't spoken a word to Shy in hours.

Things would only be getting worse as the temperature rose with the sun. Shy had already shed his shirt and wrapped it around his head. He carried the rifle bag on his left shoulder. On his right shoulder he had the duffel bag. He'd considered ditching the duffel back by the truck, but it had been with him for so long. Since back when he and Addie found it in the middle of the ocean. How could he turn his back on it now when they'd come this far?

The freeway began leveling out, and Shy was finally able to see ahead of them. He spotted two large buses first. They were parked along the side of the freeway, near several large, colorful tents. A large group of people was gathered around the tent closest to the shoulder of the freeway. Far beyond the tents were hundreds of motor homes parked randomly on either side of the freeway.

A sign said QUARTZSITE, ARIZONA.

"Please tell me we can stop here," Carmen said. She kneeled down on the freeway and rested her hands on the concrete.

"I think I heard about this on the radio," Shy said, feeling a glimmer of hope. "They're crusaders who bus people east. I had no idea we were this close."

"You really think they could take us the rest of the way?" Carmen was looking up at Shy with pure desperation. They needed a lucky break in the worst way.

"I hope so." Shy held his hand out to her. "Come on."

As they moved closer, though, Shy noticed something else. Two helicopters sat on a flat stretch of land behind the tents. He stopped and pointed to them, more than a little concerned. "I know those could just be regular government choppers," he said. "But they could also be . . ." He looked at Carmen, waiting for her response.

She just stared in the distance with a face of disappointment.

Shy scanned the entire scene in front of them again. The buses and tents and helicopters. The people milling around. And then he noticed a small group of people sitting at a picnic table about a hundred feet to the right of the tents. They had an umbrella set up to protect them from the sun. And there was a Jeep parked next to them.

"Maybe we can go get a feel for things from those guys," Shy said, pointing them out.

Carmen shrugged and started walking.

Shy pulled his shirt off his head, slipped it over his shoulders and followed her.

Turned out it was a group of four old men. They were sitting around a rusted picnic table, playing cards, their faces half hidden under baseball caps. "Excuse me," Carmen called out to them as she and Shy approached. "We don't mean to bother you, but can you tell us what's going on with those buses?"

The men looked up from their cards. "I suggest you get yourselves down there pronto," a man in a Yankees cap said. "They're vaccinating people and taking them east, to Avondale."

"But it's first come, first served," a guy in a Cubs hat added. "So I'd get a move on."

"They have the vaccine already?" Shy asked. "I thought it was gonna take a while to circulate it." When Carmen shot him a confused look, Shy realized she didn't know about the vaccine yet. She'd been sleeping when he heard it on the radio.

"They brought the very first batch here to Quartzsite," the Yankees guy said, pushing up his shirtsleeve to show Shy and Carmen a Band-Aid.

"The people running the bus line are connected to the drug company everyone's talking about," another man said. He had a bushy gray beard and a generic blue cap. "That's why we were lucky enough to get it first."

LasoTech, Shy mouthed to Carmen.

"Where'd you all just come from?" the Yankees guy asked.

"Over by Blythe," Shy told him.

"You *walked?*" The Cubs fan shot a frown at all his buddies before turning back to Shy. "I'd get on over there now. They're giving out food and water, too. They'll take care of you."

Shy and Carmen thanked the old men, then cautiously moved closer to the buses to get a better look. They ducked behind an abandoned tractor-trailer, and Shy crouched next to Carmen, with no idea what to do next. He assumed anyone affiliated with LasoTech would know what he and Carmen looked like. But then again, maybe the lower-level employees wouldn't. And it's not like they could go dig up disguises. How were they going to get on that air-conditioned bus without getting caught?

Shy focused on one girl who was carrying a cooler toward the second bus. Blond ponytail swinging back and forth. Long, tan legs shooting out of a pair of jean cutoffs.

She was far enough away that it could've been anyone, but Shy turned to Carmen, his stomach filling with butterflies.

"Is that who I think it is?" Carmen asked.

He swallowed hard. "I don't see how."

Carmen's eyes filled with rage. She climbed to her feet without another word and started walking toward the bus.

Shy grabbed her wrist and pulled her back down. "Hang on," he said. "We need to figure things out first."

"Lemme go, Shy. It's that fucking Addie chick and you know it."

"There's no way." Shy studied the girl for a few seconds. It really did look like her, though. And then he realized something that made him feel incredibly guilty. He *wanted* it to be her. He wanted to look in her eyes again. And talk to her again. Because maybe she had absolutely nothing to do with her dad's company.

"Let go, Shy," Carmen said again.

"Just . . ." He studied the girl for a few more seconds, then turned back to Carmen. "Just hang on. We have to be smart."

58
Once This Is Over

It was a good thing they waited.

A few minutes later, Shy spotted a group of three men dressed in black leaving one of the tents. LasoTech security. He was sure of it. They climbed into one of the helicopters and closed the door behind them. Soon the blades began spinning, blowing dirt everywhere, and the chopper slowly lifted into the air.

Shy and Carmen rolled underneath the tractor and watched the helicopter dip its nose slightly and fly right over their heads, heading west. Maybe the security guards' mission was to find *them*. Shy shifted so he could watch the helicopter grow smaller and smaller in the sky.

"That's three of 'em we no longer have to worry about," Carmen said. "For real, Shy. I'm not hiding under a stupid tractor all day. Bust out those rifles."

"What do you wanna do?" Shy said. "Roll in there like damn Zorro?" He glanced at the second bus, the one the blonde had boarded. "We're trying to get to Avondale, Carm, not start a shoot-out."

"Why?" Carmen fired back. "You heard those old dudes. Laso-Tech made a vaccine. Who cares if we get to Avondale anymore? All that matters now is getting revenge."

"We got the letter, though," Shy argued. "They'll all go to jail. We can make sure that shit happens." He realized he was trying to convince himself, too.

Carmen pursed her lips and glared at him.

Truth was, Shy wanted to check out the bus, too. There were so many things he needed to ask Addie—if it was really her. And after hearing her on the radio, he was convinced she was looking out for him. She'd warned him that LasoTech was coming after him. And she claimed she had the last page of the comb-over man's letter, which had the missing portion of the vaccine formula. Maybe this no longer mattered to scientists in Avondale, but it mattered to *him*.

He turned to Carmen. "The second we spot another security guy, we're out, all right? I'm serious."

"Fine," Carmen snapped. "Now gimme one of them damn rifles."

"Wait till we get there," Shy said.

They climbed out from under the tractor and hurried over to an RV parked less than twenty feet from the closest bus, both the rifle bag and duffel slung over Shy's right shoulder. He didn't see any more LasoTech security. At least not by the tent closest to the buses. It was just regular people waiting in line to get vaccinated by two Asian women wearing doctor smocks.

While they were standing there, the first bus started up and slowly pulled out onto the freeway. Shy watched it maneuver around a stalled car and move cautiously down the fast lane. The blond girl had boarded the second one, Shy told himself. She was still here. The butterfly feeling grew stronger.

What would he do if it really *was* Addie? He honestly didn't know.

Carmen suddenly bolted from behind the RV. Shy grabbed for her wrist but missed. "Carm," he called to her in a loud whisper.

He followed her across a short stretch of desert, straight up to the remaining bus and climbed on after her. They pushed their way past a handful of people looking for seats. Shy watched in disbelief as Carmen marched right up to the blonde and shoved her onto the laps of two women already sitting down. "Did you know they were gonna shoot everybody?" Carmen shouted.

Shy watched the blonde scramble to her feet in shock. And when he could finally see her face, his stomach dropped. It really *was* Addie. He was suddenly so dizzy he backed up without looking and dropped right into an empty seat by the door, the gun bag and duffel falling into his lap.

"What?" Addie said. "Who are you?"

Carmen cracked her in the jaw, and Addie went down again. This time a few people got between them as Addie looked up, holding a hand to her mouth. Shy saw a look of recognition wash over her face. Addie remembered Carmen, and her eyes immediately started darting around the bus, looking for *him*.

"On the island!" Carmen shouted. "Did you know they were gonna kill everybody?"

Everyone was staring at Carmen. One man tried to calm her down, but that only made Carmen flip out even more. She pushed him down and kicked him in the legs, shouting: "Mind your business, asshole!"

He scrambled away from her in a hurry.

When Addie spotted Shy rising up from his seat, her eyes grew wide and she shouted his name.

He gave a subtle nod but didn't say anything.

"Oh, hell nah, *puta*!" Carmen shouted. "Pretty boy's not here to help *you*! Now answer my damn question. Did you know?"

Addie covered her face with her hands, then dropped them and looked at Shy again. "My dad told me everything," she said. "They accidentally spread the disease in Mexico. It was the biggest mistake of his life. But instead of getting help, he tried to make it right himself. Which led to all this."

Accidentally spread the disease? Shy couldn't believe his ears. Addie was still buying her old man's lies.

"He's promised to turn himself in," Addie went on. "As soon as all this is over. But first he has to try and save as many people as he can."

"He's trying to *save* people?" Shy shouted. "Are you shittin' me, Addie?"

"I swear to God," she said. "He's setting up clinics like this all over the West Coast. He's giving medicine to sick people. And once the vaccine's approved, he'll make sure no one else ever gets the disease. He's paying for everything out of his own pocket."

"Fuck your dad's clinics!" Carmen shouted. "Where's that asshole now?"

"Not here," Addie said.

Shy couldn't stand it. Addie was too smart to be brainwashed like this. "Why'd you go on the radio, then?" he shouted. "Why'd you warn me he was coming after us?"

"My dad *told* me to do that!" Addie cried. "He doesn't want anyone else getting hurt. The men coming after you were hired by LasoTech investors. He has nothing to do with them."

Shy was so frustrated he felt like smashing his fist through the closest window. Addie was blindly following anything her old man told her. But what pissed Shy off even more was the tiny kernel of doubt that had crept into his mind. What if Mr. Miller really *had* told Addie to warn him? What if he really *wasn't* responsible for everyone shooting at them?

The people on the bus were now shouting over one another, sticking up for Addie. "Leave her alone!" they barked. "Get off the bus!"

One woman shouted: "She's here to save our lives!"

"I asked you about the island!" Carmen yelled over all of them.

Addie shook her head, clearly scared. "I have no idea what you're talking about."

"They were all shot down!" Carmen shouted. "Every single person on the island! And you knew about it! You had to know!"

Addie was crying now. "No! I swear!"

When he saw tears streaming down her face, Shy felt bad for Addie. And he felt bad for feeling bad. "Do you really have the last page of the letter?" he asked, coldly.

"Yes!" Addie cried. "I've been carrying it with me this whole time."

"Does your dad know about it?" Shy asked.

Addie shook her head and turned to Carmen. "Just let me get it from my tent."

"We need to follow her," Shy called out to Carmen. "It's important we have this."

Carmen glared as Addie moved past her, back through the narrow aisle.

59
The Manila Envelope

Shy stepped off the bus ahead of Addie, trying to get shit straight in his head. If Addie hadn't showed her dad the last page of the comb-over man's letter, maybe she wasn't following him as blindly as Shy thought. Unless she was leading them into some kind of trap.

Shy pulled the two rifles out of the bag and tossed one to Carmen. He slung the duffel over his shoulder and studied their surroundings as he and Carmen followed Addie into the cluster of tents. There was still a line of people waiting to get shots. But the crowd had thinned now that the first bus was gone. The scattered motor homes to the east seemed farther away now. The dry air was hotter, too, and Shy kept wiping sweat from his forehead.

Addie stopped at one of the smaller tents in back. She unzipped it and ducked inside.

Shy held the flap open, watching Addie dig through a small suitcase. After a few seconds she pulled out a manila envelope and held it out to Shy. "I knew you'd come looking for this. It's important, right?"

Shy had to crouch down to step into the tent, and he stayed hunched as he moved across the tent toward Addie. "It *was*. I don't know who needs the vaccine formula now." When Shy went to grab the envelope out of Addie's hand, though, she held on tight. There was a desperation in her eyes he'd never seen before, not even when they were stranded.

"You have to leave here right away," she said in a quiet voice.

"What?" he said, startled. "Why?"

"Just trust me." She let go of the envelope. "You shouldn't have come here."

Shy nodded and slipped the envelope into the duffel bag, his heart suddenly pounding. Just as he was spinning around to leave, though, a man's voice came from right outside the tent. "Addie?"

Shy froze, staring at the man he'd been obsessed with since the moment he'd left the torched island on Shoeshine's tattered sailboat.

Addie's dad.

Mr. Miller.

Behind him was a second man, who was holding a gun to Carmen's head.

Cold fear shot through Shy's veins as he watched Carmen slowly drop her rifle and hold up her hands.

60
Two Wrongs

"Dad!" Addie shouted. "What are you doing here? Everything's fine."

Mr. Miller gave Shy a subtle grin as he pulled a handgun from the back of his waistband. "Why don't you drop the rifle, son, and we'll all take a walk outside and have a civilized conversation."

Shy stared into the barrel of the gun. Who was this guy calling "son"? It made Shy want to throw up. But he couldn't do anything about it with a gun pointed at Carmen's head. He let his rifle fall to the ground and glanced at Addie. She'd lied about her dad not being here. But she'd also warned him to leave.

So which one was it?

Mr. Miller led Shy and Carmen out of the tent and into a small clearing. "This will do just fine."

"We should go, Dad," Addie said, tugging on his arm. "There are people waiting for us on the bus."

"Hang on a minute, honey." Mr. Miller pulled free of Addie's grip and pointed his gun at the duffel hanging off Shy's shoulder. "What's in the bag?"

Carmen spit in Mr. Miller's direction. "None of your business, asshole!" She fought to get out of the LasoTech guy's grasp, but he had her in a headlock from behind. When she continued struggling, he cracked her in the back of the head with his gun.

"Get off her!" Shy shouted. He then turned to Mr. Miller and told him: "You know exactly what's in here."

Shy was surprised at how calm he felt in Mr. Miller's presence. He hated that Carmen had a gun to her head, but as long as he focused on Mr. Miller's beady eyes, he was okay. All the death he'd experienced over the past month made the threat of it now seem less intimidating. "Tell your guy to let Carmen go and I'll show you."

Mr. Miller shook his head. "I'm not sure you're in a position to be making demands."

"Dad, come on," Addie pleaded.

"They're gonna fry your ass!" Carmen shouted at Mr. Miller. "And I'm gonna sit right up front watching that shit with fucking popcorn!"

Mr. Miller grinned at her. "I've made some mistakes," he said. "I'll be the first to admit it. And as soon as this is over, I'm happy to have everything sorted out in the courts. But right now . . . people need me." He turned to Shy. "Hand me the bag, son."

"Better watch it with that 'son' shit," Shy said, holding the man's gaze.

"Give him the bag!" the LasoTech guy shouted.

Shy wished he hadn't torn open Shoeshine's extra pocket.

Now the syringes were right there for anyone to see. Not that it mattered anymore. LasoTech had its *new* vaccine. The letter was all that he should be worried about. His proof.

"Hurry up!" the LasoTech guy shouted.

Shy pulled the bag off his shoulder and reluctantly handed it over.

"What are you doing?" Addie said to her dad. "You promised to focus on the clinics."

"That's what I'm doing, sweetheart." Mr. Miller unzipped the duffel and reached inside. He pulled out two of the four remaining syringes and looked at them. "You know, Shy," he said. "You and I are actually quite alike. We're both survivors. Just when people think they can count us out, we find a way to reappear."

"We're not *anything* alike," Shy fired back. He glanced at Carmen, who was so angry she was shaking.

"Dad!" Addie pleaded again.

Mr. Miller finally turned to look at his daughter and held up one of the syringes. "I need Chris and Gary to reproduce this immediately, Addison. Go find them in the lab, tell them to stop production on the A4 and fly back to Avondale."

Addie took the duffel bag and stood there for a few seconds, looking back and forth between Shy and her dad. Then she hurried off in the direction they'd come.

Shy watched her go, feeling helpless. He and Carmen had nothing else left. And the odds of these two men letting them go weren't good, either. He tried to imagine what Shoeshine would do. But Shoeshine was gone.

Mr. Miller waited until Addie was out of sight before saying: "It won't be long now, friends. As soon as my second helicopter team is ready, I have a little treat for you. We're going to tie you both up and push you out in the middle of the desert somewhere."

"Fuck you!" Carmen shouted.

The LasoTech guy cracked the butt of his gun against the side of her head again.

Shy saw a little bit of blood trickling down Carmen's cheek, and he lost it. "Why don't you come over here and try that shit on me!" he shouted at the guy. "Watch what happens!"

"Take it easy," Mr. Miller told Shy with a sly grin.

Shy opened his mouth to talk more shit when he saw movement out of the corner of his eye. He turned and saw Addie running from behind the tent, gripping one of the rifles. She raised it up over her head and slammed it into the LasoTech guy's back while shouting through tears: "They didn't do anything!"

The man dropped to his knees and his gun went flying. He reached for his back.

When Mr. Miller spun around to see what was happening, Shy instinctively kicked the gun out of his hand and shoved him out of the way.

Addie picked up her dad's gun and pointed it at him, then pointed it at Shy. She was so hysterical Shy couldn't make out what she was screaming.

"Addie, honey," her dad said from the ground, reaching out to her. "Please. You have to trust me."

She wiped her face with the back of her free hand, whimpering: "They didn't do anything."

"Of course they didn't," Mr. Miller said in a calm voice. "But we need to take certain precautions. I'm doing this for you, honey. For *us*."

Shy saw Carmen furiously tinkering with the rifle, which must have jammed. And he saw the LasoTech guy crawling toward the handgun he'd dropped.

Shy sprinted past Addie and dove on the guy, tackling him onto the hot dirt. The two of them rolled over, throwing wild haymakers. Shy ended up on his back and caught a fist in the mouth, and another in the ear. He summoned all the strength he had left to flip the guy over and pin his arms to the ground. He reared back and landed three consecutive jabs to the left side of the guy's face, until the man appeared dazed.

When Shy looked up again, he saw Carmen stalking toward Mr. Miller, the rifle raised in front of her. "Let's get out of here, Carm!" he shouted. He turned to Addie. "Where's the duffel?"

She was pointing the gun right at him. "Get her to stop!" she screamed.

"Carmen!" Shy was struggling to keep the LasoTech guy pinned down. "Let's go! Now!"

"I'm not going anywhere," Carmen said with a snarl. She had the rifle aimed at Mr. Miller's face.

Shy pulled in short, quick breaths, taking in the scene. It was all happening so fast. No time to think. Carmen had her rifle pointed at Mr. Miller, and Addie now had her gun pointed at Carmen, and Shy had a man pinned to the dirt.

The other handgun lay just a few feet away.

Shy now spotted the duffel bag, shoved up against the tent behind him.

When the LasoTech guy pushed out from under Shy, he reared back and blasted him in the side of the head. Shy lunged for the gun and scooped it up, while at the same time taking a crushing blow on the back of the head. He spun around, disoriented, and saw the man was about to kick him a second time. Shy rolled away just in time and aimed the gun at him, shouting: "Don't fucking move!"

The man froze, sucking in breaths and glaring.

Shy struggled to his feet and hurried over to retrieve the duffel bag, never taking his gun off the man. He noticed a small crowd of onlookers, half hidden behind another tent.

Carmen cocked her rifle and told Mr. Miller: "You killed my dad."

Mr. Miller shook his head. "It was all a mistake. I'd give anything to go back and change things. You have to believe me."

"I don't have to believe *shit*," Carmen said.

"Tell her to drop the rifle, Shy!" Addie shouted.

"Drop it, Carm!" Shy called out. "I got the duffel! Let's just get outta here!"

Carmen shook her head and took another step toward Mr. Miller. "You killed my dad," she repeated.

"Get her away from him!" Addie screamed.

The LasoTech guy took a step toward Carmen, but Shy turned his gun on him, shouting: "Don't move!"

"Please, put the gun down," Mr. Miller told Carmen.

Addie shouted: "Get away from him!"

Shy swung his gun toward Addie, then back to the LasoTech guy, fragments of thoughts flooding his brain. Shoeshine's journal and the bubbling river and his grandma's funeral and the look on Marcus's face before Shoeshine snapped his neck. And then Shy remembered his mom's face the last time he'd seen her. Before he left for the cruise ship. This last image hit him so hard his knees nearly buckled. He'd never see her again.

"That's it," Mr. Miller was now saying. "Just put the gun down."

"Shy?" Carmen called out to him. She was still staring at Mr. Miller, but she seemed to be having second thoughts. The anger had mostly vanished from her eyes.

"I got you!" Shy called to her.

"That's it," Mr. Miller said, holding his hands up. "Two wrongs don't make a right, do they?"

Addie crouched down, looking exhausted, her gun still aimed at Carmen's back.

"It's not in your nature," Mr. Miller told Carmen, looking relieved. But Shy thought he detected something else on the man's face, too. The beginnings of a sly grin. "You've never killed anyone, sweetheart."

"But I have," Shy blurted out, and he swung his gun toward Mr. Miller and fired two shots directly into the man's chest.

The crowd of onlookers gasped.

Addie screamed at the top of her lungs and turned her gun on Shy but didn't shoot.

Mr. Miller's face went ghost white as he reached up toward his blood-splattered, white-collared shirt. He opened his mouth to say something, but no words came out.

Shy stood there not even breathing hard. His gun still pointed at the man, watching him die.

61
Shy's Path

Carmen picked up her rifle and took the duffel from Shy and grabbed his wrist and started pulling him away.

When the LasoTech guy started after them, Shy turned and aimed his gun at the man's chest. When the guy didn't stop, Shy lowered the barrel slightly and shot him in both legs instead, watched him collapse to the ground writhing in pain.

"Let's go, let's go!" Carmen shouted, yanking Shy's arm again.

He turned to Addie, who was still aiming her gun at him. When he saw she was trembling, with tears streaming down her face, his heart broke for her. She dropped the gun and moved toward her dad, kneeling down and trying to lift his body into her arms.

As much as it hurt Shy to hurt Addie, he didn't feel an ounce of emotion about anything else as he and Carmen sprinted back through the tents, toward the remaining bus. There was no sense of revenge, like he'd once imagined. And no remorse. No fear. He felt nothing at all. He'd simply found himself on this path, like Shoeshine once told him, and he intended to see it through.

When they neared the bus, Shy spotted another LasoTech guy sprinting down the road toward them. The man stopped and fired at Shy and Carmen, the bullet sparking off the cement to the right of them.

A small crowd that had gathered around the bus quickly dispersed in a great commotion.

Shy pulled Carmen behind the tent where the doctors had been administering shots. He peeked his head out, and the guy fired a second time, shooting wide.

"I'll cover you!" Shy shouted at Carmen. "Run to one of those motor homes, and I'll catch up!"

Carmen stared at him.

"Go!" he said.

The second she took off running, Shy ducked out from behind the tent and fired three consecutive shots in the LasoTech guy's direction. The man dove into an SUV. Shy pulled the trigger again, but the gun clicked like it was out of bullets, so he dropped it and took off after Carmen.

As Shy caught up with her, the SUV suddenly screeched out onto the freeway. Shy turned and saw it bearing down on them. Two men inside. Even if he and Carmen went off the freeway and booked it toward the closest motor home, they'd never make it. They were too far away.

He looked at her and they both slowed down.

Then, without a word, they stopped and turned to face the oncoming vehicle together, Carmen raising her rifle, Shy gripping the duffel and swallowing.

They'd almost made it, he told himself.

There were no regrets.

As the SUV bore down on them, Shy spotted something coming up behind it.

A motorcycle.

Metallic gray.

Just as the passenger in the SUV leaned out his window, aiming a gun at Shy and Carmen, the guy on the bike fired several rounds at the truck, puncturing its two back tires and shattering the rear windshield.

The SUV swerved out of control and skidded to a stop in front of an abandoned Volkswagen van. The two LasoTech guys hopped out and started firing at the guy on the motorcycle, who lost control and fell off his bike. Both the man and his motorcycle went skidding across the freeway.

Carmen grabbed Shy by the arm and they took off again.

As they raced down the freeway, Shy looked over his shoulder. He saw the guy scrambling over to his bike for cover, saw him take aim and begin firing at the LasoTech guys again.

Shy spun back around, sucking in breaths as he continued running alongside Carmen, toward the scattered motor homes.

62
Final Days in the Desert

Shy and Carmen sat next to each other on a cushionless couch, still catching their breath, eyeing an older white woman with a buzz cut as she limped around a pile of dusty books and shoe boxes carrying two glasses of ice water. As soon as Shy got ahold of his he put the rim to his lips and started guzzling so fast he had a serious case of brain freeze. It didn't slow him down. He emptied his glass in seconds, then set it down and studied the inside of the motor home.

The place was trashed. Random papers and magazines everywhere, rolled-up rugs, dirty dishes and pizza boxes stacked to the ceiling. A couple cats were asleep against each other on a dusty treadmill. Three other cats were curled up on a partially folded beige blanket that was caked with cat hair.

The old woman was one of those hoarder people.

Not that he was judging.

She'd saved his and Carmen's asses after the shoot-out. They had tried knocking on six or seven motor home doors before hers. No one answered, even though Shy saw a few people peering out at them through their blinds. But this old lady didn't even wait for a knock. She saw them coming and flung open her door and waved them inside. Not five minutes later, while the woman was tending to the gash on the side of Carmen's face, Shy peeked through her old-people curtains and spotted the man on the gray motorcycle coasting down the street, his helmet swiveling back and forth as he looked for them.

Carmen finally finished her water, too, and set her empty glass on the newspaper-covered table, next to Shy's.

"Refill?" the woman asked.

Shy shook his head. "No, thanks, ma'am."

"We appreciate what you just did for us," Carmen said, touching the skin around her newly applied bandage.

The old woman waved her off, like it was nothing. "So what exactly happened back there? I heard all the commotion. And the gunshots. Did it have anything to do with those weirdos running the buses?"

Shy started to answer, but the woman held up a hand to cut him off. "You know what? It's none of my business. I'm just an old widow living out my last few days in the desert. The less I know, the better."

Shy glanced up at the old-style framed pictures hanging on the wall by the door. In one, the woman was standing beside a heavyset old man in a cowboy hat. He pointed at it. "Was that your husband?" he asked, figuring it was best to take his mind off things for now.

"Yep. Two weeks after that picture was taken, he kicked the bucket."

"Oh," Shy said, taken aback. He glanced at Carmen. "Sorry for your loss, ma'am."

"Don't be," the woman said matter-of-factly. "He lived a long, long life. Too long, if you ask some people."

Shy heard a helicopter passing over the motor home. Laso-Tech was already out looking for them. He was sure of it. He had the urge to peek through the window again, but something told him to stay put this time, to be patient.

"Here's a better question," the old woman said. "Where are you two going from here? I mean, you're welcome to stay awhile, if that's what you need, but something tells me you're on the move."

"We're heading east," Carmen said.

"Lemme guess," the woman said. "The Avondale border?"

Shy and Carmen both nodded.

The old woman sucked her teeth. "It's a long walk, I'm afraid. About another hundred or so miles."

Carmen looked at Shy. To his surprise, her eyes were droopy, like she was fighting sleep. But extreme stress could do that to you, he was learning. Push you off to la-la land only seconds after a gunfight.

"Follow me," the woman said, standing up. "I want to show you something." She limped around the empty birdcage sitting on the floor and headed toward the hall.

Shy nudged Carmen. "What are the chances she's got a wood chipper in there?"

"Shut up, Sancho. She's nice." Carmen got up from the cushionless couch and followed the woman. Shy glanced at the curtains again. Then he got up, too.

A few seconds later, all three of them were standing in front of a pristine dirt bike. Shy was beyond confused. The motor home was in complete disarray, yet the motorcycle was spotless.

"Either of you know how to ride a dirt bike?" the woman asked.

"I do," Shy said.

"You *do?*" Carmen asked.

Shy nodded. At least, he *thought* he remembered the Cliffs-Notes tutorial his old man had given him at the Sony lots.

"Well, I want you to take this with you to Avondale," the woman said. "Put it to good use."

"Wait," Carmen said. "Are you serious?"

"Of course I'm serious," the woman said. "I was going to ship it off to my bastard grandson, but who knows what kind of criminal activity *he'd* use it for."

Shy couldn't believe she'd actually give the bike to them after five minutes together. He looked at the bike and then looked at the woman. "Was it your husband's?"

The old woman laughed. "No, it wasn't my husband's. It's *mine.* I used to zip all over this godforsaken place. My favorite time was right after it rained. Spraying mud into people's yards. Of course, that was before my stupid hip went out. Now I just come in here every once in a while to polish it."

As the woman and Carmen continued talking about the motorcycle, Shy went to the bedroom window and peeked through the blinds. He didn't see a helicopter anywhere. Or an SUV. Or a motorcycle. Didn't hear anything, either. He felt bad taking something that obviously meant a lot to the old lady. But it would definitely beat walking the rest of the way under the desert sun.

His mind flashed on Mr. Miller when he shot him. Addie's face when he and Carmen fled the scene. He could still feel his finger on the trigger even though the rifle was back on the freeway somewhere. He reached into the duffel and pulled out the manila envelope. He unfolded the single handwritten page Addie had given him. And there it was in the comb-over man's familiar scribble, the rest of the vaccine formula.

Shy shoved everything back into the duffel and turned to the old woman. "We can't thank you enough, ma'am. Seriously, we owe you big-time."

"You don't owe me jack shit," the woman said. "Now go on, get out of here. Before I make you clean my kitchen."

63
Freedom of the Open Road

Ten minutes later, Shy and Carmen were speeding east along the 10 Freeway. Shy squinted into the wind, concentrating on the feel of Carmen's hands around his middle. Her breath on his neck. He was shocked that he'd somehow soaked in most of what his old man taught him about operating a motorcycle. It had taken a couple of minutes to get used to, but now he was flying down the two-lane freeway, shifting effortlessly, operating the clutch, maneuvering around the occasional stalled car or buckle in the freeway. The handlebars were set sort of high, which made him feel like one of those Mexican Harley *vatos* from back home.

"A hundred miles at this speed?" Shy called back to Carmen. "We should be there in two hours, max!"

"What?" Carmen shouted back. Shy was realizing how impossible it was to communicate over the rushing wind. And the old woman must have done something to the muffler because the roar of the dirt bike's exhaust was mind-numbingly loud.

"I said we should be there in *two hours*!" he tried again.

Carmen only shook her head this time. She couldn't hear a word he was saying.

Shy concentrated on the road instead.

He thought about what had happened back by the tents again. Carmen getting clubbed with the butt of a gun. Addie defying her dad and cracking the other guy with the rifle. The look on Mr. Miller's face when Shy stepped up and fired those two bullets. Shy wondered if what he did made him a bad person. What if he was more like Mr. Miller than he wanted to admit?

If only Shoeshine was still around so Shy could ask his opinion. He tried to imagine the riddle he'd get in response. Man, what Shy would give for one of those riddles right about now. Then Shoeshine would probably go off and write about Shy's question in his journal.

But Shoeshine was gone.

Shy would have to come up with his own riddles from now on.

After a while he cleared his mind, which was surprisingly easy to do while racing down the freeway on a dirt bike. There really was a freedom to being on the open road, like people said.

Soon he and Carmen would be in Avondale, standing in front of the border, holding a duffel bag that contained syringes full of a Romero Disease vaccine and the comb-over man's letter— including the last page. But for the first time since they'd landed in Venice Beach, Shy wasn't in such a hurry to get where he was going. For now he just wanted to concentrate on this moment with Carmen. Her hands linked around his waist. The warm feel of her chest against his back.

He glanced back and nodded to her, and when he saw the bandage near her right temple a strange feeling swelled in his chest. A feeling he couldn't put into words.

"Your head okay?" he shouted.

"What?" she shouted back.

He looked forward and laughed a little. And then he thought of something else. He turned to her again and shouted: "Know what's crazy, Carm?"

She shrugged. She still couldn't hear.

"I think I love you!" he shouted. "And I think it's been this way from the second we first met!"

"I can't hear a word you're saying!" Carmen shouted back. At least he was pretty sure that's what she said. His ear was only inches from her mouth.

"And no matter what happens with your punk lawyer boyfriend," Shy continued shouting, "I'm gonna keep on loving you! Even if you go on to have mad punk lawyer kids! Nothing's ever gonna change what I feel!"

Carmen didn't even shout back this time. She just shrugged and shook her head.

Shy faced forward again, smiling into the wind.

It felt good to finally get the truth off his chest.

64
Second Chances

About an hour into their ride, Shy looked at his side mirror and his breath caught. There was a motorcycle coming up quickly behind them. It took a few seconds before he was able to make out that it was the metallic gray one from earlier. The driver wasn't pointing any kind of weapon at them, though. In fact, he seemed to be waving them to the side of the freeway.

There was no way in hell Shy was pulling over. He sped up instead, looking all over for a good place to pull off the freeway and try to lose the guy. But there was nothing on either side of the freeway except wide-open desert, as far as the eye could see.

Shy kept watching the motorcycle in the side mirror.

Carmen started looking back, too.

But the more Shy thought about it, the less worried he felt.

Back near the buses, the biker had been shooting at the SUV, not Shy and Carmen. And Shy remembered the biker who'd shot out the tires of the Hummer at the gas station. He was on a gray motorcycle, too. It had to be the same guy.

There was no way Shy's tricked-out dirt bike was going to out-run a street bike anyway, so he slowed down a little, allowing the guy to catch up. In a minute or so they were riding side by side. The man kept waving for Shy to pull to the side, and Shy kept shaking his head. "What do you want?" he shouted.

"Pull to the side!" the man barked through his helmet.

At this slower speed, the muffler wasn't quite as loud. Nor was the wind. Shy could actually hear himself think again. And an odd suspicion started creeping into his brain.

Carmen was gripping Shy a little tighter, staring at the man beside them. He was wearing a dented and badly scuffed helmet with a reflective visor. Ripped-up jeans and a blue hooded sweat-shirt.

"Who are you?" Carmen shouted at the man.

The driver lifted up his shiny visor and pointed at his face. Shy saw a familiar scraggly-looking beard peppered with gray. And he saw that half the man's face was badly burned. Shy nearly drove the dirt bike right off the road.

He was right. It was his old man.

He couldn't believe it.

"Pull over!" his dad shouted at Shy and Carmen again. The man reached up to undo the strap under his chin, maintaining pace with the dirt bike, and yanked off his helmet.

Shy had no idea what to think or feel. All he could think to do was keep driving.

"What are *you* doing out here?" Carmen shouted, clearly rec-ognizing Shy's dad now, too.

"What do you think?" the man shouted. "I'm watching my son's back! Like I said before, this is my second chance! And I'm not letting it go!"

A strange feeling began bubbling up inside Shy as he shifted his gaze from his dad to the road. It wasn't pride, so much. Or happiness. It was more like a sense of security. A recognition of loyalty. He recalled all the different times they'd seen a random motorcycle along their journey. And he remembered the look he and his dad had shared just before Shy left the Sony lots. His dad must have jacked the SUV from the LasoTech guy waiting outside and followed them into the desert.

His dad shouted something Shy couldn't quite make out, so he slowed down a little more and yelled, "What?"

"Can't say I never taught you anything now!" His dad pointed at the dirt bike. "Looks like you've been riding your entire life!"

Carmen squeezed Shy's middle.

Even *she* sensed the weight of what was happening.

Shy concentrated on the road for a stretch, but there was one thing that still confused him. He turned back to his dad, shouting: "Why'd you wait till now to catch up?"

"That man you were with before!" his dad shouted. "He said to hang back until he was out of the picture!"

"You talked to Shoeshine?" Shy shouted. "When?"

"In the mountains! Outside that beat-up resort place you were at!"

Shy remembered hearing a motorcycle by the front gate when Mario was giving them a tour. And then he remembered something else. One of the last things Shoeshine had told Shy near the Intaglios. "You can't even see it, can you? You have no idea who else you're leading." Maybe he was talking about Shy's dad.

All these years Shy had held a grudge against his dad. Especially after the year he'd lived with him in LA. But the fact that

338

he'd followed Shy all the way into the desert, and tried to protect him . . . maybe Shy had it wrong.

Or maybe the earthquakes really *had* changed him.

Shy motioned for his dad to follow him and Carmen, and then he sped up a little, ready for whatever came next.

65

The Avondale Border

Miller Road marked the first sign of civilization. Shy studied the few gas stations and fast-food spots off the right side of the freeway. A large cluster of tents filled what had once been a major construction zone.

Just after a sign announcing the town of Goodyear, Shy began seeing groups of people. They were arranged in half-circles, talking, or they were lined up in large parking lots, waiting to receive relief packages from crusaders. Anywhere there was shade, people were packed in together. Families were living in half-finished housing developments, and on commercial rooftops, and in tents erected right up against the freeway. The only thing Shy could compare it to was a series of *National Geographic* photos he'd once seen of Third World slums.

Carmen rested her chin against Shy's back as they moved

slowly down the freeway, maneuvering around stalled cars and empty crates and tons of trash. Shy's dad rode slightly behind them, swiveling his head around as he took everything in.

They passed huge grassy fields covered by tents and hordes of people. Many turned to watch the noisy dirt bike sputter by. The closer they got, the more government vehicles they saw parked along the shoulder of the freeway. Cop cars. Ambulances. Fire trucks. All stranded, Shy assumed, when the border went up.

Tingles ran up and down Shy's arms and legs when he saw the first sign for Avondale, Arizona. Soon after, they passed a sign for the Agua Fria River. Shy remembered DJ Dan describing how the border was built on the east side of the river, which meant they were close.

There were hundreds of people packed along the sides of the freeway here. Thousands, even. Shy had to slow to a crawl to get through without hitting anyone. Some people shouted at him. Others grabbed at the handlebars or took swipes at the duffel bag. Shy held the bag closer to him and lurched forward whenever he came to a pocket of open space. He kept looking back at Carmen and his old man, happy they were still with him.

Shy took the next off-ramp and moved through the crowded side streets, following the signs for the river. There were tents set up everywhere. And swarms of people. "Excuse me!" Shy had to keep calling out in order to maneuver past them. He inched the dirt bike forward a few feet at a time, until Carmen smacked him on the shoulder and pointed ahead.

Shy looked up and saw it.

He stopped the bike and planted a foot on the asphalt. Then he cut the engine. Carmen put a foot down, too. His dad coasted up beside them and flipped up his helmet's visor. "Shit, there it is," he said over the commotion of the crowd.

They were right at the edge of the Agua Fria River, which was twenty, twenty-five yards wide at most. On the other side was the makeshift border Shy had been hearing about since the day they left the island. But it wasn't anything like he'd imagined. Instead of some intimidating wall that reached up into the sky, it was just a crappy-looking little fence that extended as far as he could see in either direction. What kept people from charging the fence was the river standing in front of it. And all the armed military people standing guard.

A two-lane bridge that had once stretched across the river appeared to have been blown up. Only the two jagged sides remained.

Shy turned to his dad and Carmen. "This border looks kind of weak, doesn't it?" The crowd had closed in tighter around them, making Shy feel claustrophobic.

"They didn't have a whole lot of time," his dad said, leaning his bike on its kickstand and pulling off his helmet. "What's up with that key around your neck?"

Shy reached up to touch Shoeshine's black key but didn't answer.

"I guess the guys with assault rifles make up for the shitty fence," Carmen said. She leaned over to stretch her back after the long ride, but some haggard-looking woman backed up a step just then, nearly knocking Carmen over.

Shy watched his dad check out all the people surrounding them. Most were either looking out at the river or staring at Shy and his crew. His dad cleared his throat. "I guess this is a good time to ask what we're doing here."

"You probably want to get to the other side," a nearby man said, "but it's impossible."

A college-aged guy with no shirt on laughed in Shy's face. "We all came to cross the border, dude. But here we still are, stuck in this bullshit."

"Now that the vaccine failed all the tests," the first guy said, "nothing's going to change anytime soon."

"Wait, the vaccine doesn't work?" Shy asked.

A bunch of people shook their heads. "It was announced this morning," the man said. "They're back to square one."

Shy and Carmen shared a look, and Shy clutched the duffel a little closer.

Shy's dad leaned toward Shy and Carmen. "So are either of you gonna tell me why we're here?"

Shy stared across the river again, at the guards pacing along a platform just beyond the walls. "We have to get this duffel to the other side," he said, low enough so that only his dad and Carmen could hear.

"What for?" his dad asked.

"Trust us," Carmen said. "We just have to."

Shy's dad nodded, gazing out over the river. "Then we'll make it happen," he said. "Do you guys have a plan?"

Shy shook his head.

"We haven't really worked that out yet," Carmen said.

Shy's dad glanced back at his bike and then nudged Shy with an elbow. "'Cause I got an idea if you're interested."

66
Leap of Faith

They waited until just after sunset to enact the plan.

Shy and Carmen were crouched at the edge of the river about a hundred yards south of Shy's old man. All they had with them was the duffel bag, and they huddled with it underneath a second blown-up bridge. As far away as they were, though, Shy could still hear the loud roar of the muffler-less dirt bike, especially when his dad revved the engine. And just like the man promised, Shy heard at least a few hundred people hooting and hollering for him, creating a bit of a spectacle.

Shy smiled as he listened to the crowd roar. His dad had always had charisma. Normally he used it on women, even back when he was married to Shy's mom. Tonight he'd found a more admirable use for his charm.

"Your dad was right," Carmen said, pointing at the guards directly across the river from them. They were all migrating toward the commotion.

Shy shook his head. "Dude, if this actually works . . ."

"You think he has any chance of actually making it?" Carmen asked.

"Zero."

Carmen looked back at the closest group to them. But they were all hovering around a bonfire in a metal trash can. "I don't know," she said. "The way he saved our asses in the desert those couple times?"

Shy shrugged. In reality, he was incredibly nervous. His dad's plan was to rile up as many people as he could with the Evel Knievel–type stunt he was going to attempt. If the guards focused on him, like he promised they would, Shy and Carmen would attempt to swim across the dark river, toward the base of the wall. From that point forward it was on them.

But it was his dad's stunt that worried Shy most. A day ago he wouldn't have given his old man's well-being a second thought. Now Shy was genuinely nervous.

Just then there was a swell in crowd noise. Shy and Carmen craned their necks to try to see as far north as they could. Shy spotted his old man racing the dirt bike through a mass of people that had formed a narrow corridor all the way to the stunted bridge, and all Shy could see over the tops of their heads was his dad's helmet moving down the line, picking up speed.

"They're all running over there." Carmen pointed at the guards positioned along the border. "We should go now, right?"

"Hang on," Shy said. He rose from his crouch and watched his dad hit the lip of the mangled bridge and launch himself and the dirt bike into the air, the crowd roaring behind him, the guards sprinting toward that section of the border.

A few shots were fired at Shy's dad, and when he was at the

peak of his jump he let go of the handlebars and kicked away from the dirt bike and fell from the sky like a man with a failed parachute, landing in the river face-first, creating a splash almost as high as the dirt bike.

"Come on, Shy!" Carmen yanked Shy toward the water.

Just before they dove in, Shy saw a mass of people storming the edge of the river, cheering wildly. But he wasn't able to make sure his dad surfaced, because he was now underwater himself. He held his breath and closed his eyes as he and Carmen swam through the cold water as far as they could without lifting their heads. When he finally had to come up for air, he began dog-paddling toward the stretch of unguarded border.

They swam in silence, Shy looking up every few seconds to make sure they were still on track. There was another commotion in the distance. Shy lifted his head, saw a motorboat with two military guys racing through the water, toward the spot where his dad had landed, the crowd jeering them from the river's edge.

Shy wanted to stop so he could try to see what was happening with his dad, but he couldn't. He had to keep swimming before the guards made it back to their post.

Soon he locked into a rhythm. He kicked his feet furiously underwater and paddled underwater, too, so he wouldn't splash. And as he made it past the halfway point a thought occurred to him: this was how it had all started. The cruise ship sinking and him thrust into cold water, searching for Carmen. Except she was beside him now. And they weren't in the Pacific, they were in the Arizona desert.

By the time Shy and Carmen made it to the other side, Shy's shoulders were burning. He and Carmen climbed up onto the riverbank and moved to the wall, which was only a few steps from the water. It was slightly taller up close, but Shy managed to boost Carmen high enough for her to grab the top, and she pulled herself over. Then he leaped as high as he could, catching the top with his right hand, and he slowly pulled himself up. He hooked his leg over the side, rolled over the lip and fell to the dirt on the other side.

Two guards started toward them immediately, one shouting through a megaphone, the other aiming an assault rifle. But he didn't shoot.

Shy and Carmen dropped to their knees.

Shy reached down and unzipped the wet duffel and quickly took out all the remaining syringes and the comb-over man's letter and held them over his head and locked a few fingers and looked all around the other side of the border. They were in some sort of park, full of lit-up trailers and parked cars and well-groomed people milling around in a civilized way or sitting around barbecue pits.

"Don't move!" a guard shouted from fifteen yards behind them. He wore a dry suit. A second suited guard emerged from a trailer in front of them. The rest kept their distance. Carmen put a hand on Shy's shoulder and then held her hands up, too.

"I said don't move!" the guard shouted.

Shy turned to Carmen and locked eyes with her as they waited for the guards to descend upon them.

Day 53

67
The Other Side

Shy slept through most of the next day.

When he finally cracked open his eyes, the sun was already setting. He could see it through the small window of his room inside the medical trailer. He sat up and sucked in a deep breath and studied the intense colors swirling around the sky. They gave him chills. Because he wasn't supposed to still be here.

As he climbed into his dirty jeans, which had been left folded beside his cot, details from the night before came trickling back into his consciousness. He and Carmen had spent several hours in the "disease control" holding cell while scientists tested the contents of the syringes. And when the vaccine came back as legitimate, everyone in camp suddenly wanted a piece of them. Reporters begged for interviews. The police needed official statements. Doctors insisted on thorough physicals complete with blood work.

Shy refused to do any of it until he knew what was going on with his dad.

Minutes later, the deputy director of the FBI led Shy into an unmarked trailer and sat him in a metal folding chair. They were in the middle of a thorough search of the river, the man explained. Every resource would be exhausted. They'd find Shy's dad. And no matter what condition they found him in, they'd bring him directly into camp. At the end of their short conversation, the man stood up and gave Shy a firm handshake, saying: "Thank you for everything you've done, son."

Shy nodded, thinking how surreal it was that people were now thanking him. As opposed to trying to kill him.

"We'd eventually like you to write out what you've been through. As much as you can remember. Can you do that for us?"

Shy nodded.

There was a long pause then, and Shy noticed that the FBI man's eyes had become glassy. "I have family near LA myself," he finally said. "My sister and her two daughters. All of us over here . . . we just want this nightmare to end."

Shy must have fallen asleep soon after he left the FBI trailer because he didn't remember anything else.

Without the duffel bag, Shy felt naked as he began searching the camp for Carmen and someone who could update him about his dad. Authorities had taken nearly everything from him, including the comb-over man's letter. All he had left was the diamond ring in his pocket and the key around his neck. *Shoeshine's* key. It didn't seem right that the person most responsible for them getting the vaccine into the hands of scientists wasn't here to take credit. Then again, Shy couldn't imagine Shoeshine putting up with all the attention.

Shy slowed near a group of nurses sitting at a picnic table, huddled around a radio. The volume was low, but Shy was still able to recognize DJ Dan's voice. He moved closer and bent down to retie his shoe so he could listen.

". . . and as most of you know, that first version of the vaccine turned out to be ineffective. Which is why these new rumors are so encouraging. To recap, a group of teenagers allegedly snuck across the Avondale border last night carrying a briefcase containing a second Romero Disease vaccine. We still haven't confirmed whether the teens created the vaccine themselves or acquired it some other way. Perhaps even more important than the vaccine, they also handed over to scientists a written chemical formula, which will allow for much quicker production and distribution. Some are saying the Avondale border could come down in as few as three days.

"In a strange twist, we're also hearing that LasoTech, the pharmaceutical company responsible for the original vaccine, is now under investigation, although we still don't know what for. . . ."

When Shy noticed that the nurses had begun whispering and pointing at him, he moved deeper into camp.

He felt incredibly relieved at what he'd just heard. The formula, including the last page from Addie, was in the right hands. And they were taking the comb-over man's letter seriously enough to investigate LasoTech. But that was nothing compared with the relief Shy felt when he spotted his dad. He was standing beside a food truck, eating a taco and chatting up a female reporter.

Shy hurried over and gave his dad a quick, awkward hug before stepping away. "You're alive," he said excitedly.

"Of course I'm alive," his dad said. He glanced at the female reporter, then focused on Shy. "See, boy? My plan worked to perfection. I was just telling Sarah here how I came up with it after what, ten minutes of being in Avondale?"

"It's true," Shy said. He wasn't surprised the reporter was pretty. Even after everything that had happened in California, his dad still couldn't resist dropping game on a good-looking woman.

"You've been through so much," the reporter said to Shy.

"My son's a hero," his dad blurted out.

"Do you think we can sit down and talk?" the reporter asked. "I understand you started out on a boat? Tell me what *that* was like."

"Maybe later," Shy said coldly. He wasn't trying to be mean, but he'd just spotted Carmen across the yard. She was standing with some GQ-looking dude in a blazer who was reaching for her hand.

Shy's stomach began to cramp.

His dad nudged him with an elbow. "Hey, don't sweat that. Like I said, you're a hero now, son. There'll be plenty of women. I promise."

Shy shrugged. "It's not like we're together or anything." Secretly, though, he felt kind of stupid for rushing out here to find Carmen. Actually, he felt like a punk.

"She the one you were traveling with?" The reporter had a notebook out and was jotting things down.

"Anyways," Shy said, backing away from his dad and the reporter. "I'm happy you're good, Pop. How about I find you later. Right now I'm supposed to check in with some FBI guy."

"Hey, Shy," his dad said, locking eyes with him. "We did it, boy. We made it."

"We did," Shy said. And when he actually stopped to think about it, he got chills again. He felt proud.

Shy's dad pulled him in for another quick hug, and this time when Shy tried to push away, his old man held him for a few long seconds. When they finally separated, Shy's dad turned back to the reporter. "It's my second chance with my boy. I told him way back in Cali, everything's gonna be different now."

Shy nodded as he slowly backed away. "It really was my pop's plan that got us over here," he told the reporter.

Before Shy was able to duck out of the courtyard, he heard Carmen calling his name. He pretended not to hear her and kept going, but a few seconds later, she grabbed him by the arm.

"Hey," she said, spinning him around. "Didn't you hear me calling you?"

"Oh, hey," Shy said, acting surprised. "Actually I can't hear too good right now. I think my ears got plugged up from all that swimming last night." He knocked the side of his head a few times, noticing an older man and woman now standing with Mr. GQ. The three of them looked related.

"See that guy over there?" Carmen said, pointing.

Shy nodded. "It's your boy Brad, right?"

"Brett."

"That's what I meant—"

"I know what you meant." Carmen crossed her arms and let out a little sigh.

"I see it's one big happy family again."

"Shy," Carmen started, but then she didn't say anything else.

He took a breath and told himself to chill the hell out. He'd known all along this day might be coming. And after everything they'd been through, it seemed stupid to get hung up on this one little detail. "Look," he forced himself to say. "I'm happy for you, Carm. For real."

"Oh yeah?"

He nodded. "But only 'cause I know *you're* happy."

It was Carmen's turn to nod. She looked back at her man, then focused on the ground in front of her.

"Anyways," Shy said. "I'm supposed to go talk to this FBI guy—"

"I *am* happy," Carmen said, cutting him off. "But I also found out he basically left my family behind."

"He told you that?"

Carmen shrugged. "Right after the earthquakes, I guess, his parents arranged for him to get helicoptered out of San Diego." Carmen paused to smooth her reckless hair behind her ears. "My mom's place was only two blocks away. He didn't even check on them."

"Damn," Shy said. He wanted to sound supportive, though, so he added: "I'm sure shit was pretty messed up at that point, though, right?"

Carmen looked at her fiancé, standing there with his parents. All three of them were now watching Shy and Carmen. "Yeah," she said, turning back to Shy. "But you know me. Family means everything."

Shy knew.

"Look," Carmen said, taking Shy by the wrists. "Brett and his folks have a hotel like twenty minutes away. They're letting me shower there. And I promised I'd get something to eat with them after. But can we meet here later and talk?"

Shy shrugged. He wasn't so sure Carmen would make it back. *He* wouldn't come back if he didn't have to.

Carmen looked at her fiancé again. She held up a finger and mouthed, *One minute.*

"Anyways," Shy said. "I gotta go."

Carmen turned back to him. "The FBI guy, right?"

She knew Shy was making stuff up. "Something like that," he said.

"So are we *not* gonna meet up later, then? To talk?"

Shy gave another shrug. "We'll see if you actually show up."

"Hey," Carmen snapped. "Why you acting nasty?"

"How am I acting nasty?"

Carmen rolled her eyes. "You know how you're acting, Shy. I thought you were gonna love me no matter what."

Shy froze.

Those were the exact words he'd shouted at her on the dirt bike. "You heard me?"

Carmen grinned. "Every single word, Sancho."

Shy lowered his head, embarrassed.

"Anyways," Carmen said, chuckling a little. "I'll find you later. I promise." She turned to leave, but then spun back around, holding out her right hand.

"What?" Shy asked.

"My ring."

Shy stared at her, confused.

"Maybe if I take my ring with me, you'll believe I'm coming back."

Shy pulled the ring out of his pocket, butterflies stirring in his stomach. "But you said you'd never take it unless—"

"I know what I said."

"So does this mean . . . ?"

"Just give me the ring already," Carmen told him. "The sooner I go, the sooner I can be back here with you. 'Cause maybe . . . I feel the same way."

Shy dropped it in her palm, his brain spinning as he watched her turn and start back toward Mr. GQ and his parents. He felt hopeful all of a sudden. Not just about Carmen, but about everything. The wall coming down. The vaccine being distributed. The government sending teams of people into California to begin the rebuilding process.

Shy felt his empty pocket. The ring was finally with Carmen, where it belonged. But at the same time, he didn't want to leap to any conclusions before they talked. He pushed all Carmen-related thoughts out of his head and moved back over to his old man, who was still talking to the reporter.

"Hey, Pop," Shy said. "You think you'd wanna get something to eat with me later?"

His dad glanced down at his half-eaten taco. "Sure," he said, dropping the taco back onto his Styrofoam plate. "Yeah, that sounds great. Just come get me whenever you're ready."

Shy turned to the reporter. "Any chance you have an extra notepad I can borrow?"

The woman smiled, pulling her satchel off her shoulder and unzipping the front pouch. "I have about *five* extra notepads, actually." She pulled a brand-new pad out and handed it to Shy.

"Thanks," he told her.

The woman nodded and dug back into her bag, saying: "I'm assuming you'll need a pen, too."

68
The Hunted

Twenty minutes later, Shy was sitting on top of the makeshift border, between two armed guards in military fatigues, staring at the blank notepad in his lap. He was supposed to write stuff down for the FBI director. But there was so much. He had no idea where to start.

He lifted his head and looked out over the river. The sun had fallen behind the desert to the west, but the sky was still light enough that Shy could see the calm waters and the masses of people still suffering on the other side. They were sitting in groups around bonfires near the river's edge, waiting for the vaccine to be distributed, waiting for the wall to come down. But it wasn't only the survivors Shy saw now, it was those he'd lost, too. Friends from the ship like Rodney and Kevin and Marcus. His entire family, aside from his dad. Miguel. His sister and grandma.

A lump climbed into Shy's throat as he pictured his mom waving goodbye to him from the couch.

Shy suddenly didn't feel so good about being on the safe side, removed from all the suffering. He may have dogpaddled across the night before, but he'd left his heart on the other side. He glanced at the camp behind him. People dressed in clean clothes and moving leisurely around large tented areas. People eating and drinking at picnic tables near the food trucks. Talking.

Shy pushed away the guilt and uncapped his pen and held it over the first page of the pad, trying to imagine how Shoeshine had decided what to write. He remembered the title that started the man's journal, and he wrote down two simple words of his own and stared at them. Then he wrote about the ocean's whispering, and the sailboat, and the excitement he felt when he first spotted the California shoreline. And he wrote about Carmen and Marcus and Shoeshine.

Soon he had filled half a page, and he looked it over, fingering the key around his neck. He glanced up at the people stooped over fires on the other side, then stared at the river again. It was about twenty-five feet below where he sat, but he could still hear its subtle whispering. Something Shoeshine told him popped into his head. All along, the man had said, people had been following Shy. It still seemed pretty hard to believe, but what if Shoeshine was partly right?

Shy pulled Shoeshine's map out of his pocket and stared at the spot just outside of Blythe where they'd left the man behind. He drew in a single line where he and Carmen had continued on. Then he smoothed out the map and stuck it inside his pad and looked at his words again. They didn't seem quite right. But like Shoeshine had said about his own words, no one person can own the truth. Shy looked at the two guards. And he looked back at camp. Then he did something that surprised even him. He tucked the notepad under his arm and stood up and peered down at the river, butterflies suddenly flapping around in his stomach and chest.

"Hey!" one of the guards shouted.

They both started lumbering toward him.

Shy sucked in a deep breath and held it and leaped off the fence.

And on his way down he could hear the guards yelling, and he could smell the bonfires, and he could still picture Carmen's hand reaching out for the ring, which he knew was important. He had no idea what he was doing, or how he'd explain it, or what he planned to do once he got to the other side. He just knew it was where he had to go. To see if anyone would follow. To see if anyone would help fix this. And suddenly his body slapped the river's surface and he let go of the notebook and pen and concentrated on the familiar cold that spread its arms out around him, pulling him home.

Acknowledgments

Much gratitude goes out to the folks who've helped me turn a bunch of rough ideas into an actual book. Krista Marino, who's been my editor, friend and artistic guide for a full decade now. Steve Malk, the most creative, thoughtful, loyal, badass agent in the business. All the supportive and passionate people at Random House, especially Beverly Horowitz, Dominique Cimina, Monica Jean, Lydia Finn, Lauren Donovan (still), Lisa Nadel, Adrienne Waintraub, and Lisa McClatchy (I love you, Random House!). Matt Van Buren, for always being my first reader. Celia Perez, for double checking my español. My amazing wife, Caroline, for her incredible support and belief (and for making me smile every single day!). The rest of my family: Caroline, Al, Roni, Amy, Emily, Spence, the Suns and the newest addition, Luna Grace de la Peña, our beautiful daughter who showed up in the middle of this book and stole my heart (and my sleep!). Last but not least, I'd like to thank all you educators and booksellers out there who make a special effort to get great diverse literature into the hands of not only diverse readers but every reader.

About the Author

The Hunted is Matt de la Peña's sixth novel and the sequel to *The Living*, for which he received the Pura Belpré Author Honor Award. He attended the University of the Pacific on a basketball scholarship and went on to earn a Master of Fine Arts in creative writing at San Diego State University. He lives in Brooklyn, New York, where he teaches creative writing. Look for Matt de la Peña's other books, *Ball Don't Lie*, *Mexican WhiteBoy*, *We Were Here*, *I Will Save You*, and *The Living*, all available from Delacorte Press. Visit him at MattDeLaPena.com and follow @mattdelapena on Twitter.

Turn the page for a look at how Shy's story began in *The Living*—the companion to *The Hunted*.

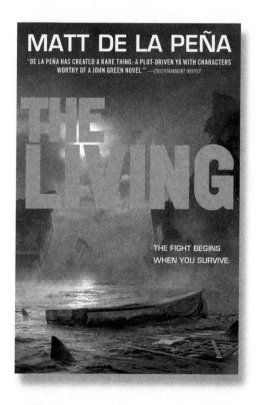

"De la Peña has created a rare thing: a plot-driven YA with characters worthy of a John Green novel."   —*Entertainment Weekly*

Shy stands alone on the Honeymoon Deck. Cooler full of ice-cold water bottles strapped across his chest.

Waiting.

It's day six of his first voyage as a summer employee of Paradise Cruise Lines. Towel Boy at the Lido Deck pool by day. Water Boy at night. But the money's good. Like, game-changing good. He calculates again how much he'll have pulled by the time school starts back up. Three eight-day voyages, plus tips, minus taxes. Be enough to help his mom out and still score some new gear and a pair of kicks, maybe take a female out to dinner.

Shy moves to the railing, picturing that last part.

Him with a girl on an actual date.

He'd get a reservation at a nice spot, too. Cloth napkins. Some fine girl sitting across from him in the classy-ass booth. Maybe Jessica from the volleyball squad. Or Maria from down the street. All eyelashy smiles as whatever girl glances at him over her menu.

"Get whatever you want," he'd tell her. "You ever had surf 'n' turf? For real, I got you."

Yeah, he'd play it smooth like that.

When it's overcast at night, the moon above the cruise ship is a blurry dot. The ocean is black felt. Can hardly tell where the air ends and the water starts up.

You can hear it, though.

That's another thing Shy never would have thought before he landed this luxury cruise gig. The ocean talks to you. Especially at night. Whispering voices that never let up, not even when you sleep.

It can start to mess with your head.

Shy spots a passenger stepping out of the Luxury Lounge. The thick glass doors motor open long enough to let out a few notes from the live orchestra. Inside there's a formal event going on called the Beacon Ball. Harps and violins and all that. Hundreds of dressed-up rich folks drinking champagne and socializing. Shy's job tonight is to offer water to anyone who steps outside for air.

Like this dude. Middle-aged and balding, dressed in a suit two sizes too small.

Shy moves in quick with his cooler, asking: "Ice-cold bottle of water, sir?"

The man looks at the sweating bottle for a few seconds, like it confuses him. Then a grin comes over his face and he digs into his wallet. Holds a folded bill toward Shy between two veiny white fingers.

"Sorry, sir," Shy tells him. "We're not supposed to—"

"Says who?" the man interrupts. "Take it, kid."

After a short pause, for show, Shy snatches the bill and buries it deep inside his uniform pocket. Like he always does.

The man uncaps the water bottle, takes a long swig, wipes his mouth with the arm of his suit jacket. "Spent my entire life trying to get to this place," he says without eye contact. "Top scientist in my field. Cofounder of my own business." He looks at Shy.

"Enough money to buy vacation homes in three different countries."

"Congratulations, sir—"

"Don't!" the man snaps.

Shy stares at him for a few seconds. "Don't what?"

"Don't tell me what you think I want to hear." He shakes his head in disgust. "Say something real instead. Tell me I'm fat."

Shy glances at the ocean, confused.

The guy's definitely fat, but if Shy's learned anything during his first six days on the job, it's that luxury cruise passengers don't want anything to do with real. They want a pat on the back. "Tell a dude how great he is and get paid." That's his roommate Rodney's motto. But this guy isn't fitting the formula.

The man sighs, asks Shy: "Where you from, anyway, kid?"

"San Diego."

"Yeah? What part?"

Shy shifts the cooler from his left side to his right. "You probably never heard of it, sir. Little place called Otay Mesa."

The man laughs awkwardly, like it pains him. "And you're trying to *congratulate* me?" He shakes his head. "How's that for irony?"

"Excuse me?"

He waves Shy off and re-caps his bottle. "Trust me, I know Otay Mesa. Right down there by the border."

Shy nods. He has no idea what the guy's getting at, but Rodney warned him about this, too. How eccentric luxury cruise passengers can be. Especially the ones whose front teeth have already turned pink from too much red wine.

It's quiet for a few seconds, Shy readying himself for his exit, but the man turns suddenly and points a finger in Shy's face. "Do me a favor, kid."

"Of course, sir."

"Remember this cowardly face." The man taps his own temple. "It's what corruption looks like."

Shy frowns, trying to find the logic.

"This is the face of your betrayer. Me, David Williamson. Don't you ever forget that! It's all in the letter I left in the cave."

"Not sure I'm following, sir."

"Of course you're not following." The man uncaps his water bottle again and turns to the ocean. He doesn't drink. "I've made a career out of hiding from people like you. But tell me this, kid: how am I supposed to go on living with all this blood on my hands?"

Shy abandons his search for meaning and focuses on the guy's comb-over. It's one of the more aggressive efforts he's ever seen. The part starts less than an inch above the left ear and dude's expecting a few wiry strands to cover a serious amount of real estate.

Maybe that's what he means by "hiding." Down to three defiant hairs and still believing he has that shiny-ass dome fully camouflaged. It reminds Shy of little-kid logic in a game of hide-and-seek. How his nephew Miguel used to bury his face in a couch cushion, thinking if he couldn't see you, you couldn't see him either.

Shy hears flutes and harps again and turns his attention to two older women who've just come out of the lounge in sparkling party dresses. They're both laughing and holding their high heels in their hands.

"Hello, ladies," he says, moving toward them. "Care for an ice-cold bottle of water?"

"Oh yes!"

"Honey, that sounds marvelous!"

He hands over two bottles, amazed that wealthy women can get so worked up over free water.

"Thank you," the taller one says, leaning in to read his name tag. "Shy?"

"Yes, ma'am."

"Now, that's a curious name," the other woman says.

"Well, my old man's a curious guy."

They all laugh a little and the women open their waters and take well-mannered sips.

After the Paradise-recommended amount of small talk, Shy steps away from the women and goes back to looking at the dark sea that surrounds them. Thousands of miles of mysterious salt water. Home to who knows what. Big-cheeked bottom dwellers and slithering electric eels, whales the size of apartment buildings that swim around all pissed off they don't have real teeth.

And here's Shy, on the top deck of this sparkling white mega-ship. Two hundred thousand tons and the length of a sports arena, yet somehow still floating.

He remembers his grandma's reaction when she first learned he was applying for a summer job on a cruise ship—two weeks before she got sick. She ducked into her room, came out seconds later with one of her scrapbooks. Turned to several articles about the rise in shark attacks over the past decade.

Shy had to take her to the local library and pull up an image of a Paradise cruise liner on the Internet.

"Oh, *mijo*," she breathed, all excited. "It's the biggest boat I've ever seen."

"See, Grandma? There's no way a shark could mess with one of these things, right?"

"I don't see how." She looked at the screen and then looked back at Shy. "I have pictures of their teeth, though, *mijo*. They have rows and rows. You don't think they could chew right through the bottom?"

"Not when the bottom's like eighteen feet thick and made of pure steel."

Shy is staring blankly at the ocean like this, remembering his grandma, when out of the corner of his eye he sees a blur climbing the railing.

He spins around.

The comb-over man.

"Sir!" he shouts, but the guy doesn't even look up.

Shy cups his hands around his mouth and shouts it louder this time: "Sir!"

Nothing.

The two older women now see what's going on, too. Neither moves or says a word.

Shy rips off the cooler and sprints across the width of the deck. Gets there just as the man lowers himself over the other side of the railing and goes to jump.

Shy reaches out quick, snatches an arm. Grabs for the man's collar with his other hand and balls the material into his fist. Holds him there, suspended against the ship.

Everything happening so fast.

No time to think.

This man dangling over the edge, twenty-something stories up from the darkness and too heavy for one person, slipping through Shy's fingers.

He hooks his right leg through the railing for leverage so he won't get pulled over, too, and shouts over his shoulder: "Get help!"

One of the women hurries toward the lounge, through the glass doors. The other is shouting in Shy's ear: "Oh my God! Oh my God! Oh my God!"

The comb-over man locks eyes with Shy. Shifty and bugged. Up to this point his hand has been gripping Shy's forearm. But now he lets go.

"What are you doing!" Shy shouts at him. "Grab on!"

The man only looks below him.

Shy tightens his grip. Grits his teeth and tries pulling the man up. But it's impossible. He's not strong enough. Their positioning is too awkward.

He looks over his shoulder again, yells: "Somebody help!"

The second woman shuffles backward, toward the lounge. Hand over her mouth. The water bottles from Shy's cooler rolling around the deck behind her.

Shy can feel the man's elbow starting to slip through his fingers. He has to do something. Now. But what?

Several seconds pass.

He lets go of the collar long enough to clamp on to the man's arm with his left hand, too. Just below the elbow. Both of his hands in a circle now. Fingers linked. Shy's whole body shaking as he holds on. Sweat running down his forehead, into his eyes.

His leg in the railing beginning to cramp.

A few more seconds and then he hears a ripping sound. The man's suit coming undone at the arm. He watches helplessly as the seams pull apart right in front of his eyes. Slow-motion-style. Black threads breaking, dangling there like tiny worms.

Then a loud tear of material and the man drops, screaming. Eyes wild as he falls backward. Arms and legs flailing.

He disappears into the darkness below with hardly a splash.

Shy! someone calls out.

But Shy's still staring over the railing, into the darkness. Trying to catch his breath. Trying to think.

Shy, I know you can hear me.

Other passengers moving out onto the deck now. The hum of hushed conversations. A spotlight snapping on above him, its bright beam of light creeping along the surface of the water. Revealing nothing.

Stop playing, bro. We need to hurry and get to Southside.

The ocean still whispering, same as before. Like nothing whatsoever has happened, and nothing will.

Shy glances down at his hands.

He's still gripping the man's empty sleeve.